SOMETHING EVIL COMES

A. J. CROSS

Severn House

This first world edition published 2017
in Great Britain and the USA by
SEVERN HOUSE PUBLISHERS LTD of
Eardley House, 4 Uxbridge Street, London W8 7SY.
Trade paperback edition first published
in Great Britain and the USA 2018 by
SEVERN HOUSE PUBLISHERS LTD.

British Library Cataloguing in Publication Data
A CIP catalogue record for this title is available from the British Library.

ISBN-13: 978-0-7278-8739-9 (cased)
ISBN-13: 978-1-84751-853-8 (trade paper)
ISBN-13: 978-1-78010-913-8 (e-book)

All Severn House titles are printed on acid-free paper.

Severn House Publishers support the Forest Stewardship Council™ [FSC™],
the leading international forest certification organisation.
All our titles that are printed on FSC certified paper carry the FSC logo.

Typeset by Palimpsest Book Production Ltd.,
Falkirk, Stirlingshire, Scotland.
Printed and bound in Great Britain by
TJ International, Padstow, Cornwall.

ONE

The jemmy moved forward and back within the narrow space between door and jamb, followed by a pause, quickened breathing and a brief inspection which indicated only minor dents in the wood. A second application plus inspection ended in a series of low expletives, its operator sending a furtive glance around the immediate area.

His accomplice's broad face turned to his. 'I don't like it here, Col. I don't like the graves over there. Can we go home now?'

Col raised his finger to his lips in the kind of gesture Barney understood best, his head filling with yet more expletives, this time directed at his own mother. She was the reason Barney was here at all. She was always going on about him and when his mother got started on something she stuck with it: 'Take Barney out with you,' she'd said countless times that day, not knowing where he was going. 'Go on, it's a shame for him. He's got no mates.'

If Col hadn't realised before why Barney had no mates it was now blatantly obvious. His nerves were jangling from Barney's constant questions and he'd had enough of this place with its owl hoots and quick scurryings. Plus, he didn't like the graves any more than did Barney.

'Just shut up and follow me.' He held out the jemmy. 'Here. Carry this.'

Col left the shadow of the massive door and made a sharp turn, following the line of the building, sticking close to the wall, Barney padding after him.

'Where we going, Col?'

'Home.'

They continued on in the building's shadow for a few metres until Col stopped dead, Barney bouncing off him. Midway between two wall buttresses, unnoticed till now despite Col's recce of the place, was a flight of stone steps leading down to a door. A fraction's hesitation, a quick look around the dark open space around them and he was down the steps, running his hands over the door, searching for a handle, finding only a keyhole. He looked up at Barney.

'The jemmy. *Quick.*'

Barney came down the steps one at a time, like a child, and held it out. Snatching it from him Col applied it to the side of the door, near to the keyhole. A few back-and-forth applications and he got that satisfying sound of splintering wood. This wasn't going to be a waste of time after all. A few more energetic manipulations of jemmy on wood produced a cracking sound. The door separated from its jamb. A few seconds' of listening in case his efforts had attracted undue attention and hearing nothing, Col was inside, the blackness only marginally alleviated by moonlight. He turned to Barney close by his side.

'I can't see nothing. Turn the bloody torch on.'

A sudden click and the torch emitted a wavering pinpoint in the blackness.

He snatched it from his cousin. 'Give it here.'

'I thought we were going home, Col? I don't like it here.' The voice became a whine. 'I wanna go *home.*'

'*Shut* it.'

Low on his heels, the torch balanced upright, Col struck a match in its feeble light. The match flared. Reaching into his jacket pocket he brought out candles and held them to the match. The tiny flames created delineation and shadow out of the blackness.

'Here. Hold these. Hold them up high, like this. Yeah, that's right.'

Col's eyes moved around the room. No wonder it was freezing down here. All he could see was bare stone and the same for the floor. What he wanted was a door to what was above. On the move, Barney following close behind with the candles, he scanned the walls. There was no door except the one they'd come in by. Frustrated, he gestured to Barney to raise the candles some more and got his first sight of yet more stone made into a large box shape. He'd seen something like it in a film a couple of months before. He'd made Barney watch it with him because Barney was just this side of better than nobody when you

watched vampire hunters at work. Frowning at a faint smell of
burning, he jumped at the childlike voice directly in his ear.

'Col?'

'*What*?'

'I think my glove's on fire.'

'Oh, for—' He grabbed the candles, then the woollen fingers,
pulling at them and squeezing them, then blowing on his own
hands.

'You *idiot*. Take 'em off!'

He glared at his cousin whose round face in the jack-o'-
lantern lighting was as artless as a five-year-old's. Shaking his
head, he moved forward with the candles, reluctant to abandon
the place after his efforts to get inside and not about to pass
up whatever there might be down here for the taking. He reached
the waist-high stone structure and looked down at old wood
illuminated by candlelight.

'Here. Hold these while I work out how to get this lid off.'
The flames became two pairs. He ran his hands over smooth
wood, Barney's voice intruding into his thinking.

'Remember that film, Col? The vampire went to sleep in a
thing just like this, didn't he?' A brief silence. 'Is this where
they hide all the stuff, Col?'

Col slipped his fingers into the narrow space between stone
and wood and gripped the lid, then stopped, ears straining, brow
furrowed. He'd heard something. Something coming from
outside.

'What's up, Col—?'

'*Quiet.*'

A chill running across his shoulders, he lowered his head,
looking towards the steps and up. Whatever it was had stopped.
He glanced at Barney. No point asking him if he'd heard it. If
you asked him what day it was you risked getting two different
answers. He listened again. Nothing. This place plus Barney
had got him jittery.

He grabbed the wooden lid and pulled, eyes squeezed tight,
rarely used muscles screaming. It moved a few centimetres. He
gripped it again, pulled some more, then manoeuvred it to one
side and stared down into the small triangle of blackness.

'Bring the candles here. I can't see nothing.'

The flickering light fell into the triangle. Sunken eyes in dark sockets regarded Col, the nose below them a dark wedge, the lips pulled back in a crazy grin above a gaping hole . . .

Col reared, fell backwards, candles falling and rolling around his feet as he shoved Barney aside and lunged for the steps. Erupting into the cold night, breath exploding in great clouds, Barney on his heels, he came to a stop, leant against the wall, his heart filling his throat, cold sweat on his forehead, clutching the torch like some puny weapon.

'You two! Stop right there—'

They fled without a backward look.

The uniformed man reached the spot where they had been, looked down at the open door, the flight of steps and started towards them.

TWO

Spreading moisturiser onto her damp face, Kate Hanson was lost in her own head. *Gym class was hard tonight. Glad when it finished. A lot to do tomorrow.* 'Mom?' *Need to get the post-grad research students moving with the—*

'Mom!'

Hanson started and looked up at her thirteen-year-old daughter's aggrieved reflection behind her in the mirror. 'I called you. Twice. Didn't you hear? You were looking dead weird.'

Hanson eyed Maisie via the mirror. 'I was doing some para-cosmic thinking, actually.'

'Yeah, right. Old Mrs Hetherington looks exactly like that when she's doing what she calls "wool-gathering" and she's, like a hundred and three.'

'Why aren't you asleep? You went to bed an hour ago.'

Hanson got the pout-and-shrug combination which had become a standard response from Maisie to most inquiries over the last couple of months. 'Have you got a headache? Stomach cramps?'

The blue eyes rolled. 'Just *leave* it.'

Hanson studied this slightly shorter version of herself: dark red hair in lush, natural curl, large blue eyes in a heart-shaped face and, in Maisie's case, a sour expression.

'Grandpa's going to make hot chocolate. Would you like some?'

'Please.'

A couple of minutes later Hanson followed her downstairs and into the kitchen where Maisie was now sitting, elbows on the table, head propped on her hands. Hanson got an inquiring look from Charlie. She raised her shoulders. *Whatever's going on with her, I do not have a clue.*

'Have you and Chelsey had an argument?'

'*No.*'

OK. Leave it there. Hanson assembled mugs and Charlie dispensed chocolate powder.

'Mom?'

'Mmm . . .?'

'How old were you when you decided that you wanted to be a forensic psychologist?'

As Charlie poured hot milk onto chocolate Hanson considered the question. 'I don't think I did decide, at least, not in the way you probably mean. I suppose I slowly gravitated to it.'

'Right,' said Maisie, managing to put a morose twist on the single word.

Hanson pressed on. 'You're thinking about what you'd like to do eventually?'

'That's already decided isn't it? Something with maths.'

Hanson suppressed a sigh. Tuesday evening. She'd already done two very full days at the university, she needed sleep and right now she could do without a discussion which had all the makings of a minefield.

'No. Nothing's decided. You can keep your options open until you identify whichever area really interests you.' She understood Maisie's comment about her future. Maisie had a prodigious mathematical talent. Twice weekly during the previous academic year it had taken her across the road from her high school to the university where her mother lectured, to join undergraduates at least five years her senior in maths lectures. She'd appeared to thrive and in October the arrangement had been upped to thrice weekly.

'Maisie if there's a problem with your university lectures . . .?'

'I didn't say that! Did I *say* that?'

Experience telling her she was on a hiding to nothing, Hanson took the tray of drinks and carried them into the sitting room, Maisie trailing her. Setting it down, she handed one of them to her father. 'Here you go, Charlie.'

He took it from her. 'Thanks, Kate.' He glanced at Maisie now on the sofa, well-shaped brows low, then at Hanson who shrugged. Within five minutes Maisie finished her drink, jumped up, put her mug on the tray and headed for the door, omitting the usual kisses. 'G'night.'

Charlie watched her leave then glanced at Hanson. 'What was that about?'

'You know as much as I do. Whatever it is she'll tell me, possibly you, in her own time.' Maisie was some months into her teenage years and so far, so . . . OK. Hanson recalled Maisie's toddler years, distance lending them a rosy glow. In reality, much of it had been a difficult time. She and Kevin had separated, followed by divorce and lone parenthood for her. Maisie had become increasingly challenging. Hanson had blamed herself, then Kevin and finally both of them for not being able to hold things together. Testing and the revelation of Maisie's high IQ had stopped the self-blame, the other blame. Maisie was now old enough to tell Hanson what was troubling her. If anything. Eventually.

'OK, Kate?'

She looked across at Charlie, aware that she was smiling. 'Yes. Everything's fine.'

THREE

Early morning chill on her face, Dr Connie Chong glanced ahead to the spire of St Bartholomew's Church jabbing November cloud, laying odds that where she was heading was as cold inside as it was out. In October she had left Birmingham for eighty-degree days in the place she still thought of as home. Her return to bone-chilling damp two days ago had prompted her to add a fleece beneath the forensic suit she was wearing. The choice had perturbed her. It was something her elderly mother might do. Now she didn't care. Without it, she'd be cold to the bone and likely to stay that way for the next several hours. She smiled, knowing the life-enhancing power of such small positives when it came to her job. She walked onto the wide swathe of land, the massive church now in full view.

Acknowledging the scenes-of-crime officers watching her approach, she went under the blue-and-white tape. Her first task was to get information. She waved a hand at one of the young uniformed constables from headquarters, idly noting that he looked about fifteen. He came towards her, breath preceding him in clouds.

'The chief was frugal in what he told me,' she said. 'What do you know?'

'A community support officer on the night shift rang it in.' He pointed. 'He was coming along that side of the church when he heard noises, came to investigate, and saw two figures running out of there.' He pointed again, this time to a flight of stone steps disappearing downwards. He looked back to Chong.

'He went and had a look. It's in there.'

It. 'Nobody else has been inside so far?' She got a swift headshake.

'SOCOs have been waiting for you to come. I was instructed to guard the scene until you arrived.'

'Is the community support officer still here?' Another headshake.

'After he phoned it in, he waited. I was first here. He told me he'd gone down and seen it. I didn't ask any questions. He looked like he was about to puke,' he finished, adding a quick 'ma'am'. 'He went straight to headquarters to make a statement.'

This was shaping up to be Chong's kind of scene. No disturbance. No exposure to the elements. And so far, thanks to the chief's tight lips, no media interest. She looked at the youthful officer, wondering when she'd acquired the gravitas to cause nervousness in the ranks. Well, among the very young and inexperienced. 'No doubt it will all be in his statement. Has an official of the church been informed?'

He flicked open his notebook, the small act lending him stature. He pointed to a large Victorian residence some distance away, where the land rose, a dark shale path among nearby headstones leading to its dark bulk outlined against the overcast sky.

'That's Church House. A Father Anton Delaney lives there. He's sort of the vicar here. Before the CSO left I told him to guard the steps and went over and rang the bell. Got Delaney out of bed. He was all for getting dressed and coming to have a look but I told him to stay indoors and that somebody would get to him in due course.'

'Well done.' She beckoned to one of the SOCOs who came at a quick clip.

'Let's take a look at what we're facing here.'

They followed the constable to the flight of stone steps. Reaching them he moved to one side, starting at a sudden owl hoot.

'It's down there,' he said, adding an unnecessary, 'you can't miss it.'

Slipping on shoe covers handed to her by the SOCO, she approached the steps, three of his colleagues also following, each carrying a portable light source. As she reached the last step one of the lights was activated, throwing bright white light onto splintered wood along the edge of the few-centimetres-open door. She pushed at it. It creaked, squealed in protest then swung wide.

They came inside, keeping to the walls, the white light flooding the low-ceilinged stone chamber. The distant sounds of early-morning traffic barely audible above ground were now silenced. Chill air closed around them. She looked across to the single feature of the place: a rectangular stone structure around a metre-and-a-half in height and approximately two metres in length. She waited as two of the SOCOs made a quick examination of the floor, followed by headshakes. Nothing for their own footfalls to disturb or destroy.

'Let's get started,' she said.

As SOCOs attached metal stands to the lights, she set down

her case and walked to the stone structure. A heavy-looking wooden cover, a little askew, was resting on it. She leant against the structure to peer inside, feeling the cold from the stone seeping through her clothing and onto her lower body. Straightening, she turned and gestured for lights to be brought, tapping the wood. 'This has to come off.'

Two SOCOs lifted and carried it to a corner, one of them returning to it with fingerprint powder, brush and a roll of clear tape.

Chong gazed into the stone structure at what was now fully visible, the reason she and her colleagues were here. A few seconds to size up the situation and she turned to the senior SOCO.

'He has to come out but before he does I need to get inside for a closer look. We'll start with photographs.'

The SOCOs worked around each other in silence, movements coordinated, punctuated by the whir of cameras. She fetched her own from her case, hung it around her neck by its wide strap. Clipboard, pen and a small recording device in hand she returned to the structure. As the SOCOs moved away she approached it, raised the large camera and focused it downwards, firing off several shots in rapid succession, giving each a critical appraisal as she went. Getting a confirmatory nod from the senior SOCO she raised herself to a sitting position on the wide stone edge and swung her legs over the side.

Crouched inside the chill, confined space she studied what had to be the best preserved human remains she'd ever seen, the damage to the throat the worst. She activated the recording device. 'Initial observations: deceased young male in excellent state of preservation lying in supine position within a stone sarcophagus located in a semi-basement room of St Bartholomew's Church, Moseley. Age estimate: eighteen to twenty-five. Dark hair. Clean shaven. Appears to be of average height and build. Dressed in dark-coloured overcoat, zig-zag blue-and-green patterned scarf, black jeans, black boots. Nothing further visible at this time. Frontal aspect of throat appears to have been . . .' She searched for a neutral alternative to the two words in her head. None came.

'. . . torn out.'

Stopping the recorder she stared down at the damage wrought to the front of the neck, then moved to the right side of the remains. Crouching, she noted a mark just below the ear. Reaching forward she gently pulled down the overcoat collar and gave what was revealed close scrutiny. It was sizeable, darker than the leather-like, grey-to-brown flesh surrounding it and formed from straight lines which nature would never have created.

'Deceased has what appears to be a tattoo on the right side of the neck. Design not yet identifiable.'

Straightening, she clicked off the recorder, sat on the side of the structure and swung her legs over. Taking out her phone, she selected her assistant's number. Her call was picked up on the first ring. He was an early bird.

'Igor. Run a data search of MISPERS, please.' She repeated her initial findings.

'If you find a good fit, tell the chief, let me have the ID details and I'll take a DNA sample and send it over for final confirmation.'

An hour later the body had been removed from its resting place and was lying on a white sheet spread over a fully-open body bag. Legs braced, her body angled above it, Chong steadied the large camera and took several shots. They would be added to the ones she'd taken of the body in situ, all of them assembled into a crime scene album. She idly wondered about the deceased's family if he had one. They probably had photo albums. Evidence of happier days.

Feeling a presence at her elbow she turned to a SOCO who was holding a shallow cardboard box towards her. She looked down at candles, one flattened and broken, the others intact, their wicks burnt.

'These fit with the community officer's report of intruders in here,' he said. 'We'll test for prints.'

As he took them away, Chong picked up voices coming from outside. Eyes on the steps beyond the damaged door, she watched large, outward-pointing feet in blue shoe covers coming downwards, followed by the rest of a tall, heavyset officer, his broad face set. Detective Sergeant Watts. He nodded to Chong, came to where she was standing and got his first sight of the remains. 'Bloody *hell*.'

A dark-haired, younger officer followed him, look down at the remains then up at Chong. She noted that his face had a light tan despite the bright white light which had everyone, apart from Chong herself, looking washed-out. Aware of the blue eyes turned on her, not for the first time she wished away a decade. Pure, light-hearted fantasy. Maybe not so pure. Lieutenant Joseph Corrigan had also taken leave at around the same time as she had, his choice the eastern seaboard of the United States rather than the Far East.

She nodded at each of them and to Corrigan, 'How was Boston?'

'Homely. How'd you find Hong Kong?'

'Turned left after India and waited.'

His thick arms folded, Watts was eyeing the remains lying on the sheet-covered body bag. 'Some pilfering types got a nasty shock when they came down here.'

'It looks that way,' said Chong. 'They left candles behind. SOCO will process them.'

He gave her an appraising look. 'The chief says you already know who this is.'

She glanced towards the remains. 'I phoned initial examination details to Igor. He found a likely MISPER: Matthew Flynn, resident of Erdington, Birmingham who disappeared in October of last year. Twenty years old.' She gazed down at the wreckage lying on the sheet. 'I've sent a tissue sample to headquarters for final DNA confirmation. You'll have to be patient for the result.'

'I can do that,' said Watts, looking anywhere but at the remains.

Chong eyed Corrigan, saw the dark brows rise. 'You don't say?' She glanced at her watch. 'I'm hoping we'll have it by late today.'

Watts looked at her. 'How come you're so confident who it is?'

She hooked a finger at both of them. 'Time for the guided tour.' They followed her and stood in silence, gazing downwards as she waved a hand over the remains. 'This is as good as it gets in terms of preservation.'

'Take your word for it,' murmured Watts.

She crouched. 'See here – and here? Those faint lines?' She looked up at them, finger-pointing the neck. 'Nature doesn't do straight lines. This is the ID clincher so far. According to a statement by a work colleague of Matthew Flynn's, he had a tattoo on the right side of his neck.'

Watts got down on considerable haunches, his eyes travelling quickly over the remains, wincing at the ragged hole to the front of the neck. He pointed. 'Apart from that, he looks to be in relatively good nick.'

Chong raised her hands to the walls and low ceiling. 'We've got this place to thank for it.' She stood, walked to the stone construction and patted it. 'Plus, he was inside this. More stone to keep him cold.' She pointed to a distant corner. 'That wooden lid kept out the light. Not that there is any down here, even in daytime. There's no indication of blood spillage or other stains so he wasn't killed here. Take a look inside his sarcophagus.'

Corrigan went to it, peered inside. 'Real cosy.'

'When do we get the rest?' asked Watts, sounding casual.

She shot him a reproving glance. 'Give certain people all you've learned from two hours of dedicated work in what feels like a fridge and they're still not satisfied.' She walked back to him. At times like this she was as amazed as everyone else at HQ at the simple, off-duty friendship between her and Watts. 'One of your defining characteristics is that you never disappoint. I was waiting for your Sergeant Pushy alter ego to show up. Listen, because this is how it's going to be: Mr Matthew Flynn will go back with me to the PM suite. I'll do a thorough examination of him, the results of which you'll have in due course.' She watched his eyes move over the walls and floor of the room. 'I take it this is the Unsolved Crime Unit's next cold case?'

'According to the chief, once DNA is confirmed. I've emailed Hanson so she knows.'

They heard a low buzz. Chong reached inside her forensic suit for her phone and took the call, her eyes fixed on both officers. 'Yes? That was quick. Thank you.' She looked up at them. 'DNA confirmation: Matthew Flynn, initially missing, now known to be deceased. The Unsolved Crime Unit is officially in business.'

'Do we know who's in charge at the church?' asked Corrigan.

'The officer guarding the door can tell you. Go and ask him. It'll get both of you from under my feet.'

They came up into weak, early light, Watts briskly rubbing his big hands together.

'I've just realised how cold it is down there. It goes straight to my feet and – *Hey*. You!'

The young officer leaning on one shoulder against the exterior wall, his arms folded around himself leapt to standing.

'Sarge!'

Watts came close, looking down at him. 'Who runs this place?'

'A Father Delaney. I told him somebody would be wanting to talk to him. He lives in that big house over there.'

Watts and Corrigan looked in the direction he was pointing. The church itself occupied an extensive island of land surrounded by suburban roads. The house was beyond an expanse of grass, along a wide path cut through the graveyard. Except for one upstairs window it was in darkness.

'Nice piece of real estate,' said Corrigan.

Watts glanced at his colleague. 'Surprised to hear that from you, Corrigan.'

'Back home, religion's a big deal but so is finance. We're kind of realistic.'

The constable's excitable voice broke into their conversation. *'That's* him, Sarge. See that big chap heading over here? The one in the long—'

'Settle down, lad. We see him,' said Watts.

He and Corrigan started walking, their eyes fixed on the man coming towards them, vast in girth, jowls spread over his collar. When he reached them he topped both officers by a good five centimetres.

'Who is in charge here?' he asked, his voice rich yet soft.

Watts looked at the priest in his long black robe. He wasn't exactly a non-believer because his mother had chivvied him and his several brothers and sisters to Sunday school. But he wasn't a believer either. What he was right now was uncomfortable. He held up identification.

'Detective Sergeant Bernard Watts. This is Lieutenant Joseph Corrigan. Full name, please.'

Notebook out, pen poised, Watts waited then looked up. The big man was staring at a couple of white-suited SOCOs coming up the steps leading from the frigid room beneath the church.

'What's going on here? What are those people doing? What's happened? I've been waiting at my house for somebody to come and tell me but . . .' He caught Watts's facial expression, pen still poised. 'Father Anton Delaney. This is my church. Is anybody going to tell me what's happening? All I was told in the early hours was that there had been an incident and to stay inside.'

'We were just coming to find you.' Watts jabbed his pen in the direction of the steps. 'What's that room down there and who has access to it?'

Delaney looked from him to the steps then back. 'It's the crypt. It's not used. Hasn't been for the twenty years I've been here. It's kept locked.'

'Where's the key?'

'There isn't one to my knowledge. There's a small office at the back of the church. It might be somewhere in there but as I said, the crypt is never used . . .' Delaney stopped, his eyes on the SOCOs again, his forehead creasing. He looked from Watts to Corrigan. 'You're not here about the vandalism and the other things, are you?'

Watts eyed him, wondering what it was that got a man to take up a life of celibacy. He thought about his own situation. Given what wasn't happening in his own life, he and the big man in the long outfit had something in common. 'We're here to investigate a murder.' He watched Delaney's plump face drain and his mouth open, forestalling any further words with more of his own. 'We need you and whoever else works here to keep away from the church building until that room – crypt – and the grounds around it have been fully processed. It's likely to take most of today.'

Face aghast, Delaney shook his head several times. 'No, no. That's quite impossible. We have a morning service scheduled.'

Watts stared up at the fleshy, reddening face, thinking that a

Lord who was all-seeing would already have concluded that a service scheduled for today was off. This was the problem with civilians in his experience, or one of the problems, anyway: they wanted crimes investigated but not necessarily at the expense of their own plans. He repeated the gist of what he'd just said, adding detail for Delaney's benefit. 'This whole site is a crime scene. It will be guarded and visitors turned away until the crypt and surrounding area have been thoroughly processed. We'll be speaking to you as soon as we can.'

Corrigan spoke. 'We regret any inconvenience to the church, sir.'

Watts gave Corrigan a meaningful head tilt and moved away. Corrigan was a good officer and he brought added benefits, what Chong called 'social skills'. A big plus right now was that he knew about churches like this.

Recalling Delaney's earlier words he turned back. 'And when we do speak to you, you can tell us about this vandalism you mentioned.'

Delaney looked at him, then at Corrigan and walked away in the direction he'd come. 'He can wait,' said Watts. 'Our priority today is the post-mortem results.'

Hanson looked out of her window at the chill autumn campus. November, now. Did that qualify as winter? It was cold enough. Something about the approach of the year's end invariably made her reflective. She looked down at the small stone grotesque perched on a ledge just below her window, its little fangs displayed, its wings unfurled, about to launch itself into cold space. *Stay on your ledge where you're safe.*

Her assistant's voice drifted from the adjoining room and Hanson thought of Maisie and whatever it was that was bothering her. Something definitely was. Or maybe it was the onset of teenage years? *The onset of adolescence, so help me.*

'Yes, I'll ask Professor Hanson then get back to you with her response. Bye.' Crystal appeared in the doorway, blonde hair spikey, lips crimson. 'Somebody from the local radio station is asking if you'd like to give an opinion on air about offender profiling. Are you interested?'

'No.'

Crystal grinned. 'Didn't think so. Want a refill?'

Hanson shook her head. 'No, thanks.'

'Anything else I can do for you?'

'No, I'm fine.'

Crystal returned to her room and Hanson's attention went back to the view beyond the window. She watched two female students, members of her first year tutorial group chasing an errant hat being buffeted across the grass by a sudden stiff breeze. She was fine. Her promotion to professor had arrived towards the end of the last academic year in recognition of the courses she taught, the psychological assistance she gave to police headquarters and the resultant well-received research papers published in numerous high-profile academic journals on the place of forensic psychology in modern policing, co-authored by Hanson and her three PhD students, principal among them Julian Devenish. She regretted the reduced student contact that promotion brought, but it gave her and her PhD students time to devote to further research which would bring additional financial benefits to the university and kudos to the psychology department. It was how academe worked.

She left the window for her desk which held several neat piles of papers. Eight weeks into this academic year and she was on top of her new job. Life was good and not only on the work front. Earlier in the year there had been a reconciliation between her and Charlie Hanson, the man she regarded as her father. After several months, the fact that they weren't biologically related still remained unsaid between them, an elephant she'd thought too big for any room, yet in practice surprisingly easy to ignore. Those had been months of happy familial discovery for her and Maisie. Charlie Hanson was kind and considerate and her father in all the ways that mattered. Later in the summer he'd had a bad bout of bronchitis, which he hadn't seemed able to shake off. It had worried Hanson, led her to insist that he move into her home until he recovered. He'd arrived, frail, drained and apologetic. Over recent weeks he'd gradually improved, regained his strength. Lately, he'd begun making comments about going home. She wanted him to stay. Maisie was equally delighted to have her grandpa living with them. Hanson knew she would experience his leaving as a wrench.

She looked across the campus. From this window she could see a corner of the School of Mathematics. She'd dropped Maisie there this morning, watched as she trotted into the nondescript modern building lugging her school bag crammed with textbooks, dark red curls bouncing, her mood of the previous evening seemingly gone. Hanson had lingered, searching for friendly overtures towards her daughter from the few early students straggling inside, evidence that Maisie was finding her niche among these undergraduates. She hadn't seen any. She told herself that those students might not be in Maisie's lectures. She took a deep breath. *Stop worrying. Life's good.* She heard the phone again, took another sip of coffee, picking up Crystal's quick laugh, then: 'Kate? It's Detective Sergeant Watts calling.'

She reached for the phone, heard the familiar voice. 'Quick. Write this down: St Bartholomew's. Postcode, B—'

'*Wait.* I don't happen to have a pen grafted onto my hand.'

'What's got you so tetchy?'

'I was fine three seconds ago. You work it out.'

She wrote the details and brought his earlier email onto the screen. 'You've got confirmation that this is our next cold case?'

'Yes, with the emphasis on cold. We need you over here, soon as. When can you get here?'

She needed to make adjustments to her morning. 'As soon as I can. What do you know?'

'Victim is a twenty-year-old male who somebody thought deserved to have his throat ripped out, poor sod. Hope you've got something warm on.'

FOUR

Those working at the body recovery site paused briefly as the petite figure came under the scene tape and headed towards them, backpack slung over one shoulder, hands thrust deep into the pockets of an olive green parka, sudden winter rays turning her hair to fire.

'Aye-up. Rapunzel's arrived,' said Watts.

'Say that to her face,' murmured Chong. 'Go on. I double dare you.'

'Dream on. I like living too much.'

They waited for Hanson to reach them through lingering morning mist. 'Morning, doc! Or should that be prof-*ess*-or?'

'Whatever makes you happy,' she said easily, joining them. 'What exactly have we got?'

Chong pointed to nearby steps. 'Follow me and I'll show you.'

She followed Chong down into the frigid, half-subterranean room and stood, giving it a searching once-over. There was little to search or see except for stone floor, stone walls, stone everything. Eyeing the rectangular construction to one side, she pointed.

'What's that?'

'It's a sarcophagus,' said Chong. 'Probably quite old and unoccupied until our victim was placed inside it. Come and have a look at him. His name is Matthew Flynn. You'll understand the present tense when you see him.' Hanson followed Chong to a temporary screen erected in a corner of the room and gazed down at the body. It gave her a jolt. She'd seen the many states and stages of decomposition. This was like nothing she'd ever seen. He lay on his back, thick, dark hair mostly in place, if a little dusty, but it was the face which squeezed the breath from her chest. Getting her breathing under control, she let her eyes drift over it. It was pale grey in places, light brown in others, the eye orbits a dark amber. She made herself look at the eyes. They were open, looking into hers with an impatient expectancy, an urgent wanting that completely wrong-footed her.

Wrenching her attention away from them, she looked at the discoloured nose and on to the mouth. Not exactly a smile, nor a grimace. The jaws appeared to be slightly agape as if to allow an intake of breath. Between the well-defined, drawn back lips she could see strong, regular teeth. The combination of eyes and mouth gave the face a living, avid aspect. A few nights ago Hanson had found Maisie watching a horror film. She'd switched it off, causing yelps of annoyance. Gazing down at Matthew Flynn's face she recalled Chong's 'present tense' comment. *He doesn't look dead. Dead but not dead. Undead.*

She looked at the front of the neck. Whatever Matthew Flynn's face had conveyed, what she was seeing now was indisputable death. In the heavy silence her words sounded harsh. 'That looks deadly.'

'I think it probably was,' said Chong. 'Unless I find something even more deadly once I strip him. This afternoon I should at least be able to confirm the cause of death.'

Hanson's attention lingered on the neck. Around the cavernous hole, the flayed edges of flesh were thickened and dried, dark red to black in places; below it a heavy overcoat, a loose scarf, the legs covered in black denim and ending in black boots. She lowered her voice, as if fearful of waking him. 'I've never seen anything quite like . . . him.'

Chong nodded. 'This level of preservation is rare. He's been waiting here a year or so, not exactly lovely to look at but we all know it could have been a whole lot worse.'

Hanson turned from the body, its image now fixed inside her head, took out her phone and headed for the steps, picking up Watts's voice outside.

'When I get back to headquarters I'll fetch the original investigation files out of storage.'

Hanson emerged into relative warmth, Chong following. 'No need. I'm ringing Julian. He's already at HQ. He'll sort it.' He and Corrigan listened as she spoke to her research student who used the between-case quiet of the Unsolved Crime Unit to catch up on his reading. 'Julian, I'm sorry to break into your doctoral time but I need you to go to the basement and locate all the data on a MISPER case dated October of last year. MISPER's name: Matthew Flynn, F-L-Y-N-N.' She looked at Chong who nodded confirmation. 'Aged twenty when he disappeared. Date of birth . . .' She read it from the clipboard Chong was holding out to her. 'Get his file photograph and all biographical information into the Smartboard and check for any criminal antecedents, too, please.' She ended the call.

'Tote that barge, lift that bale,' murmured Watts to Corrigan. They watched two SOCOs go down the steps, one carrying a lightweight metal and canvas stretcher.

'Ready when you are, Dr Chong,' said one.

'Give me a minute. We won't rush it. He's intact so far and

I'd like him to stay that way.' She turned to Hanson and her colleagues. 'I'll start his post as soon as I'm back at head-quarters, hopefully in the next half hour.'

Hanson looked at her watch then at Chong, her university commitments pressing now. 'Any idea when you'll be in a position to tell us about him?'

'I'm hoping for a three o'clock completion time.'

'Nice to know,' said Watts. 'Any chance of some prelims before that?'

'No, but I'm planning to get some lunch in the canteen at around twelve thirty if you'd like to join me in social chitchat.' He shrugged. 'I'll have the case details in my head by then and nothing better to do. I'll see you there.'

Hanson caught Corrigan's amused look and rolled her eyes. Chong squinted up at Watts. 'You do know that your personal charm is only exceeded by your physical beauty?'

'Yeah. You've said.'

Hanson regarded his broad back as he headed towards a couple of uniformed officers. She turned to Corrigan. 'Why is he edgy and red-faced?'

'The chief's too busy to oversee the case so he's made him acting manager of UCU.'

'Ah. That would do it.' She walked to where Watts was standing, his eyes moving over the immediate area, a hint in the bulldog features of some serious thinking. 'Isn't it a bit early in a case to be stressed?'

He didn't look at her. 'Right now, I'm searching for traces of a killer, like you're always on about. And who's stressed?'

'I'm guessing you might be. How's your blood pressure?'

'Fine. How's yours?'

'Same, but I'm not overweight and pushing—'

'What do you think of this place, doc?' She followed his eyes to the church as Corrigan joined them. 'It's . . . impressive.' Watts huffed. 'Religion never helped me when I needed it.' She looked away from him, aware that he'd struggled after his wife's death some years before. 'It was a time we were desperate for a Villa win. Just one goal would have been enough but did they pull it off? Not bloody likely.'

She looked up at his grinning face, the small gap between

the two front teeth. 'Do you know that you're at your most annoying when you're playing the professional Brummie?'

'Wha'?' He looked at Corrigan who was laughing. 'What did I say?' He turned towards the distant Range Rover. 'My feet died half an hour ago. See you later at headquarters.'

She watched him go, aware that he'd managed to divert her from health issues. Watts didn't welcome personal comment. Particularly the kind which sounded like it might come from concern and carry advice. Going down the steps again she took another look around the chill stone space, alert to subtle indicators which might tell them why Matthew Flynn had had to die. Even at this early stage she found herself searching for traces of his killer's thinking, his or her choices, behaviour and needs. Watts was right in his observation of what she routinely did. She shook her head. This cold cell was telling her nothing. She went back up the steps. Corrigan was outside, his gaze moving from the crypt across the expanse of open land. She followed his gaze to what she'd been told was Church House. It looked solid, imposing. Self-contained.

'Did you enjoy your time back home?' she asked.

'Sure did.'

Corrigan was a man of few, invariably polite words. Which is why it had come as a surprise several months before when he told her of his interest in her. She'd already known, of course. She'd even been tempted to tell him how she felt about him but she hadn't. It was too complicated. Not him. The situation. They had to work together. *Maybe it's me who complicates things?* He looked tanned and rested. She smiled up at him. 'Your mother's been indulging you, hasn't she?'

'Yup. Somebody has to.' She searched his face for signs of a hidden point, found none. Knowing him, she wouldn't have expected to.

Good. I'm too busy for complication.

At three-fourteen that afternoon the post-mortem technician let them into the quiet of the pathology suite where the stripped remains of Matthew Flynn, shrunken and dry, lay bathed in white light on the steel examination table.

'Relatively pleasant to be near, isn't he?' said Chong,

emerging from the distant corner she had made into her office space. She waited as they pulled on forensic gloves then passed an A4 sheet to Watts. 'Take a look.' He did, Hanson and Corrigan either side of him. 'That's my rendition of the tattoo on the right side of his neck. It's an inverted crucifix.'

'The Cross of St Peter,' said Corrigan. 'Symbol of humility for Catholics.'

Watts looked less than impressed. 'A few years back we had a spate of domestic pet killings here in Birmingham. A cross like that was daubed around the remains. We called in an expert who told us it was probably an indication of some type of occult shenanigans.' He glanced up. 'I prefer your version, Corrigan.'

Chong placed a shallow tray in front of them. 'Matthew Flynn offered up this little gift when I stripped him. Three hundred pounds in consecutively numbered fifty-pound notes. Except for one which is missing.'

Hanson looked down at the money. 'Where was it?'

'Inside his right boot.' She left the table and returned with several small clear plastic items in transparent sealed bags, individually labelled. 'When I began the search for trace evidence I found multiple fragments on the sheet I'd wrapped around him before transportation. I vacuumed his clothes and his body and got more. Have a look.' She held up one of the small items. They peered at it through plastic.

'This filter contains what I collected from his heavy wool coat.' She pointed at another. 'That one has all I got from the right-hand pocket.' She spread her hands over them. 'All of what's inside these filters looks to me to be the same plant-based material. I'm hoping forensics will identify it.' Hanson gazed down at tiny brown to black bits of something, understanding Watts's often expressed impatience with forensic science. They'd have to wait. Chong gathered up the plastic bags. 'I'll let you know when I've got an identification. I'm also sending the money to them. They're processing the candles found at the scene.' She glanced at Watts. 'They're overstretched so don't expect or pester for results today. Or for several days, come to that.'

Watts was looking gratified. 'Know what the money and the stuff you collected from him is telling me?' He paused for effect.

Hanson was feeling the impact of her day's early start. 'That you need to pop to the bank and the cleaners?'

'No, clever clogs. It's saying "drugs", loud *and* clear.'

Chong regarded him for a few seconds. 'At the risk of raining on your parade, whatever's in those filters doesn't look like any substance I've encountered. I can tell you now, it isn't marijuana.'

Watts was undeterred. 'New pharmaceuticals are constantly cropping up.'

'What's in that envelope doesn't look pharmaceutical,' said Hanson.

He remained upbeat. 'Some of the new pharmaceuticals are semi-synthetic. Extracted from natural materials. For all we know, what's in these filters might be a new kind of mix. It was on his coat, in his pockets, so it's obviously something he regularly carried on him. That and the concealed money are giving me a strong message: Matthew Flynn was into drugs.' He glanced down at the remains. 'He was expecting trouble.' His colleagues were silent. 'And by the look of him, he got it. Our first line of inquiry when we see the family is the people he socialised with.' He shifted his attention to the ravaged neck, then up to Chong. 'Any ideas on what caused that?'

She shook her head. 'Not yet, but as soon as I got back here I requested assistance from the forensic reconstruction artist. He's had a look at the injury. What he comes up with might answer your question. As soon as I have it I'll send you a copy.'

They were inside the Unsolved Crime Unit, Hanson's attention fixed on a photograph of Matthew Flynn in life. It radiated from the Smartboard screen, the face amiable and smiling, attractive yet too fine-drawn to be regarded as handsome. It was undoubtedly the face she'd seen in that chill stone room and just now in the PM suite. Yet it wasn't. The face which had gazed up at her in the crypt had had a beseeching quality. She left the board, tuning into Julian going through the basic facts of the original investigation.

'Matthew Flynn. Younger son of Brad and Diana Flynn.' This produced glances of sudden recognition. 'Brad Flynn. One of this city's entrepreneurs. Owns several businesses: a car dealership, fitness centres, an employment and training agency with offices in the city and a portfolio of properties he leases out.' Julian paused for breath.

'Got form, has he?' asked Watts.

'No, I checked.' He pointed to the photograph. 'Matthew was employed by an agency and living independently on the city side of Erdington at the time he disappeared. Parents live in Sutton Coldfield. Elder son, Dominic lives a couple of miles from them and works in the family businesses. Updates on this information as recent as two months ago indicate no change.' With a glance at Watts he changed the screen to one showing official data.

'The system indicates that one family member had form. Matthew Flynn himself. One caution for Class A drug possession when he was fifteen.'

Unsettled, Hanson stared at the details, recognising her own disappointment. She gave a slow headshake. *Rule One: do not create false personas. They can blind you to facts.*

'Well, well, well. Who'd have thought it?' said Watts.

Hanson glanced at him. 'At a guess, you're about to remind us that you did.'

Corrigan was looking doubtful. 'A caution at fifteen doesn't mean he was still into drugs at twenty.'

'A reasonable point, Corrigan, but then I'm not as reasonable as you and right now, as far as I'm concerned, it fits with the trace evidence we've got.'

'What was his caution for, specifically?' asked Hanson.

'A very small amount of magic mushroom,' said Julian. 'His only recorded offence.'

'Which probably isn't his whole story,' said Watts. 'We don't know what else he was into.'

Hanson knew she couldn't say otherwise. Watts had thirty-plus years' experience in the job. She rested her cheek on one hand. 'Is there any more information about his family?'

Julian nodded. 'There's a bit relating to the brother, Dominic. He contacted headquarters several times after Matthew disappeared, demanding action, plus progress on some street hassle he'd reported on Matthew's behalf – after he'd disappeared. Maybe he thought they might be connected.'

A sharp bleep from the Smartboard got their attention. He turned to it, tapping one of several icons. 'Information from Dr Chong.' The massive screen filled with a 3D, high-resolution, full-colour image which silenced them. An anatomical illustration: a human head upturned, the line of the lower jaw an inverted 'V', the neck below it fully extended. Around the elongated neck were finely executed labels indicating the internal features of the throat: vagus, glossopharyngeal nerve, hypoglossal nerve, carotid artery, all neatly arrowed within the surrounding ripped, flayed flesh worked in fine lines of brick-red, black to grey.

Corrigan broke the silence. 'Matthew Flynn's neck wound reconstructed to show how it looked at the time he was killed.' Julian stared at it wide-eyed, the light and colour from the screen reflected onto his own face.

'Jeez.' The reality inside the crypt and the PM suite had not prepared Hanson for this gashed horror. An image of a fleshy, mashed peach slid into her head. She learnt closer, noting tiny pinpoints of severed blood vessels. The mashed peach image was extinguished by another: a hacked-up fig. In the shocked hush she looked at her colleagues, their facial expressions mirroring hers.

The door opened and the chief's voice followed by his bulk came inside. 'Good. You're all here because I wanted to tell—' Seeing their faces he stopped, turned and stared at the technicolour horror. 'What the devil's *that*?'

'The forensic recon artist's impression of how Matthew Flynn's neck injury probably looked at the time he was killed,' said Corrigan.

Lips compressed, the chief looked from it to Watts. 'This Flynn case needs wrapping up, quick as you can. I've been with the chief constable all morning. He's still smarting over comments in the press last week about unsolved cases in this city being allowed to stagnate. Now, he's overreacting. Demanding reviews of three just for starters which I've sent Upstairs: a series of rapes of adult women going back to the nineties, two child abductions from years back, and three pensioners beaten senseless the year before last, *plus* any other ideas he might be having as I speak. We're already six officers short because they're out searching for the Building Society

Bandit who's struck again in Smethwick after a gap of twelve months.' He shook his head. 'A quick "solve" of the Flynn case means we won't get Dominic Flynn demanding progress like he has since his brother disappeared. For all I know, he and the rest of the family might be behind the press criticism we're getting. The father's got clout in this city. Seven days from now I want to know what you've got on this case and it needs to be enough to satisfy the chief constable that it's well under way.' He was through the door, passing Chong on her way in.

'I'm guessing that wasn't a happy visit,' she said.

Watts pushed his hand through his hair. 'A *hint* about the weapon used on Matthew Flynn might help.'

'I can only try and lighten your mood on that.' She walked to the board and looked up at the depiction of the destroyed neck. 'In my years as a pathologist I've seen countless neck injuries inflicted by knife, razor, ligature, gun, you name it. I don't recall seeing anything remotely like this.' She pointed at various places. 'See how the flesh is torn, here, here and here? If you look closely, there's a similarity in their positioning on each side. I don't think they were caused by individual strikes. I think whatever inflicted them was something with cutting edges on both of its sides.' She saw confusion. 'I know. It's hard to visualise what kind of weapon would do that. One possibility is that it was home-made.' Getting more frowns she came to the table. 'If it isn't something the killer put together himself, the nearest I've come up with is a Swiss army knife.' She pointed at the sketch. 'Imagine such a knife with all of its various tools extended and you'll get some idea of what I'm saying.'

Corrigan was the first to speak. 'A complex weapon like that would be real risky to whoever wielded it.'

'Exactly what I'm thinking. I'll be testing Matthew Flynn's clothes for blood which isn't his.' She headed for the door then turned. 'With the chief on the rampage, what can I say, except good luck? Soon as I have anything else, I'll let you know.' The door closed on her.

'You free later on, Corrigan?' asked Watts.

UCU did not have a monopoly on Corrigan's time. The main

reason for his being in the UK was his role as headquarters' armed response trainer. Getting a nod he reached for the phone. 'I'll contact the Flynn family. Let 'em know we need to see them sometime this evening. We don't want them finding out from tomorrow morning's telly or radio what happened to their missing son.'

Hanson pulled on her coat, her eyes still on the sketch on the screen, trying to decide what it might be saying about this killing. She looked at the gross mutilation, focusing on the specific lacerations pointed out by Chong. Without any indication yet as to motive, what she was seeing suggested massive anger. Malice, even. The concealment of the body indicated that whoever did it was capable of planning. This didn't look to be somebody committing mindless violence for its own sake. She went closer. So, what had twenty-year-old Matthew Flynn done to arouse this degree of rampant viciousness in another person sufficient to provoke such rage and loss of control? Planning. Loss of control. It made little sense. She needed the 'why'. Another question sidled into her head. One she should have asked sooner. She looked at her two colleagues. 'I need to get back to work and do some catching up. A question before I go: Why were his remains left inside St Bartholomew's crypt?' She didn't get a response. She hadn't really expected one.

Hanson came onto her drive, parked behind Charlie's dark saloon and pulled at her seatbelt, all that she had seen and heard today in relation to the case still vivid inside her head. A small line formed between her brows. Matthew Flynn's body might have lain in that sarcophagus, surrounded by cold stone and secrecy for decades, but for the actions of two inefficient, would-be thieves. She glanced at the dashboard clock. She was an hour later than she'd planned. She'd left the house in early-morning darkness. Now it was six thirty and dark again. She got that familiar surge of filial guilt. *Charlie isn't your babysitter.* Beyond tired, she got out of the car, collected her belongings from the boot, hurried towards the house and let herself in. 'I'm home!'

Dropping her bag and briefcase on the hall chest she caught a muffled greeting drifting downstairs. The day's post in her hand she headed for the kitchen, breathing in an inviting aroma. Charlie had insisted on preparing some meals: 'I eat so I should cook.' Finding dinner underway when she came home was still a welcome novelty. She crossed the large, square kitchen to the tall, sixty-plus man stirring a saucepan on the range. She gave his arm a gentle squeeze. It felt frail still. 'Hope you're not overdoing it, Charlie.'

He smiled down at her. 'That would be difficult. This is practically all I've done today beyond a sedate walk to the High Street.'

'Which is as it should be, according to the doctor.' She resolutely closed down her thinking on his recently expressed intention to return to his own home soon. She glanced at the table set for one. 'You and Maisie have eaten?'

'I hope that's OK. She was hungry and she's been given an assignment by one of her maths professors which she has to submit tomorrow so I decided to feed us both at around five thirty. I didn't know if you might be going out.' The last few words were an oblique reference to an evening she'd had a few nights previously, a date with someone uncomplicated but too boring to even contemplate a no-strings relationship with. She shook her head, peering into the full pan. 'Mmm . . . that looks hearty.'

'Beef stew with root vegetables.'

She looked up at him. 'Did Maisie eat some? She isn't crazy about vegetables.'

'Two helpings.' Seeing her facial expression, he laughed. 'Less to do with my cooking than an expressed aim to be taller: five-eight is the goal, apparently. Or not five-three, whichever way you look at it.'

Hanson rolled her eyes. 'Not that again. She's almost as tall as me now and I've told her that either of those heights is genetically unlikely. Why this rush to be different from our parents? Or more accurately, me.' She caught his quick head-shake and grinned. 'That was rhetorical. I'll just go up and see how she is.'

'She's fine, she's busy and she'll be down now that she knows you're home. Sit.' He filled a deep plate, carried it to the table and pointed at it. 'Eat.'

Hanson was five minutes into her dinner when Maisie's feet sounded on the stairs. She came into the kitchen, hair unruly, wearing bear-claw novelty slippers and a sweater Hanson recognised as hers. She dropped onto a chair next to Hanson, a large notebook in her hand.

'Hi, have a good day?' asked Hanson, searching Maisie's face for shadows of whatever had been bothering her and getting nothing. She glanced at the notebook. 'Grandpa says you've got an assignment.'

Maisie looked up. 'Yeah. I wanted you to look at it.'

Heart sinking, Hanson watched the open notebook arrive next to her on the table, both pages a mass of hieroglyphics. No slouch at maths herself, Hanson knew that Maisie's ability was already way beyond hers. 'It looks complicated,' she said, aware of Charlie making himself scarce on the other side of the kitchen.

'It's just problem-solving,' answered Maisie with a shrug. 'But you're missing the point, Mom. Just . . . look at it.'

Hanson looked. Most of the symbols conveyed little to her. Relieved, she spotted numbers separated by a symbol she did understand. She pointed. '*Aha.* That's about probability distribution.'

Maisie gave her a patient look. 'I *know* that, but don't you see how beautiful it is?' She picked up the book, gazed at the pages then back to Hanson. 'I just remembered something.' Hanson caught a glance from Charlie, guessing that what Maisie had to say wasn't about maths. 'Daddy rang.'

'He did?' Hanson was back on familiar but not necessarily welcome territory.

'He said can you ring him. He wouldn't say anything else so I reckon he's got something he wants to say that you won't like.'

Hanson sighed. 'Thanks for that.'

'How about I put this in the microwave,' said Charlie, taking Hanson's plate as she stood and headed for the door, Maisie's voice following her. 'Tell him I'm bringing my certificate to show him on Saturday!'

In her study at the front of the house, the door firmly closed Hanson sat at her desk and tapped her contact list, running through a number of possible scenarios prompting her ex-husband's call.

Or rather, one scenario with variations: he wouldn't be able to have Maisie to stay on Saturday.

He picked up after two rings. 'Hi, Kate! Thanks for calling back. I really appreciate it. How's it going? Everything OK with you?' Hanson pictured Kevin's broad face and stocky build as the conciliatory words flowed into her ear. *Conciliatory: stock-in-trade for a lawyer.* She rubbed her eyes. *Cut the cynicism. Give him a chance.*

'Now that you ask, I'm concerned that Maisie might be struggling socially at the university.'

'Give her time to settle. She's only been doing three days since October. She'll adjust. She's a smart kid.' She waited out the pause, picking up the drop in his voice. 'Listen, Kate. Things are a bit tricky for me right now. I'm really overstretched. I'm being pulled in all directions.' *Here we go. Again.*

'Sounds painful. What do you want, Kevin?'

His tone underwent an abrupt change. 'Why do you always assume . . .?'

'It's not assumption. It's called learning from experience.'

A long sigh drifted into her ear. 'OK, OK. I need a favour. It's about this weekend.'

'You want to change Maisie's contact arrangement.'

'Exactly,' he said, sounding relieved.

She sank back in her chair. 'Maisie is looking forward to it. She's bringing the certificate she won at the Stats Olympiad to show you.' She listened to his exasperated sigh.

'That's right, Kate. Pile it on! Do what you do best. Make me feel bad.'

She ignored the words. 'What's the reason this time?'

'Stella's moving out.' Hanson sat up, taking a few seconds to absorb the news. Stella was the current in a long line of girlfriends Kevin had had in the decade or so they'd been divorced. In addition to those she'd discovered he'd had during the time they were married. She'd come to like Stella, a mature young woman who handled Kevin well. Maybe too mature? Kevin could wear pretty thin for anyone with maturity and awareness. *Unlike me, back then.* Hanson shook her head. In the years following their divorce she'd learned to tolerate how he chose to live his life. He wasn't about to change. Which did not mean that Maisie had to bear the fallout.

'Sorry to hear it but why would that affect your weekend with Maisie?' She waited as he searched for a tack to change to, listened as he softened his voice and selected 'Poor me'.

'Look, allow me some slack, here. I've got a big case on at work and, well, I'm upset about Stella. I really thought she was the one. That I wouldn't be on my own any more. That we were going somewhere. I'm finding this whole situation very difficult.'

Barely registering the flow of words, the possibility now crossed Hanson's mind that Stella might still be at the apartment during the coming weekend. She did not want Maisie going into a negative atmosphere. 'OK. We'll leave it for this weekend but I'll get Maisie to call you. You can give her an explanation. Make it honest, please, as well as age-appropriate.'

'What do you think I am, Kate?'

She shook her head. 'Like I said, I'll get Maisie to call you.' She stared down at her phone. Her ex-husband could not be faulted on the basis of consistency. With him, there was always a let-down.

FIVE

Watts drove, details of the next day's weather drifting from the radio: 'So, listeners in London, Manchester, Edinburgh you might be lucky enough to enjoy some sun tomorrow. And now . . .' He flicked it off.

'Hear that, Corrigan? We're not allowed weather in the Midlands in case we get to enjoy it, just the occasional shower of frogs.' He glanced across at his colleague in profile. 'Nice at home, was it?'

Corrigan nodded. 'It was the fall. Sure was beautiful.'

Watts navigated his way off Spaghetti Junction. 'Family all right?'

'Yep. Took my daughter out for dinner to celebrate her twenty-second birthday and my sister just had her third baby.' He looked out of the window. 'Cute little critter.'

They continued on to Sutton in silence. Watts wondered if Corrigan was homesick. He rejected the idea. Yes, he had a big family in Boston and yes, he missed them but he'd put down roots here. Bought a house. He gave the quiet American a swift sideways glance, wondering if he was missing Rupe? Corrigan had taken on the dog following a case they'd had a year or two back. That dog had become his shadow but Corrigan, being a bit on the soft side about some things, had decided during recent months that it wasn't right to leave it on its own while he worked long hours at headquarters. He'd given Rupe to a keen neighbour who already walked him when Corrigan was working. Following that, he'd given Watts regular updates about his visits and Rupe's progress. Watts smiled to himself, shook his head. No. Whatever was up with Corrigan, it wasn't homesickness. He'd sensed that something had happened when the Unsolved Crime Unit last worked together earlier in the year. He didn't know what the something was because Corrigan was tight-lipped on personal stuff, but Watts had an idea it involved Hanson. Around three years back, she'd had a relationship with an officer who once worked at headquarters. It had ended before she joined UCU. For all he knew, she could be seeing somebody else. He thought about his own situation. He had his own house to go back to whenever he finished work which now felt like part of his DNA after so many years and which more than filled his time, but . . . He swore to himself as the car in front slowed without warning and made a leisurely left-hand turn. He drove on, thinking about the news he and Corrigan had to deliver to a family about its youngest son. At least they weren't going in cold. Matthew Flynn had been missing for a year. The worst situation was when a front door was opened by a mother or father who had no idea that a son or daughter was never coming home. Part of the job. Which didn't make it any easier.

After several more miles he slowed and turned into a wide drive, tall metal gates open, halting the Range Rover at the top of it. They looked at the house in front of them with its wide frontage, all dormer windows and complex roof levels, its facade subtly illuminated in the darkness. It was as immaculate as the dark blue Bentley parked in front, next to a small red sports car. He guessed the house would set anybody back two million-plus. Which probably wasn't a problem for Brad and Diana Flynn. 'Right, Corrigan. They're expecting us and they'll be anticipating it's about Matthew. I'll confirm the lad's death and outline what we know, leaving out the detail then ask some general questions. I want you to lead with the mother. We'll keep it brief.' They got out of the Range Rover into chill darkness. 'Let's get it done.'

Watts guessed that the tall, mid-forties man who opened the door, shook their hands and invited them inside, was Brad Flynn. They declined his offer of drinks as he showed them into a lounge as big as the whole ground floor of Watts's place. A woman was sitting there. She said nothing in response to their greetings, just stared up at them. Diana Flynn. Mother. The similarity to Matthew was there in the fine features. Offered seats, Watts chose the sofa, Corrigan a chair close, but not too close, to Diana Flynn. Watts got down to it. 'Thank you for agreeing to see us.' The atmosphere inside the room was drum-taut. 'We have some news about Matthew and—'

'Just tell us,' said Brad Flynn. His wife had drawn a sharp breath and was looking at them now with a mix of fear and hope, one hand at her mouth. 'You've found him?'

'Yes,' said Watts, guessing from what he was seeing that Brad Flynn was the realist.

'He's . . . all right, isn't he?' she asked. Her husband turned away, running a hand over his head. Watts made himself look directly at her. 'Mrs Flynn, there's no way to make this easier. I'm really sorry to have to tell you: Matthew is dead . . .' She was at the door and out of the room. They listened to her feet on the stairs, heard a door on the upper floor close with quick force. In a silence heavy enough to weigh, they waited for a response from the man in the expensive formal suit standing at the window, looking out at a rear garden which was probably a riot of colour in summer but now had November's cold hand all over it. He'd made no move to follow his wife and had spoken only to refuse Watts's offer of the services of a family liaison officer. Leaden seconds ticked on in the thickly carpeted room.

Flynn turned to them. 'Where was he?'

Watts cleared his throat. 'The Moseley-Kings Heath area.'

'I know it. Where, exactly?'

'Close to a church. St Bartholomew's.' Watts decided that other details could wait. 'Both Lieutenant Corrigan and I are sorry to have to bring you such bad news, Mr Flynn. We'd be grateful if you'd convey that to Mrs Flynn. I'll contact you soon and arrange to see you again.'

Flynn shook his head as Watts half-rose. 'We've got the face time now so let's use it.'

Face time? Watts waited as Flynn walked to a nearby suede sofa and sat, pale but composed. 'Whatever you want to ask, do it now. Diana's been in denial these last twelve months. I warned her. I always knew this wouldn't end well.'

'We'll keep it brief. Can you confirm the last time you saw Matthew?'

'The last time he came here for a family dinner, which would have been the Wednesday.' Watts asked for a date and wrote it down. 'Was it a special occasion?'

'No. We had the boys round to eat with us once a week, time and work permitting. His mother tried to contact him on the following Tuesday to confirm he was coming for dinner on the Wednesday evening. She couldn't reach him.'

'Both your sons lived locally back then?' asked Watts, already knowing what the file had to say but wanting it confirmed.

'Dominic, my eldest had his own place a couple of miles away from here. Still has. Matthew had a flat in Erdington.'

'Can you recall anything of that Wednesday evening when Matthew was here? Was there anything about him, the way he was, what he said which you now think might be relevant to what happened to him?'

'The police asked us at the time. No. It was the usual family get together. Good food. Diana's a first-rate cook. Good conversation. A bit of heated discussion.'

Watts looked up from his notes. 'Heated discussion?'

Flynn nodded. 'The usual business talk between Dom and me, mainly.'

'Matthew didn't work for you?'

'No. Dom is the one with the business head, the organisational skills. He gets that from me. Matthew was creative, open, idealistic.' He looked away from them. 'A bit too open and idealistic. If he'd toughened up he would have done well with us. I offered to put him in charge of our gym business but he refused.'

'So what was he doing at the time he disappeared?' asked Watts.

Flynn shrugged. 'He got a place at Aston University the previous August then decided it wasn't for him. He struggled after that to decide what he did want. He signed up with an agency and worked temporary jobs while he tried to make up his mind. He was still doing that when he . . . went. Excuse me.' They watched him go to a tray of bottles and glasses on a low table, pour himself a drink and swallow it in one.

'You and Mrs Flynn supported his decision to do what he was doing?'

'Yes. Matthew had to make his own life in his own way.'

Watts continued his note-taking. From his early impression of Flynn, this acceptance of his younger son's choices came as a surprise. 'Matthew wasn't part of the "heated discussion" you mentioned?'

Flynn turned, stared at Watts. 'If you're looking at this family for an explanation of why Matthew decided to leave it, you're looking in the wrong place.'

Watts arranged his face into an expression intended to sooth. Obviously, Flynn's view was that Matthew had disappeared by choice. He might have done. But whatever he'd had planned back then, he hadn't had long to enjoy it. Chong's view was that his body was placed inside the crypt not long after he disappeared. Not scientific but as a guide it was the best they had.

'What about Matthew's belongings, sir?' asked Corrigan. 'Are they here?'

Flynn stood, turned to him, four-square and Watts felt his own muscles involuntarily tense. 'His belongings? There aren't any. Your records should tell you that he took his few clothes with him in a backpack when he left.'

True, thought Watts. But clothes didn't signify a life. 'What about the things he kept at the place where he lived? His books, computer, personal papers, all of that?'

Flynn gave him a steady look. 'There's a box here with a few papers in it. He took his laptop with him. He'd bought books for the course he didn't take up. His mother gave them to the university.'

Watts eyed him. 'I want that box, Mr Flynn.' He saw the first sign of weariness in Flynn and felt a surge of sympathy. Until he heard Flynn's next two words.

'You *people*.'

Watts's feelings were now on hold. He wanted to tell this man that *these* people had been working on his son's case from the early hours when his body was discovered, work which hadn't stopped. He'd read up on the family history: Mrs Flynn had been her husband's secretary from when he'd started his first business, bankrolled by his father to the tune of five hundred thousand on reaching his twenty-first birthday and which he'd developed over several years into what might now be described as a business empire. He glanced around the room. It whispered wealth. Watts recalled his occasional spats with Hanson when she first joined UCU. He hadn't immediately taken to her academic background and what he regarded as her posh southern accent. To him it said privilege. Her response had been that his chip was showing. 'You *people*.' The chip was back.

He chose his words. 'We'd be grateful if you'd let us have the box before we leave.' Somewhere just beyond the house there was the thrum of a powerful car then a short silence punctuated by a door slam.

'That'll be Dom,' said Flynn. 'I phoned him to say you were coming. He was out running.' The sound of a key in the front door was followed by footsteps across the wood floor of the hall. The sitting room door opened. If Watts and Corrigan hadn't known who this man was they would have guessed. He had the same dark hair and large features as his father, only the merest hint of his mother. Her small, regular features were visible on the remains now stored in the pathology suite's walk-in refrigerator. Dominic Flynn looked to be in his late twenties, possibly early thirties, muscular in running gear. Watts's attention was on his hair which was pulled back and secured behind his head.

'What's happened?' he asked. Flynn went and laid his hand

on his son's shoulder. Dominic Flynn didn't respond, his eyes fixed on Watts and Corrigan. 'Matthew?'

Watts nodded. 'Yes. We're very sorry.'

Now he looked at his father. 'Where's Mom?'

'She's upstairs.' He watched his son head for the door. '*Leave her.*'

Dominic was still on the move. 'I'm fetching the dog in.'

'No! Leave it in the car. These officers need our help. They want information about Matthew.'

Dominic Flynn turned, took a few steps closer. 'You don't say?'

Picking up more than a hint of antagonism, Watts gave him a direct look. 'We need to know everything about your brother's life. What he was doing around the time he disappeared. Who he was friendly with. Who he was seeing.'

Dominic held Watts's look. 'Matthew and I didn't spend a lot of time together. Now I've got a question for you: why weren't the police interested in my calls to check on progress after he disappeared? Or the time I reported him having trouble with a couple of local thugs?'

'Stop it, Dom,' said Flynn.

Watts had seen a report in the case file of harassment of Matthew made by Dominic Flynn following his brother's disappearance. The report described the information he had provided as 'brief and undetailed second-hand knowledge' relating to three incidents which had occurred in the area where Matthew was living at the time. The report also indicated subsequent inquiries by the local force but nothing substantive coming to light.

'It was investigated,' said Watts.

The sitting room door swung slowly open. Watts and Corrigan got to their feet.

The woman in the doorway gestured them back to their seats. They'd seen Diana Flynn only briefly before she'd become upset and left the room. Watts was no good on women's ages but now he guessed she was of similar age to her husband, mid-forties. She looked good in the figure-skimming pale grey dress, blonde hair well groomed. Her face told a different story. Efforts had been made to reduce the effects of crying but they were still there. Flynn went to her. 'I've told these officers we'll answer their questions now.' He ignored Dominic's snort.

Diana Flynn pulled her hand from her husband's and sat, her face turned to Watts. He listened to subdued words from which the Birmingham accent had been smoothed away. Almost. 'I'm sorry about earlier. It's just that the thoughts in my head are just too awful to think about.' She looked down at her hands gripped together in her lap. Diamonds flashed in the room's low lighting.

Corrigan spoke. 'Ma'am, if you feel able to talk to us, we'd appreciate any details you have of Matthew's social life, his friends, work colleagues and anything else you can tell us about him and what he was doing prior to his disappearance.'

She nodded, drawing herself upright. 'As far as I know, most if not all of Matthew's friends were people he worked with at the various places the agency sent him. Do you want the agency details?' Getting a nod from Corrigan she got up, went to a small desk, located a printed sheet after a search of its drawers and brought it to him. 'Most of the friends he had from when he was at school had gone to university so they were no longer around. I think Matthew found that hard to deal with but he was a real people person and he enjoyed working in the coffee shops.' She paused, bringing her voice under control. 'It didn't pay much but he was happy. He said he didn't want the kind of work which carried a lot of responsibility.'

Watts shot quick glances at Flynn and the elder son. Both were staring straight ahead, their faces closed. Diana Flynn continued. 'My two boys were very different. Dominic was always robust and Matthew didn't have his intellect but he was a sweet boy.' She looked away from her husband as he spoke.

'Dom thrives on business. He's willing to put in the hours, upskill himself where needed. I spent more time with Dom than I did with Matthew. I had to. I knew he had what it took to succeed in business, grasp opportunities, become my full partner.'

Dominic stared out of the window. 'Eventually.'

'Not the time or the place,' snapped Flynn. He paused. 'The boys were always poles apart in temperament. Matthew was never interested in business so I didn't force it on him.'

Corrigan looked to Diana Flynn. 'Ma'am, can you add anything about Matthew's life away from his work?'

She shook her head. 'No. Young people like to do their own thing, don't they? I didn't ask questions.'

'How about you, Mr Flynn? Can you tell us anything about Matthew's social life?'

'My wife's just told you all we know.'

Feeling Corrigan's eyes on him, Dominic Flynn looked up. 'There was nearly eleven years between Matthew and me so we didn't have that much in common.'

Corrigan transferred his attention back to Diana Flynn. 'Matthew was working for low pay, yet he was able to live independently?'

Dom Flynn glared at him with a muttered, 'Bloody cheek.'

His mother gave him a look then up at Corrigan. 'Matthew was living rent-free in a house we own.' She hesitated. 'The area is a little . . . urban, but it was convenient for Matthew to travel into the city. Most of his jobs were in the Bull Ring or close to it.'

'Did he live there alone?'

'No. He had two housemates. They're still there.' She gave details which matched what Corrigan had already seen in the file. 'Did he have his own transportation, ma'am?'

'No.' Brad Flynn spoke. 'I offered to give him a car. He refused. He said public transport was good between where he was living and working. He didn't want the hassle and cost of parking in the city centre.'

Diana Flynn looked at both officers. 'Matthew never gave us a moment's worry. He was a sensible, good boy. Rather conventional for his age.'

Watts's eyes narrowed. Corrigan nodded. 'Were you surprised when he got his tattoo?'

All three stared at him. 'His *what*?' demanded Brad Flynn. 'Matthew didn't have a bloody tattoo.'

Mrs Flynn was on her feet, staring at her husband, her eyes huge. 'I *knew* it. I told you this was all wrong. It's all some ghastly mistake. They've got the wrong person!' She whirled on them, the atmosphere in the room charged. 'Whoever you've found, it's *not* my Matthew.'

Corrigan spoke, his tone measured. 'I'm sorry, ma'am, but we wouldn't have brought you such terrible news without a DNA match.'

She stared at him for several seconds then sank down onto her chair.

Watts diverted his attention to Dominic Flynn. 'What can you tell us about the two individuals who were causing problems for your brother near where he lived?'

There was a brief silence as Dominic appeared to gather his thoughts. 'The first incident Matt told me about was when they knocked him down and stole his bag.'

'He didn't report it?'

'No, and by the time he told me about it there was no point me doing so.'

'Why do you think your brother didn't report it?' asked Watts.

'He probably also thought there was no point.'

'What else?'

Dominic's eyes moved between Watts and Corrigan. 'He told me about a couple more incidents after that, involving the same two people.'

'And?' prompted Corrigan.

He shrugged. 'They just appeared. Coming along the street. They shoved him around. Demanded money. The third time they hit him around the head as they walked past.'

Watts looked up from his note-taking. 'The same individuals each time, you say?'

'That's what Matt told me.'

'This incident when they took his bag. Any money in it?'

He shrugged again. 'Matt said not.'

Watts studied his notes. 'Did they get any money during the incident when they shoved him around?'

'I'm not sure. I don't think so.'

'Your brother definitely confirmed it was the same two individuals each time?'

'That's what he said.'

'Did he give you a description?'

Dominic nodded. 'Around eighteen. White. Baseball caps, low-slung jeans. Look, the police know all of this—'

'And your brother didn't report any of the incidents,' said Watts.

Dominic Flynn gave him a cold look. 'I just told you he didn't. Maybe he didn't bother because nothing was taken.'

Watts eyed him. 'What about his bag?'

Dominic was looking impatient now. 'He told me there was nothing of value in it. He probably knew the police wouldn't be interested.'

Watts let the comment go. 'Did your brother offer any reason as to why these two individuals would victimise him three times?'

'No.'

'Do you have any ideas about that?'

Dominic gave him an angry look. 'Do lowlife like that need a reason? This is my kid brother we're talking about. Only twenty years old. He hadn't done anything with his life, yet you're making it sound as though it was his fault!'

'Cool it, Dom.' Brad Flynn glared at him then looked at Watts and Corrigan. 'You'll have to excuse him. He and Matthew were very close despite the age difference and Dom's been working hard this last few months. The employment and training agency I own is his pet project.'

'*Business*, Dad.'

Flynn turned to his wife. 'I need to get moving. I've got a meeting in an hour so I need to eat.'

She stared up at him, eyes wide. 'You're going out again? After what we've just been told?'

'Just make me something simple.'

'Surely you don't have to go?'

He gave her a direct look, his tone flat. 'You're not listening to me, Diana. I need to eat before I leave. I won't get a chance later. Just see to it. Like I said, something simple.'

Watts glanced at Corrigan and they stood. 'Thank you for your time. We appreciate it. We'll be in touch.' On their way to the door, Watts turned, anticipating that the question in his head might worsen the tension here. It had to be raised. 'We understand that Matthew was given a caution for drug possession when he was fifteen. I'm asking about it in case it has a bearing on what happened to him.'

Brad Flynn shrugged. 'I don't see how. It was five years ago. Just youthful curiosity. It was nothing.'

Diana Flynn nodded agreement. 'Many youngsters dabble, experiment, which is what Matthew did. He never bothered again.'

Her husband looked at her. 'Diana? Food?' Then to Watts. 'I'll fetch that box you want.'

All four of them left the room, Watts and Corrigan continuing on to the front door.

Back in UCU in the relative evening-quiet of headquarters Watts was looking at the case file. He tapped his pen as Corrigan brought coffee to the table. 'It says here the last time the family saw Matthew was on the Wednesday for a family dinner, like Flynn told us.' He gripped one of many Post-its and turned to another page. 'And by the following Tuesday, mid-morning, this agency Matthew was working for is on the phone to his parents' house because they can't raise him on his mobile, wanting to know why he hadn't shown up at work the previous day and' – another page-turn – 'by the end of that week he was officially reported missing.' He frowned at Corrigan. 'His mother wasn't able to contact him either. What happened to his phone? Did these two types Dominic Flynn reported take it? Surely a young bloke like Matthew would have reported the theft of a phone?' He sighed, shook his head. 'By the time it was real-ised that Matthew had gone, it was regarded as a twenty-year-old employed male with money and the freedom to do what he wanted doing exactly that.'

Corrigan read the information on the complaints over Watts's shoulder. 'I'm looking for indications of the motivation of the two guys who harassed him. Three incidents suggests they were local to where Matthew was living.' He pointed. 'The first and second incidents were in the evening, after which they targeted him again, this time in daylight. That was a helluva risk to take. Matthew could have identified them.'

'But he never reported any of it,' said Watts. 'I'm wondering why he didn't.'

Corrigan was at the board, looking up at Matthew Flynn smiling out of it. 'Why did he hide money inside his boot?' He shook his head and came back to the table. 'It would be easier to understand if his two attackers believed he was in some way a vulnerable individual. Yet Matthew Flynn was anything but: he was a good-looking, twenty-year-old guy, smart enough to get a university place.'

Watts gulped coffee and shrugged. 'Maybe they knew him. Knew something about him.'

'Like what?' asked Corrigan.

'Like I said, there's a possible drugs angle here. Maybe he owed them.' Watts dropped his pen onto the table and rubbed his face with both hands. 'This "maybe" phase of an investigation gets me down.' He looked at the information spread on the table, then up at Corrigan. 'I don't recall anybody mentioning that Matthew Flynn had a girlfriend, do you?'

'Nope.' Corrigan studied his colleague's pensive expression and gave a quick headshake. 'If I'm onto your line of thinking here, you're way out of time, my friend. It's all 'Out-and-Proud' now. A lot of that bad hassle has gone.'

Watts returned his look. '*That*, Corrigan, depends on where you live. I want to know a lot more about these two street types and I've got somebody in mind who might help. While I do that, how'd you fancy a trip to church early tomorrow morning? More up your street than mine.'

'I can do that,' said Corrigan. 'What did you think of the parents?'

'The mother seems like a nice woman.'

'What about the father?'

'A man who knows what he wants and gets it,' said Watts. 'Came across as on the controlling side to me.'

Corrigan gave a slow nod. 'You mean his demand that Mrs Flynn fix him something to eat straight after being told their son was dead. I thought the same but it could have been the stress of the moment: folks can say and do some odd things at those times.'

Watts stared at the details on the Smartboard then across at Corrigan. 'On the other hand, a willingness to push people around could explain how he comes to be where he is: head of a business empire worth a few million.'

Corrigan moved to the desktop and opened databases. After a few minutes' search he turned to Watts with a headshake. 'No allegations of violence, domestic or otherwise against Brad Flynn.'

Watts nodded at the box they'd brought back from the Flynn house which Corrigan had gone through. 'Anything useful?'

'Some timesheets and other stuff relating to his agency job is all. If there ever was anything, you can bet it was inside his long-gone laptop.'

SIX

The door of Church House swung wide, the huge man who had responded to Corrigan's ring seeming to fill the space. Smiling, he waved him inside and reached out his hand.

'I'm Father Delaney. Lieutenant Corrigan, I assume?'

Corrigan took the soft, plump hand in his. 'I appreciate your time, father.'

Delaney inclined his head. 'Come inside. We'll use my study.'

Corrigan followed him across a wide hall, stairs directly ahead and along a dark passageway into a square, high-ceilinged room.

'Have a seat,' said Delaney going to the high-backed chair at the desk and settling himself down. 'I was just putting the final touches to a sermon. I can't offer you anything because my housekeeper hasn't arrived yet.'

'That's not a problem, sir.'

Delaney smiled again. With his fleshy face and light brown curly hair he had the look of a massive cherub. He folded thick arms over his wide frontage, looking conspiratorial. 'You're *American*.'

'Yes, sir. From Boston.'

Delaney's face was rapturous. 'What a wonderful city! I was there, you know. Many years ago, of course. Before I came here.' He gave Corrigan some good-natured scrutiny. 'I assume you're familiar with churches like mine and that you're not here for my theological background. You've come to tell me what occurred here the other night. Or should that be early yesterday morning?'

'An attempt was made to break into the church,' said Corrigan. 'We don't have any information about whoever was responsible although we believe there were two of them.'

Delaney gave a slow headshake. 'Thank goodness it was only an attempt. St Bartholomew's has many fine items of brassware and other artefacts.' He looked up at Corrigan. 'But didn't I see officers and other people in and out of the crypt?'

'A second attempt was made via the crypt.'

Delaney's face relaxed. 'They couldn't have got into the main building that way. When the church was built at the beginning of the 1900s there was some structural difficulty in providing access from it to the church proper. Don't ask me what that was. I have no idea.' He paused. 'From what you say it sounds as though they were very determined to get inside.'

'A body has been found inside the crypt, sir.'

Delaney came bolt upright, cheeks quivering. 'What! But that's impossible. The crypt has never been used to my knowledge. It was planned as a final resting place for the wife of the industrialist who funded the building of St Bartholomew's. He died first and his wife had him buried here in our churchyard. Records don't show what happened to her. As I said, you can't reach the crypt from inside the church so it had no function.' He glanced at Corrigan, looking flustered. 'You did say a *body*?'

'Yes, sir.'

Delaney stood and went to a bookshelf, reached up to a high shelf and brought down a bottle. He returned with it to the desk, took two glasses from a drawer and held one out towards Corrigan.

'No, thank you, sir.'

'I hope you don't mind if I do,' said Delaney, sitting heavily and pouring a generous measure of whisky. He lifted the glass and swallowed half of its contents. 'You'll have to excuse me. This is shocking news.' He met Corrigan's eyes. 'You're saying there was a falling-out among thieves and one of them killed the other?'

'No, sir. It seems the body could have been there for up to a year.'

Delaney stared at him, mouth agape. 'But . . .? That's not . . .? How did whoever put it there get it inside? Why would anybody leave a body down there?'

Corrigan did not respond with the most obvious answer: concealment. He watched Delaney drink more whisky, seeing his thought processes playing catch-up.

'I suppose it would be a good hiding place but there have

been no previous reports of damage to the crypt door. I certainly don't recall any in the years I've been here.'

'We have similar questions to yours, sir, and we'll be looking for answers.' Corrigan took out his notebook.

Delaney drew a hand across his forehead, gave his head a quick shake. 'Yes, of course. My apologies for being so slow, lieutenant. Please continue.'

'We know the victim's identity. His name was Matthew Flynn. Twenty years old. He lived in the Erdington area of the city. Is any of that information familiar to you?'

Delaney shook his head. 'No. None of it.'

Corrigan took a photograph from his inside pocket and held it out to him. 'This was Matthew Flynn.'

Delaney took it, looked at it, some colour returning to his face. 'So young,' he whispered, handing it back. 'I'm sorry. I've never seen him.'

'When Detective Sergeant Watts and I saw you last night, you made a reference to "vandalism". We need to know what that's about, sir.'

Delaney slow-nodded. 'I thought that was why you were here. That you'd received a report of more vandalism in progress. We're a thriving community here at St Bartholomew's with a large congregation compared to many churches in the city, but we've had our share of destructive behaviour.' Corrigan waited for more. 'Four incidents over the last eight months or so. A couple of windows broken, fortunately not stained glass – they cost thousands to repair. Graffiti on some of the headstones between this house and the church. By far the worst incident was an attack on the main door of the church: a pentagram, a circle enclosing a five-point design executed in red paint. It made a terrible mess of the door and the flagstones leading up to it – drips everywhere.' Delaney's mouth tightened, his face registering prim disapproval. 'We scrubbed off what we could, then got a firm in to remove it completely in case it encouraged similar incidents from whoever was responsible.' He hesitated. 'There were one or two other . . . occurrences. Members of the congregation here on church business reporting seeing one or two young people loitering around the grounds.' He looked at Corrigan. 'They couldn't give any useful details and this is a public space after all. People can cross it for legitimate reasons so I personally did not set much store by the sightings, but they were unnerving for our older members in particular.'

'Did you report the incidents of vandalism?'

Delaney shook his head. 'No. It was discussed in committee but one of my deacons advised that there was little point in doing so because the vandalism was inevitably the work of very young people whom the police would struggle to identify and apprehend. After all, they did occur over a fairly protracted period of time.'

Corrigan wrote quickly. 'Always best to report every incident in case they escalate.'

'Yes. I see that now.' Corrigan finished writing and looked up at him. 'You said you've been here twenty years.'

Delaney swallowed more malt. 'Around that, yes.'

'The crypt door has a keyhole.' Corrigan watched the plump face change as he got the inference.

'Surely you're not suspecting what you'd call an "inside job"? If there ever was a key I never saw it.' Delaney frowned. 'I thought you said the burglars forced the door?'

Corrigan gave him a steady look. 'I'm referring to a year ago when Matthew Flynn's body was placed there.'

Delaney shook his head, looking drained. 'Please forgive me, lieutenant. This is all very shocking and confusing.'

Corrigan nodded understanding. 'Sir, if there's been no historical damage to the door then whoever took Matthew Flynn's body into the crypt twelve months or so ago would have needed the key.'

'This is dreadful,' whispered Delaney. 'I shall have to inform the bishop!'

'Earlier, you mentioned St Bartholomew's being a large church. You don't work alone here?'

With visible effort Delaney brought his attention back to the question. 'No. I have two deacons: Deacon Richard Burns and Deacon Jeremy Fellowes. Feel free to talk to both of them, although Burns is away right now, on retreat. Has been for the last three weeks. There's also a committee made up of several members of the congregation who help to maintain the grounds, the church interior and assist in other ways, such as playing the organ. The usual chores a church like ours depends on volunteers to perform.'

He gave a handful of names, watched Corrigan note them then get to his feet. He did the same and they walked from the room, the priest looking preoccupied. 'Since the vandalism, particularly the one featuring the pentagram, some of our congregation have been pressing for a service of re-consecration. Now that this dreadful event has occurred I shall have to give it some serious consideration. When one has ministered as long as I have, lieutenant, one has heard terrible things and seen their impact. Which makes our work, yours and mine, very similar, wouldn't you say?' He accompanied Corrigan to the front door. 'St Bartholomew's will support the police in any way it can. This awful business is a coach and horses through our quiet orderly community. I trust you'll keep us updated on the investigation.' He held out his hand. 'Are you married, Lieutenant Corrigan?'

Corrigan took the hand. 'No. Why do you ask?'

'I was thinking of myself two decades ago, alone in Boston because of my calling and now you're here, also alone. Please bear in mind that St Bartholomew's is open to all, member or not.'

Corrigan inclined his head and walked away from him to the veranda steps. 'Thank you for your time, father.'

SEVEN

Watts moved along Erdington High Street, his eyes scanning passing faces. Far ahead he saw the one he was searching for coming in his direction. This was no coincidental meeting. He knew that the individual in his sights was on his way to a meeting with his probation officer. Swerving across the pavement, causing an irritable tut from a shopper close behind him, Watts ducked into a narrow alley between two shops and waited. As soon as the peak of the red-and-black baseball cap appeared, he reached out and grabbed its owner's arm, pulling the rest of him into the alley and shoving him against the wall.

'What the—!' Equal measures of shock and anger in the pinched face leached away, replaced by a look of sulky resignation. 'Wha' do *you* want?'

'Just a little chat, Desmond, m'boy.' His big hand gripped the front of the Puffa jacket. 'How about you and me move down here where it's nice and quiet, yeah?' Watts walked the youth backwards until they reached the end of the alley and he was against the chain-link fence. 'OK, Desmond. I need your expertise.'

'What you on about?'

'I'll put it another way. I want to run something by you and you as an expert in mugging are going to tell me what you think.'

'I don't do that no more . . .'

'Course you don't. This is a hypothetical little chat.'

Desmond looked resigned. 'Just tell me what you're after. I've got to be somewhere.'

Watts stared down at the narrow, closed face. 'Picture this: a kid of around eighteen or so walks along a street, a bit like the one I've just dragged you off, now that I think about it. He's minding his own business and *wham*!' Desmond flinched. 'Two other kids start to have a go at him. Before this kid knows what's happening, he's on the floor and his bag has gone—'

'It wasn't me!'

Watts shook him by the jacket. 'Now, *that's* your trouble, Desmond, lad. You don't listen. I haven't told you the whole story. OK, he's on the floor, bag gone. The next time he's out and about the same two kids stop him, only this time they demand money, but he hasn't got any. Fast forward to the next time. It's broad daylight. They hit him around the head and walk on.' He kept his voice low. 'Tell me what you make of that?'

Desmond looked along the alley then up at Watts. 'The only reason I'm saying anything to you is because you was good to our old lady in court that time, but I don't owe you nothing, right?'

'The cold's getting to me. Spit it out!'

'All right, keep your hair on.' He adjusted the Puffa as Watts released it. 'Sounds to me like a pair of amateurs. Everybody's got some money. Or cards. If you're recognised in this game – not that I'm in the game no more,' he added hastily, 'you'll have the filth at your door in no time. No offence.'

'None taken. Targeting a mark more than once isn't something you'd do?'

Desmond grinned, exposing teeth in need of a brush. 'Leave it out. It's brainless, that is, going after the same person, although . . .'

'I'm all ears, Desmond.'

'Maybe they thought this kid you're on about was an easy mark?'

The tattoo parlour closest to where Matthew Flynn had lived and which Hanson had tried to contact by phone had a closed sign on its door and a heap of dusty-looking mail lying on the floor inside. She continued along the street in mid-morning chill to the second on her list, a single-storey premises which she couldn't have missed even if she hadn't done her research. Its frontage was painted neon red, its name scrolled across the plate glass window in black: 'Tattoo Inc.', above a stylised skull. She pushed open the door.

Inside she found some of the features she had anticipated. The walls were covered in photographic examples of the tattooist's art, the place itself equipped with angled lamps and reclining chairs, plus a padded table currently occupied. Surprised at the space and the level of daylight streaming inside, she went further, looked up at a wide lantern ceiling, then down to a pristine black and chrome Harley Davidson on a stand. A talking-point ornamentation, rather than a bike in use?

'Can I help?'

Hanson turned. A woman with short green hair was looking up at her, a fleshy-looking male, face down on the table, his back bared beneath her gloved hands. Hanson held out her headquarters identification. 'I'd like to speak to the proprietor, please.'

'Hang on.' She turned her head towards a door at the far end. 'Fat Mack!'

Hanson thought she heard a low-level response. 'There's a lady here to see you!' The door opened and an averagely built man in his forties with shoulder-length hair and a beard came through it.

He approached Hanson looking amiable. 'Morning. What would you like?'

She showed him her identification. 'Information, please.'

He folded thick forearms, neither of them skin-coloured, and frowned. 'What about?'

'Have you done a tattoo like this for anyone in the last year?' She held up Chong's photograph of the inverted crucifix on Matthew Flynn's neck.

The green-haired woman also looked at it. They both shrugged. 'It's not that clear, but probably,' he said. 'A stock theme, that is.' He walked over to the wall of photographs. Hanson followed, optimism slipping. 'See?' He pointed to one of a disembodied upper arm bearing an inverted crucifix very much like the one in Chong's photograph. 'Trends come and go in this game. Inverted crucifixes are popular with some, but a bit "niche". He pointed at the photograph on the wall. 'Now, if they were really popular this photo would be nearer the door.' Hanson waited. He gave her a patient look. 'So clients with no ideas of their own would see it as they come in,' he said, in the manner of a teacher to a not-very-bright pupil. 'It's that or have them buggering about for an hour trying to make up their minds what to have.' The green-haired woman laughed.

Hanson followed him to one of the black reclining chairs where he sat. 'How many of these crucifixes have you or your colleague done in the last say eighteen months?'

'Difficult to say.' He gazed across at the green-haired woman's intent activity which looked to Hanson to be both meticulous and exacting as far as she could judge. Fat Mack caught her look. 'Sandy here specialises in artwork. See?' He pointed to the half-completed head and shoulders. Another quick glance at the customer's fleshy back and Hanson picked up an inked face which only a mother could love, plus elongated fingers. The customer beneath it twitched and grunted.

'That's Sandy's particular speciality: Freddy.'

'Who?'

'*Nightmare on Elm Street*. Look at the skill in that.' He stared at it, shaking his head.

'Mr . . .?'

'Fat Mack.'

'. . . Yes. Are inverted crucifixes regarded as artwork?'

He looked scornful. 'No. A one-session job, depending on the size. Thinking about it, I'd say I've done no more than half a dozen in the last eighteen months or so. Like I said, they're niche.' The man enduring Freddy was now grunting at regular intervals.

'Meaning?'

Fat Mack was back in teacher-mode. 'It's like this. You've got your Goths, your Satanists, even your heavy metal fanatics. They're into the inverted cross because it's two fingers at what they see as established society. It's a defiance thing. Now, for some others it's also a bit pagan. The ones who fancy themselves as a bit edgy, a little bit on the "dark side".'

None of this sounded to Hanson like it applied to Matthew Flynn. She pressed on, holding up the photograph Chong had given her. 'Does this look like your work?'

He gave her a long look then took it. 'Hard to say. The skin round it looks funny.' He gave her a sudden, direct look. 'This isn't about somebody who reckons he got an infection?'

'No. Did you do this?'

He examined the tattoo in the photograph, pursing his lips. 'Like I said, it's hard to say. It's not as sharp as I'd have expected.' He passed it back to her. 'It's possible it's one of mine. It's got the small embellishments I often use.'

She reached inside her bag again, tension climbing. 'Would you take a look at this photograph and tell me if you've ever seen this man?'

He took it from her and stared for several seconds at Matthew Flynn's face in life. 'I look at faces if that's where the tattoo is going, but mostly I look at body parts.' Hanson waited. 'Arms, legs, hands, torsos. I can tell a lot about a person from them. Take you, for example.' She narrowed her eyes at him as he continued, pointing at her hands. 'They say a lot about a person. Yours are telling me you don't do a lot of manual stuff.' *Clever, seeing that I'm five-three and you know from my ID what I do for a living.* She reached for the photograph. He pulled it away. 'Hang *on*, give us a chance.' Hanson waited, impatient, beginning to suspect she was being messed around.

'It's him.'

She stared up at him. 'What? Who?'

Fat Mack held the photograph towards the green-haired woman. 'See this?'

She looked up from her client's meaty back. 'Yeah. Looks like him.'

Hanson looked from one to the other. 'You're confirming that this man was here?'

He nodded. 'A good few months ago. Around last autumn at a guess. It was just before I went on holiday to Marbella. I remember him now because of how he was, all twitchy and het up.' Hanson frowned. He gave her a sage nod. 'Tattoo virgins are like that. Probably why he brought his mate with him.'

Hanson deep-breathed. 'He came here with someone?'

He passed Flynn's photograph back to her. 'Yeah. A kid of about the same age. Now *he* was no virgin. He already had an inverted crucifix on his neck.'

'Tell me more about the one who came to get the tattoo,' persisted Hanson.

The man getting the Freddy emitted a deep grunt. Fat Mack gave her a direct look. 'You don't let up, do you? All I remember is that he was young with dark hair, like his photo. Nothing else stood out.'

'He and his companion spoke to each other?'

'Course they did. The one who came with him was being reassuring, like. Telling him it was painless.'

'What else?'

'Give us a chance to think.' There was a brief pause. 'The one in your photo listens to what his mate has to say. He's still nervous, worried like, but now he wants it done, pronto. He even refuses a skin test. You're sure this isn't about an infection, because if—?'

'Do you remember anything that was said between them?'

'No. They stood close together and his mate did the talking. After that he was as good as gold while I did it. When I finished I gave him the usual aftercare instructions, took the money and he was all smiles. Well, more cheerful than when they came in. He seemed like a nice kid. He thanked his mate for coming with him.'

'What specific words did he use?'

Fat Mack gave her another long look. 'You are joking.'

Hanson frowned. 'Have you got any record of exactly when this happened? A receipt?'

His eyes slid away. 'I'm not that good at keeping records but I remember he called his mate by name.'

It was Hanson's turn to give a long look. 'You remember *that* from a year ago.'

'For one reason. It's the same as my son's: Callum.'

'Any surname?'

'No.' He walked her to the door and held it open for her. 'Have a card.' He handed it to her. 'I could do you a butterfly. Very popular on the shoulder, they are. Or how about a nice mouse?'

Two minutes later Hanson was heading inside the public car park when she was halted by a shout.

'Doc!'

She waited for Watts to catch up. 'How'd you get on with the "type" you came to see? Did you find him?'

'Yeah,' he said, breathing hard. 'I described the three assaults on Flynn. His opinion was they were amateurs because of the risk involved. He also suggested the same as Corrigan: they might have victimised Flynn because they thought he was an easy mark. How about you?'

'I've been to the tattoo parlour down the road. It's where Matthew Flynn got his inverted crucifix done. He had a friend with him. Somebody named Callum, no surname.'

'Good going. That's something to follow up. All leads welcome right now.' They walked into the car park together. 'You going to headquarters?'

'Briefly.'

He headed for the Range Rover parked nearby, looking upbeat. 'We might be seeing a bit of movement in this case.'

Hanson was waiting on the phone, watching her two colleagues entering data into the Smartboard. 'That about covers it for me,' said Corrigan. 'Delaney didn't recognise Matthew Flynn's name. His church has been targeted by vandals in the last year or so, the most recent damage being satanic in nature. Security is a little lax there which helped those two guys get inside the crypt. Looks like they were hoping for access to the church itself.'

Watts pointed at the board. 'We need to follow up Matthew Flynn being victimised because a couple of types reckoned he was some kind of vulnerable misfit. Problem is, we don't know what kind. According to what you were told, doc, Satanists and a few other fringe types like inverted crosses. Maybe he was seen with it and it got him killed. But, first thing we do is follow up this mate Callum he had with him.' He waited for Hanson as she replaced the phone. 'What's Mrs Flynn have to say?'

'She doesn't recognise the name Callum. She's confirmed that she and the family knew nothing of Matthew having a tattoo.' She gazed at the board. 'I'm wondering why they didn't know about it. See it.'

'Maybe he kept it covered to avoid upsetting his mother,' suggested Corrigan. 'That, or he didn't get the tattoo until after they last saw him.'

She looked at the phone, contemplating a call to the tattoo parlour but dismissed it. Fat Mack had told her it was around October last year. Without any sales records it was unlikely he could or would be more precise.

Watts pointed to the notes he'd just added on Brad Flynn: confident. In charge. In control. 'Anything you want to add about him, Corrigan?'

'What you've got about covers it. Flynn is the type who assumes he's in charge, whatever the situation.' He turned to Hanson. 'Right after we delivered the news about Matthew's death, he was preparing to leave for a business meeting.' Watts grunted. 'Suppose it fits with him being one of these entrepreneurial types. A workaholic. The other son came across as the same.'

Hanson had her own opinion of what she'd just heard. Brad Flynn sounded like an alpha male. Her colleagues' description of him as tall and good-looking added to it. She gave Corrigan a fleeting glance. Tall. Good looking. Deep voice. Alpha males tended to have more sexual partners. More affairs. She'd never known Corrigan seek to dominate situations, but . . . But.

'You all right, doc?'

'Fine. What's this about Flynn being a "controller"?'

'He told his wife to make him something to eat before he left,' said Corrigan. 'Dominic Flynn presents as a similar character although I'm not sure how deep it goes, but he sure as hell didn't like his father referring to the business he runs as his "pet project".'

Hanson gazed at the board. 'The two Flynn males sound like strong characters. Not like Matthew. Or, rather my impression of him.'

Watts flipped shut his notebook and dropped it onto the table. 'We've talked to those closest to him. They didn't have much to tell us about his friends or anything else for that matter. It's time to start working outwards.'

The door opened and Chong came inside. 'I've got a hit-and-run fatality waiting for me and two minutes to give you the results of the blood test on Matthew Flynn's clothes. Forget any hopes of a DNA identification of his killer. I've tested every item of his clothing for blood which isn't his. There is none. Not on the overcoat, the jeans, the boots or anything else he was wearing. His killer got lucky. He didn't injure himself when he ripped out Matthew Flynn's throat.'

'What about his scarf?' asked Hanson.

Chong turned, halfway to the door. 'No blood on that either.'

Hanson stared after her. 'None at all?'

'Not a trace.' She was gone, leaving Hanson still staring.

'That's odd.' She looked at her two colleagues. 'Has the Flynn family specifically identified the scarf found on the body as belonging to Matthew?'

Corrigan churned A4s on the table and held up a list. 'Mrs Flynn referred to all clothing items listed as Matthew's. Both the brother, Dominic, and Mr Flynn were a "couldn't say".'

She took the sheet from him, read it then reached for the phone.

'What you up to?' asked Watts.

'I'm going to read the description of the scarf to Mrs Flynn. I want her categorical confirmation that it belonged to Matthew.'

Watts glanced ceiling-ward. 'Doc, if there was a national award for determination in following up every angle, nobody else would stand a chance against you.'

He and Corrigan listened to Hanson's half of the conversation. 'Yes. A long cashmere scarf with a blue-and-green zigzag pattern.' There was a pause then: 'Thank you very much, Mrs Flynn. I apologise for ringing you at a time like this.' She replaced the phone. 'She's categorical that the scarf belonged to Matthew. It was a birthday present from her and her husband.' She raked back her hair with both hands and looked down at her notes. 'That makes no sense to me. That he sustained such a terrible injury to his throat yet the scarf he was wearing wasn't bloodstained.'

'He could've taken it off before he was killed,' said Watts. 'And afterwards, whoever killed him put it back on him.'

'Why?'

He shrugged. 'To make certain that when he was put into that crypt, everything of his was with him and not lying around somewhere and needing disposal.'

She was silent for a moment. 'My impression from what we've got is that the Flynn family wasn't all that aware of what was happening in the life of its youngest son. Is that how you see it?'

'Yeah,' said Watts. 'But that's not so unusual when kids don't live at home anymore.' Hanson thought of Maisie. *Still living at home but do I know what's going on with her?* She re-tuned to Watts's voice. 'They saw him, what, once a week? I remember my daughter leaving home for university. OK, Oxford was a bigger move than the one Matthew Flynn made but it's the leaving, not the number of miles. After she went there I never had much of a clue what she was up to, although her mother probably knew more. I never got told much and I didn't delve. University life was a mystery to me and it mostly stayed that way.' He glanced at Hanson. 'I know more now but back then Oxford was about as familiar as the moon. It wasn't until the day we took her to her college that I realised there was more than one.' He looked across the table. 'How about you, Corrigan? Was your daughter a bit of a stranger when she was getting her independence?'

Corrigan nodded, chair on recline, his eyes on the written-up information. 'I guess. But somebody, somewhere, knows about Matthew Flynn and his life after he got his own place.'

Hanson stood, pushing her notebook into her bag. 'We need to talk to whoever knew Matthew on a daily basis, the people he lived and worked with in the months prior to his disappearance. If we don't yet have a list of them, we need one.'

'We're onto it, doc.'

Hanson glanced at her watch for the third time in as many minutes. Seven fifty-five. Maisie should have arrived home from her youth club twenty minutes ago. She looked again. Make that twenty-five minutes.

Charlie's voice drifted across the kitchen. 'Don't worry. She'll be here soon.' Charlie wasn't worried. Or he wasn't showing it. Either way, his reassurances weren't helping. She headed for her study.

Inside, she took her phone from her bag. Her call was picked up after three rings. 'Candice, it's Kate. I was starting to wonder what's delaying the girls.' There was a brief silence. 'Kate. I thought you knew. Chelsey was off-colour when she got home from school so she decided to give the club a miss. Maisie went without her, saying she would phone you.'

The words slammed into Hanson's ear. *Twenty minutes late, she's thirteen, it's dark, it's* . . . Candice's voice came again. 'Don't worry. The club probably over-ran again like it often does. She'll be home any time—'

The front door banging shut making Hanson flinch, triggering a rush of relief which made her head spin. 'It's OK, Candice. She's here. Sorry to have bothered you.'

Maisie was removing her boots as Hanson came out of her study. 'Hi, Mom . . . What's up?'

Hanson got her voice under control. 'You went on your own to the club.'

'Yeah. So? When I got to Chel's she was like, "I'm not coming, I feel bad".'

'You told Candice you would phone me. You didn't.'

Maisie looked up, exasperated. 'I *forgot*.'

Hanson did some deep breathing. 'What you should have

done is come back here and I'd have taken you, then picked you up.' She got a sulky look. 'If I had, I'd have been late getting there. I went to the club and I came back from the club without a problem. Just . . . calm down.'

'Do *not* tell me to calm down, Maisie. You're nearly half an hour late. You should have phoned me and you know it.'

They looked to where Charlie was standing at the kitchen door. 'Hello, Maisie.' He glanced at Kate. 'I'm making toast and a drink. Any takers?'

'Please.' Maisie made her escape, two stairs at a time. Hanson watched her go, telling herself that at thirteen Maisie needed to test her independence. *Which is fine. Except she doesn't know what I know about risk and depravity and . . .* She put a hand to her forehead. *She doesn't realise that one of my jobs is to make sure she never will.*

She wandered into the kitchen where Charlie was organising plates and mugs. 'Thanks. I know I over-react where Maisie's concerned but I need to feel I'm in control. That I'm doing all I can to keep her safe.'

He gave her arm a gentle squeeze. 'I know. Just go easy on the throttle.'

The doorbell rang and Hanson went to open it. It was Watts. 'Evening, doc. You all right?' He followed her towards the kitchen.

'Why wouldn't I be?' she snapped.

He gave her a mild glance. 'It's what we say around here.' He caricatured his own accent. 'You-alroight?'

She laughed, some of the tension draining. Charlie held up a cup to Watts.

'Don't mind if I do. Two sugars in mine, ta.' He reached inside his coat. 'Here you go, doc. The names of five one-time work mates of Matthew Flynn's who worked with him in a coffee shop in the Bull Ring. Can you pay 'em a visit when you can fit it in? Me and Corrigan are visiting some others he worked at around the city centre tomorrow morning.'

She took the details. 'I can do it tomorrow.' She looked across at him. 'How do you think the case is going so far?'

He shrugged. 'Early days, doc. Early days.'

*   *   *

At eleven thirty Hanson went upstairs. Reaching the landing she saw a seam of light under Charlie's door. She knocked gently. 'You OK, Charlie?' Getting a positive response she went inside. A couple of days before, she'd noticed his suitcase out of the wardrobe and standing in one corner. Now it was lying open on the wooden chest at the foot of his bed.

He tracked her eyes. 'I'm starting to get organised.'

'So I see.' She watched as he folded a sweater, added it to the suitcase and looked across at her.

'I need to think about going home.'

'No. You don't.' She bit her lip. *Throttle back.* 'You were quite ill during the summer, you know. You've only been here a few weeks and the doctor said—'

'You need your home back, Kate.'

'No, I don't.'

He came to her. 'Before it gets too comfortable here, I need to pick up my life again.' He smiled down at her then returned to the suitcase. She watched him add another item then turned away and headed for the door.

EIGHT

Following an early-morning progress session with her research students, Hanson left the university. Within the hour she was inside the Bull Ring shopping centre stirring coffee, her eyes on the five names Watts had given her the previous evening, four of them already crossed through. This was the coffee shop Matthew Flynn had worked in most regularly but those four employees had worked different shifts and couldn't comment on him. Which left just one. She checked the clock high on the wall then glanced towards the young woman serving drinks and snacks. She'd been helpful, although not directly in relation to Matthew. She'd started work here six months ago, her knowledge of Matthew Flynn confined to what she had picked up from colleagues' conversations since they learned of his disappearance and now the news of his murder. When she'd spoken to Hanson she'd mentioned one name.

'Terri Brennan's your one hope, I'd say. She worked the same shifts as Matthew. She's a bit older than the rest of us. I heard somebody say she was a sort of mother figure to him.'

Brennan's was the one remaining name on Hanson's list. Getting a subtle signal from behind the counter she looked towards the door. A woman of around Hanson's own age, mid-thirties, was coming inside. She watched as the two employees exchanged greetings, the one behind the counter pointing in Hanson's direction. The woman looked uneasy as she walked to where Hanson was sitting and took a seat across the table. 'I'm Terri Brennan. You want to talk to me?'

'Yes. About Matthew Flynn.'

'You're from the police?'

'Yes, I am.' Hanson pushed her card across the table. The woman looked at it. 'It was on the news this morning. It's a terrible thing to have happened to Matthew but it's over a year since I last saw him. I don't see how I can help you.'

Hanson kept it brief. 'I'd appreciate your talking to me about him.'

'What do you mean?'

'Tell me whatever you recall about Matthew as a person.'

'Like I said, it's a long time since I saw him.' She fell silent, appeared to be thinking. 'OK. What I most remember about him was the nice way he had.' She gave Hanson a direct look. 'I know that charm can mean a lot of different things, not all of them good, but with Matthew there was a quiet charm that was really nice. Really natural.'

'How did that show itself?'

Brennan gave the question some thought. 'It wasn't just that he was pleasant to work with. He was kind as well. He genuinely liked people. Cared about them.' She looked down at the table. 'I had some problems last year. Relationship problems and stuff, you know. Not that I told Matthew about those, but that's what I'm saying about him. He seemed to sense when something was wrong and he would kind of cheer me up. It was like he took an interest. Wanted to help if he could. He knew I was down and he wanted to make me feel better. He usually did, just by talking to me, making me laugh.' She fell silent for a few seconds. 'I remember that last day I saw him here. He was really upbeat.'

Hanson waited. 'Why was he upbeat? Did he tell you?' She pressed.

Brennan looked up. 'He showed me. He hadn't said he was getting a tattoo. I was surprised, I can tell you. Mr "Middle-of-the-Road", was Matthew.'

'After he disappeared, did the police come here?'

'A few days after, yes.'

Hanson made a quick note, thinking of Matthew's parents who seemed to know little about their son's life. 'Did you tell them about Matthew's tattoo?'

'They asked if I'd noticed any change in him prior to his going. I said he was the same as he always was. I'm not sure I mentioned the tattoo.'

'Do you remember what day it was when Matthew came in and showed you his tattoo?' asked Hanson.

Brennan nodded. 'That's easy. It was the Monday. He must have got it done over that weekend. He didn't arrive for his shift on the Thursday and that was it. I never saw him again. I wouldn't say it annoyed me exactly, but you get used to working with certain people, particularly if you get on well with them.' She looked down at the table. 'If I'm honest I suppose I was put out that he didn't confide in me that he was leaving. But then the months went by and I suppose I didn't think about him that much. Hearing what's actually happened to him is awful.' She looked away from Hanson. 'I feel guilty now that I didn't think about him more often.'

'What did you know about his background?'

Brennan looked uncertain. 'You mean his family? Nothing much. I got the idea they were well off but Matthew never actually said so. Just the odd comment here and there. He mentioned he had an older brother who worked with their father. He also mentioned the school he went to and I recognised the name. One of those private schools. I think he'd had the chance to go to university but he never talked about that either.'

Hanson knew she had to extend Brennan's thinking if at all possible. 'OK, Terri. If you had just four words to describe Matthew, what would they be?'

There was a short pause as Brennan gave it some thought. 'I'd say . . . kind, honest . . . brave and cheerful.'

Hanson looked up. 'Brave?'

She nodded. 'When Matthew and I were working together in the summer last year, a man came in. He obviously had some problems and he was starting to get a bit loud. Talking to himself, you know. This centre is massive but the security is really good. Each retail unit has its own silent alarm. Anyway, I was all for activating it but Matthew said no. He went and spoke to the man, calmed him down and he left without causing any more trouble.'

Hanson thought about it. Brave, possibly. Also ill-advised, if you don't know what you're dealing with. 'Any idea why Matthew chose to do that?'

'He said the man obviously had problems and he didn't want to give him more by calling security and maybe involving the police. Like I said, kind. Although, I did say to him afterwards that it probably wasn't a good idea to be kind all the time.' She looked at Hanson. 'That wasn't meant to sound critical of Matthew.'

Hanson's thinking was now in overdrive. 'What did this man look like?'

'All I remember is that he was tall, around five-ten, thin.'

'Neatly dressed? Scruffy?'

'Neither. Just ordinary. That's all I can say about him. He looked OK, else security would probably have picked up on him before he got this far into the centre.'

'Did you get any sense at all that Matthew knew this man?'

Brennan eyed her, clearly surprised. 'It never occurred to me. I don't think so. No. I'm sure he didn't.'

Hanson sighed inwardly. Just another sad, lonely individual drawn to the city centre. 'What about Matthew's social life?'

'I can't tell you much about that, except I don't think he was one for going out every night.'

'Did he mention the people he shared a house with?'

'Not that I recall.'

'Did he mention any particular friends?'

Brennan gave it some thought. 'The only name I remember him mentioning was Zach but I don't think he was a friend.'

'What makes you say that?' she prompted.

Brennan shrugged. 'It was just an impression I got. It seemed to me like he didn't like this Zach.'

Hanson made swift notes. For someone as personable as Brennan had indicated Matthew Flynn to be, he didn't appear to have a lot of social connections. She recalled the information from the tattoo parlour proprietor: Matthew had a friend with him when he got his tattoo.

'Did he ever mention someone named Callum?'

'No, never.'

'Would you describe Matthew as lonely at all?'

Brennan looked up, as though searching for words. 'I wouldn't say lonely. He had his family. He told me his father had wanted him to work with him in the family business like his brother, but he wouldn't. I got the idea that Matthew didn't have a lot in common with them but he never said so.'

'What about his mother?'

Brennan thought about it. 'He didn't say much about her either, except that she annoyed him sometimes.'

'Did he say how, why?'

'Nothing much, except once or twice he mentioned that she'd visited the house where he was living and brought flowers. He didn't like that.'

Hanson made another quick note. 'Did he say why?'

Brennan shook her head. 'No. Now I come to think about it, about Matthew being a bit lonely, it seemed to me he didn't have anybody close to him, know what I mean? That's why I was really pleased when he told me he'd met somebody.'

Brennan's last three words stopped Hanson's pen. She looked up, keeping her tone casual. 'Tell me.'

Brennan shrugged. 'Nothing much to tell. Matthew was private about himself, but I know he liked her a lot.'

'How do you know that?'

'He told me she was a special girl.' Brennan's bright smile disappeared. 'How sad is that, given what happened to him?'

'Did he mention her name?'

Hanson wrote down Brennan's one-word response.

Watts had phoned to say he and Corrigan were calling into the university on their way from the city centre to headquarters.

Hanson had been back ten minutes when they arrived, Watts looking vexed. 'We spoke to the manager of the agency which employed Matthew Flynn. They had next to no face-to-face dealings with him. All done by phone or online, but described him as honest and conscientious. Then we went to four places he worked semi-regularly. All we got was that he was quiet, did his job and he was reliable. End of story. Bloody waste of time. The Flynn family owns an employment agency. Why didn't they find him work?'

'He seems to have valued his independence,' said Corrigan.

Watts huffed. 'Catch me doing that if my old man had that much money. Don't forget he was happy to live in a house his father owned.' He looked at Hanson. 'How'd you get on at the Bull Ring coffee shop?'

Hanson flicked through her notes and gave a quick summation. 'Matthew appears to have been a little socially isolated, somewhat naïve in his dealings with people, he wasn't too happy with someone called Zach and, wait for it, he had a girlfriend.'

Watts raised thick eyebrows. 'You don't say.'

'All Matthew's co-worker recalled is that he was very keen on this girl, woman. He described her as "special".'

Watts gazed at her. 'Learn anything else about him?'

'No.'

'You didn't manage to drag any more details out of her, like you usually do? The old KGB training never kicked in?'

Hanson gave him a look as Corrigan put his head back in a silent laugh. 'There was nothing to "drag". She didn't know any more about him. What she did tell me was this girl's first name.' They waited. 'It was Honey.'

'You what? That's not a name,' scoffed Watts.

'There's some crazy names around,' said Corrigan.

Watts looked dismissive. 'That's just one of them pet names. We'll never trace her on that.'

'I'm telling you what Brennan told me,' said Hanson. 'It sounds like Matthew and this Honey were pretty close.'

'One thing it does tell us,' said Watts. 'Matthew Flynn wasn't gay.'

Hanson regarded him with a slow shake of her head. She

knew he was good at his job, that he was quick-witted when needed. She also knew that he navigated his way through life guided by certainties, black-white, yes-no, which probably helped him do what was needed to uphold the law. He was still annoying. 'What a simple world you live in. I don't know how you got the idea he might be gay but his having a girlfriend confirms nothing about his sexuality. He could still be gay. Or bi, or straight. We know from the tattoo shop proprietor that he had a male friend, Callum, and before you do more conclusion-jumping, the value of this information is that it's extending the picture we have of Matthew beyond his family.'

Watts flicked through his notebook, his facial expression suggesting that whatever he was looking for, he wasn't finding it. 'I think this case is about drugs. The street attacks on Matthew Flynn could have been drug-related. He upset some-body.' He paused. 'I'm picking up that the two Flynn sons couldn't be more different: Matthew is out working minimum money jobs while Dominic is sitting nice and comfy inside his old man's business empire.'

'It seems that was a decision Matthew made,' said Hanson firmly.

Watts's phone rang. He rummaged for it and spoke. 'Yeah? Whose?' He listened, nodded. 'Thanks for that.' He cut the call, wide face creased into a smile. 'That was Chong. Results of the fingerprint testing of the candles left in the crypt has produced a name: Colin Chivers. Small-time B and E offences. He's a yam-yam but he's been living in Birmingham a couple of years and I know where to find him.'

Hanson gave him a cold look. 'I hope what you just said isn't a reference to this person being of foreign origin.'

He grinned at her. 'You've still got a lot to learn about the Midlands, doc. Chivers is from the Black Country. Salt of the earth, the people there, excluding him. It's how they speak: you-am, we-am. Yam-yam, see? When we've got hold of him and he's at headquarters I'll ring you. I want you observing the interview. Chivers is a world-class liar.'

Her colleagues had left and Hanson was gazing at the photo-graph of Matthew Flynn in life secured to the flip chart. Earlier that morning she had written just four words beneath it: 'scarf. Why no blood?' She stood, her eyes fixed on his face, absorbing its individual features, searching it for what it had conveyed to her in death inside the crypt. She took a step back, shook her head. That wasn't the kind of evidence they needed. Returning to her desk for her notes on what Brennan had said, she brought them to the flip chart and added more words: 'genuine charm, personable, honest, kind, caring. Brave. Girlfriend: a special girl.' On a new line, she wrote the single name: 'Honey'.

Pausing to survey all she had written she now saw a theme. These were all positive words about Matthew and his life. She moved down the flip chart, added: 'well-off family'. Was that a positive or a negative? Watts would say it was indisputably positive. She wasn't so categorical. She began a list of what might be construed as negative characteristics: 'not close to family. Limited social life. Too kind. Naïve – sufficient to place self in harm's way'. She added a final question: 'who is Zach who was not a friend? And if he wasn't, why not?'

NINE

Perched on the table inside the observation room the following morning, feet on a nearby chair, Hanson's full attention was on the scene playing itself out beyond the one-way glass. Watts had wasted no time in bringing in Chivers. Being no stranger to legal problems, Chivers had brought his solicitor who was now sitting next to him, pen poised, his sharp eyes on Watts, the light of the PACE machine glowing at one end of the table.

She looked at Chivers, reprising what she now knew about him: twenty-two years old, extensive criminal record for breaking-and-entering, beginning when he was fourteen, interspersed with youth custody followed by a brief stay in adult prison. He was now facing Watts across the table, shoulders hunched. Hanson was here to evaluate Chivers' reliability during interview. She'd suggested that Watts start with questions unrelated to any offence.

He'd asked Chivers about his football team. Chivers had responded freely, his face animated, supporting his responses with appropriate eye, mouth and brow movements. She propped her chin on her hand, waiting for the next question as the door opened and Corrigan came into the observation room and sat on the table beside her.

'OK, Mr Chivers,' said Watts. 'You've agreed to be interviewed and you've got your solicitor present. Let's make a start. What do you know about St Bartholomew's?'

Hanson saw shutters drop down on Chivers' face. He went straight to denial. 'Never heard of it.'

'We've got evidence that you know it very well,' said Watts.

Chivers' solicitor intervened. 'What evidence?'

'All in good time,' said Watts, his eyes not leaving Chivers' face. 'Given we've got it, tell us about St Bartholomew's.'

'I don't know anything about it.' He sat back smirking. 'I avoid churches.'

Watts slow nodded, brows raised, tone conversational. 'Do you, now? That's interesting. St Bartholomews . . . could be a school, a health centre, a community centre. What makes you think it's a church?' Chivers opened his mouth. Closed it. 'How about we get down to brass tacks?' said Watts companionably. 'Or should I say, candles?'

The solicitor shot a look at Chivers whose face was now flagging up a mix of emotions, primarily fear. Corrigan leant towards Hanson. 'Looks like gotcha time.'

'I need a word in private with my client, please,' said the solicitor.

Watts inclined his head, gracious in victory. 'Of course you do. Follow me.' A minute later he came into the observation room. 'Chivers is smart enough to work out that "candles" means we've got prints.' He dropped papers onto the table and searched them. 'What do you make of him, doc?'

'You don't need me to tell you he's defensive.'

'No, but it helps to know that you agree with me and that it's not my interviewing technique that's making him nervous.'

She recognised Watts in forward-thinking mode, anticipating legal objections before they happened because he'd heard them a thousand times. She asked, 'Are you going to tell him that he and a companion were seen running from the church?'

'Depends. Resistant types like Chivers are very reluctant to admit anything. Faced with a choice they go with denial every time and I'd rather not think of the hours I've wasted which I'll never get back on people like him.'

'What do you want from him?' asked Hanson.

'The name of his crypt-visiting mate because he'll be another source.' He looked at his watch and headed for the door.

Hanson turned to Corrigan. 'Good at this, isn't he?'

'Sure is.' They watched through the glass as Watts entered the interview room, followed by Chivers and his solicitor.

'What would you like him to get from the interview, Corrigan?' she asked.

He smiled down at her. 'Top of my list would be an admission that when they went inside the crypt they found whatever was used to kill Matthew Flynn, took it with them and they still have it.' They watched as Watts restarted the PACE machine.

'Right, Mr Chivers. What have you got for me?'

Chivers looked Watts in the eye. 'OK, I am being straight with you now, right?' Hanson picked up on two of his words: *I-am. Yam-yam.* 'Yes, I went into that place and yes, I was looking for stuff to nick but there was nothing there so I left.'

'Is that a fact? Short visit was it?'

'Yeah, in and out, ten seconds, tops.'

Watts sat back, thick arms folded. 'Let's think about that, shall we?'

'My client has given you an admission that he broke in—'

'Ten seconds to get inside, walk about a bit, light some candles, have a proper look around.' He shook his head. 'Sounds like a good few minutes to me.'

Chivers was flustered now. 'No . . . Yeah, well it might have been a minute or two but that's all.'

'What about the lid?'

Chivers' eyes darted to his solicitor. 'What lid? I don't know anything about no lid.'

'Come on, lad. The lid covering the stone structure where the body was.' He mustered patience. 'You've admitted being in there. Give it up.'

The solicitor's head was swivelling from Watts to his client and back. 'What's this about a body? If this is more evidence you've got—'

'Like I said, all in good time,' said Watts, his eyes fixed on Chivers. 'What did you see?'

'Nothing. There wasn't anything.'

'Who was with you on this little jaunt?'

'Nobody. I was on my own. I always work on my own.'

Watts gave a soothing nod, then: 'Remember the candles? Wax is good for holding onto fingerprints.'

Hanson's eyes were on Chivers' face, seeing craftiness arrive as he tracked Watts's reasoning. *Chivers might be street-smart but intellectually nimble, he isn't.* She saw another smirk, watched his mouth open. *And evidently lacking the sense to quit when he should.*

'So what? Like you said, I've admitted I was there.'

Watts gave him an unwavering look. 'What about the other fingerprints?'

Chivers looked smug. 'Don't try any of that bluff with me. I've been in situations like this since I was a kid. You can't have any more prints because . . .' He shut his mouth.

Corrigan leant towards Hanson to whisper the words Chivers had left hanging. 'He wore gloves.' He looked down at her and smiled.

Chivers' solicitor leapt in. 'I want more time alone with my client.'

Watts said, 'In a bit.' His eyes fixed on Chivers. 'Whoever was with you, I want his name.'

Chivers flopped back on his chair, his face turned away. 'My cousin, Barney. But he'll be no help. He's got special needs. If you get him in, all you'll do is frighten him. He won't be able to tell you anything. Plus, our mom will go barmy at me for getting him into trouble.'

Watts nodded. 'Let's see how well we get on in the next few minutes, Colin, and maybe we won't have to do that. Tell me everything about that night at the church, starting with why *that* church?'

'I knew security there was next to non-existent. Not over-looked. No cameras. It's a doddle.'

'You'd been there before?'

'No.' He squirmed under Watts's gaze. 'I just knew.'

'Looks like I'll be needing your cousin's address,' said Watts, arranging his face into an expression of deep regret.

'No!' Chivers bowed his head. 'There's this kid I know, right? He specialises in churches. He goes for the brassware. It was him that told me the security at St Bartholomew's wasn't that hot. Some churches have cameras and alarms but not that one. He told me it would be dead easy to get inside. We tried getting in by the main door but couldn't. I was ready to call it a night when I saw steps leading down to another door at the side and we got in that way. I thought it might be like a storeroom for valuables.' He fell silent.

'Find any?' asked Watts.

Chivers gave him a sulky look. 'I've already told you there was nothing.'

'That's when you moved the lid off the sarcophagus and saw what was inside. Didn't you, Colin?' The solicitor's head was swivelling again.

'It was horrible,' said Chivers, wriggling his shoulders, his face a study in disgust. 'At first I thought it was some Halloween thing that somebody had left down there. Soon as I realised what it was, me and Barney got out of there fast. I was already spooked by a noise—'

'What noise?' demanded Watts.

'Like somebody singing. Probably somebody who saw us go down the steps and wanted to scare us off.'

'Male voice? Female? Adult? Kid?'

'I don't *know*.' Chivers was looking agitated. 'It was soft-like. I couldn't hear it that well. Just enough for me to know what it was.'

Watts leant forward, his eyes fixed on his face. 'What was it, Colin?'

'This'll sound barmy, right, and it was only a few seconds but it was like that little kids' song, "Oranges and Lemons". We should have got out of that place, there and then. We should never have went.'

Watts was looking deeply unimpressed. 'Tell us about this kid you know, the one that's partial to nicking brass and put you onto St Bartholomew's.'

'He's just a kid I've seen around the place.'

'Name!' barked Watts.

Chivers flinched. 'I dunno his name!'

Watts sat back, giving the wall clock an obvious look. 'Take your time while I give some thought to your cousin Barney.'

Chivers sighed, his chin hitting his chest. 'Spencer Albright. But you never got it from me.'

'Address.'

Gazing upwards, voice a monotone, he supplied it.

'Right,' said Watts. 'I'll ask you again: did you or your cousin remove anything, any single item from that crypt?' Chivers gave an adamant head shake. 'I've told you. There was nothing *there*. Even if there had been, I wouldn't want anything from that place.'

They were back in UCU. Chivers had been charged with breaking and entering. Watts came from the printer and dropped a wad of A4s on the table. Hanson upside-down read the top sheet: Spencer Albright's Criminal Antecedents.

'What do you hope to gain by following him up?'

'Nothing specific. It's basic policing: follow every lead to its usually bitter end, meaning we mostly get nothing but just occasionally one or other of them gives us an angle. We won't know until we do it. None of us needs reminding that we have to get a hold of this case and quick.' He looked up at her. 'What's your view of Chivers?'

'The information you got from him sounded reliable. I think he's told you everything he knows.'

'What do you think about this singing he says he heard?'

Hanson considered it. 'Not sure. In that situation his senses would have been heightened, he was unnerved and suggestible. He could have heard something. It's equally possible he imagined it.'

Watts folded the printed information and pushed it into an inside pocket. 'Right. This afternoon I'm tracking down Albright. What did you say you'd do, Corrigan?'

'I'm visiting the house Matthew Flynn shared. I've checked. The other two guys are still living there.'

Watts looked to Hanson. 'You doing anything?'

She gave him a steady look. 'Plenty, like every woman with a job, a home, a family, a—'

'If you get a minute, go over and see Father Delaney. Ask him if the names Colin Chivers and Spencer Albright mean anything. Mention the name Callum as well.' He picked up the phone and dialled as Hanson headed for the door, his words following her.

'Thanks, Everywoman!' Walking from the room she rolled her eyes and grinned.

TEN

Hanson pointed to a specific paragraph in Julian's draft research paper. 'I've checked the stats and they're statistically significant as you've shown but—' she turned pages – 'I think you're overstating your case somewhat in the Results section.' She slid the paper across the desk to him.

He quickly read the section she was indicating. 'I see it. OK, I'll rein it back.' He gathered his papers, gave her a parting wave and headed for the door and out.

She glanced at the six other draft papers on her desk awaiting similar attention, each a ticking clock in the form of their final submission dates. She'd work on them this evening and arrange to see the students who'd researched them as soon as she could. Stretching her arms, rotating her shoulders, she checked the time. There was something straightforward she could do right now. Getting her bag and coat she called to the adjoining room. 'I'll be back in about an hour, Crystal.'

Turning off the quiet road, Hanson parked to one side of the expanse of land and looked across at the church in the weak sunshine. She recalled the early morning she'd first come here when the area had been full of forensic workers. All gone now. It was deserted and very quiet despite the suburban sprawl and roads she knew were not far away. Out of her car, heading for the church, she was startled by a sudden, loud cawing. She looked up to see magpies, several of them, dark against the sky, others rising from nearby trees and swooping downwards to walk purposefully between the headstones, unperturbed by her presence. *What's a collective of magpies? A murder? No. That's crows. Very apt, if it was.*

The church itself looked deserted. She tried the door. It was locked. She turned away, seeing Church House on the other side of the large swathe of land, sombre, solid against a pale sky. She approached it, looking up at the windows, all of them covered in heavy lace curtains. She recalled what Corrigan had said about Father Delaney: he'd worked in Boston years ago, was something of a modernist but with an eye fixed firmly on tradition and a quiet living. *Which seems to have been what he'd got. Until Matthew Flynn's body came to light.*

She reached the steps, went lightly up them onto the veranda and rang the bell, then rang it a second time. A shadow appeared against thick lace on the other side of the door. It was opened by a man in head-to-foot black. 'Father Delaney.' She delivered the name as a statement because of Corrigan's physical description of him.

The man framed in the doorway was huge. 'Yes?'

She held up her Unsolved Crime Unit identification. 'I'm part of the police investigation into the recent event here. Is it convenient for us to talk?'

He opened the door fully, standing to one side, arm outstretched, his face kindly. 'Of course it is. Come in.'

Once she was inside, he closed the door and beckoned to her to follow. She did, along a chill corridor, its walls painted a dark green, the plaster heavily embossed with a pattern of five-point palm fronds. *Or are they hands?* She idly wondered.

Delaney led her into what she assumed from Corrigan's description was his study and indicated a chair. 'Please. Make yourself comfortable.' He sat on the high-backed chair, feet planted, broad hands on his knees, his eyes fully on hers. 'How can I help, Professor Hanson?'

'You spoke to a colleague of mine recently.'

Delaney's face widened into a smile. 'Ah, yes. The estimable Lieutenant Corrigan. We discussed St Bartholomew's experiences of vandalism although I'm assuming that, like him, you wish to talk about that dreadful business involving the crypt.'

She brought her notebook out of her bag. 'Yes. I have some names I'd like to put to you to see if you recognise them, if they mean anything, no matter how incidental.'

'Of course.' Delaney glanced at the empty fireplace, a frown appearing on his plump face. 'Are you warm enough? I could light a quick fire, if not. It's no trouble.'

'No, I'm fine, thank you. The names are Colin Chivers and Spencer Albright.' She waited.

'No.' He gave a slow headshake. 'No. Neither of those names means anything to me.'

Undeterred, she asked, 'What about Callum?'

Delaney appeared to consider. 'Again, I apologise. Is there a surname?'

Hanson wasn't surprised at the question. A first name was a long shot. She chose her next words. 'You'll have had a little time over the last couple of days to think about what was found in the crypt following the break-in. Has anything occurred to you which might throw some light on it or which might help us?'

Delaney looked adrift. 'Such as?'

'It might be anything. An event as shocking as this one can trigger memory, help us make a connection, perhaps remind us of past events, people we'd forgotten?' He continued to look uncertain. She gazed at him. 'Those are just examples, Father Delaney. Has anything at all occurred to you which might help our investigation into the murder of Matthew Flynn, no matter how trivial?'

He shook his head. 'I regret to say not. Was he a good boy, this Matthew Flynn?'

Hanson was surprised and unsettled by the question. 'I don't know. I'm not sure what you mean. He was twenty years old. He lived a rather simple life, as far as we know.'

Delaney appeared lost in thought. 'I see a lot of young people these days, unfortunately not at St Bartholomew's, and they seem troubled. Always talking on their phones, detached from all life going on around them.'

Hanson recognised the behaviour he was describing. She did

it herself often enough. 'I know what you mean but it might be an unreliable assumption to make from a single observation, don't you think?'

He was looking at the floor. 'Maybe. But I'd like to bring them to God.'

A silence grew between them. Hanson heard herself filling it. 'Don't people have to do that for themselves? If they want to?'

He straightened, smiling. 'You could be right.' Despite his size, he rose suddenly from his chair. 'Oh, excuse me. I must answer that call. Take your coat off, make yourself comfortable. I won't be a moment.'

Not having heard anything, she watched him get up and head for the door and out. Another door nearby opened and closed. Hanson glanced at the few written ideas she'd brought with her, questions she would have asked if Delaney had recalled anything, none of them any use now. She glanced at his desk, covered in sheets of handwritten notes, an open copy of the Bible next to them. *Why doesn't he have the phone in here?* Her eyes drifted beyond the desk to a bookcase, its top surface supporting dried flowers under a glass dome, wallpaper the colour of old tea with a design of peacocks and . . . dragons? And on every surface china figurines: dogs, cats, a doll dressed in dark red velvet, blue eyes set in her china face. She wrinkled her nose. *Don't blame Delaney for the décor. This house and its furnishings come with the job.*

She shifted on her chair, aware now of how cold it was in the room. Obviously, Delaney didn't feel the cold. She folded her coat around herself, suddenly aware of the heavy silence inside the house. Restless, she squirmed on her chair, eyes moving over the high ceiling, then the walls with their heavy framed paintings of biblical themes and others of males wearing vestments, some in red skullcaps, others in tall white mitres, their eyes returning her look, giving her steady scrutiny. Unsettled, the skin across her shoulders prickling, she looked away. The sound of a door closing, followed by Delaney's voice as he returned made her start.

'Apologies for the interruption. My housekeeper has now arrived and I suspect you are cold. I'm going to ask her to make us tea. Or would you prefer coffee? Maybe some cake?'

She stood. 'Thank you, father, but I won't take up any more of your time. I'm grateful to you for seeing me.'

'My pleasure. I regret it wasn't fruitful.'

'If you do think of anything you have my number.'

He held out his hand in the direction of the study door. 'I need to go across to the church so I'll walk with you.'

They emerged into the late afternoon, the sky now overcast. It felt much colder than when she had arrived. She thought over what Delaney had told her. Maybe the church wasn't a dead end in terms of inquiry. 'You mentioned a housekeeper just now. Your staff here might be of help if we could talk to them. Is that possible?'

Delaney glanced down at her with a gentle smile. 'Staff sounds rather grand. I have two deacons who assist me directly in church services. You're very welcome to talk to them.'

'What role do they have here?'

'They preach, give spiritual support. They assist me at Mass and they take responsibility for serving the needy in our community. Deacon Fellowes is very much involved in outreach work, Deacon Burns less so. Most of his duties are church-based.' He looked at her again. 'In case you're wondering, they're both permanent deacons. They had previous lives before they trained.' His eyes twinkled. 'What I'm saying is that they are both worldly. They would have been accepted into the church even if married. A foot in both camps, so to speak.'

Hanson hadn't been wondering because she didn't know anything about the organisation of a church such as this. Or any other, come to that. She thought of Corrigan. He was best placed to do future visits here. He would know the sorts of questions to ask. 'What about others who assist you?'

'My housekeeper is employed by the diocese via its Human Resources Department.' The eyes twinkled again. 'I see your surprise. We're very in touch with the world, you know. The remaining demands of the ministry here are apportioned to a committee, all volunteers. We regard them as "ministers" in their own right because of their invaluable contribution to the church. Together we decide on fundraising and the outreach work St Bartholomew's undertakes, such as food banks, prison visits and so forth. Staff would indeed be a luxury.' Hanson was surprised to hear the range of work and the goodwill involved.

They had reached the church doors. Delaney turned to her, his height and bulk emphasising Hanson's own small stature. 'Fundraising is key to our survival. We observe tradition but accept that churches cannot be—' he smiled – '*solely* spiritual these days. They need strong business acumen. Several of our committee members have years of that kind of experience. They share it willingly for the good of St Bartholomew's and those whom it helps.'

Delaney's mention of tradition prompted another line of thinking related to what she'd been told about Matthew Flynn having a girlfriend. 'Is the committee made up of both male and female members?'

He gave her a direct look. 'Just male and mostly of a significant age. You're a professor of psychology?'

'Yes.'

'I don't know if you're aware, but psychoanalysis and psychotherapy are regarded by some within the church as bordering on the pagan, their purpose being to destroy a person's identity, then leave him to make himself whole.' He inclined his head. 'Or *herself*, of course.' Surprised, wondering if her reference to the gender of committee members had somehow found a mark with him, she said nothing. He continued. 'The view is that psychology does not heal.' His words provoked questions inside her head. *Whose view? The church? Yours?*

She sidestepped any potential debate. 'That kind of analysis or therapy isn't part of what I do.'

Above them the huge edifice of St Bartholomew's soared, its spire piercing the swollen clouds now gathering. Hanson was suddenly aware of daylight fading fast, despite the early hour this Friday afternoon. Delaney raised his face and both plump hands towards the church building. 'Beautiful, isn't it?' He sighed, letting his hands drop, his face solemn. 'But sadly besmirched now. As a close community here, we endeavour to look after and care for each other. My colleagues and our parishioners value the friendship that exists among us. Like all friends, we keep ourselves close. There's so much suffering in the world today, don't you find? Now it feels as if some of it has visited us, but we'll remain positive.' He raised clenched hands which to Hanson looked like hams. 'The closeness we have will provide comfort to us all.' He stopped, giving her a direct look. 'I'm guessing that our God is not your god,' he said quietly. 'But we're open to all who need our help. Do come again, if you need to. You'll be most welcome.'

A chill breeze whipped her hair across her face. 'Thank you for your time, Father Delaney.'

He inclined his head. She watched as he turned away, unlocked the church's heavy door and went inside, the folds of his black cassock swirled by another sudden, sharp gust.

Back in her room, Hanson checked the radiator, surprised to find it hot. Feeling chilled, she went into Crystal's room which was deserted and switched on the kettle, dropped a heaped spoonful of instant coffee into a mug and waited, giving her arms a brisk rub. She poured boiling water onto granules, took the mug into her room where she stood, hands clasped around it, her eyes on the flip chart and Matthew Flynn's face. He stared back at her, his eyes candid. She thought of his other photograph in UCU, his dead eyes full of want. She sat at her desk sipping coffee, her eyes still fixed on his face, the lilting tune in her head, one she couldn't seem to get rid of since she'd first heard it mentioned. *Oranges and lemons* . . . She saw Matthew's face slowly darken, the eyes hollowing out, the skin around their orbits now amber, the lips parting, pulled back in a rictus, the face ruined yet beseeching, the eyes fastened on hers, hungry, yearning despite death's hand on him. He was coming to her now, his mouth open, ready to tell her what it was he needed. *Oranges and lemons said the bells of St—*

'Kate?'

Hanson's hand jerked. Coffee flew from mug to desk. She leapt to her feet, grabbing papers, moving them out of harm's way.

'Sorry, Kate. I thought you'd heard me come in. Here, take these.' Crystal handed her paper towels. Hanson blotted her desk and threw them into the waste bin. Crystal lifted the mug as Kate sat again. 'Want more?'

'No, thanks.'

'What was so absorbing when I arrived?' Crystal's eyes followed Hanson's to the flip chart. Hanson pointed. 'Him. Matthew Flynn. Crystal, have you ever looked at a photograph and thought that the person in it wanted something? Or had something for you?'

'Can't say that I have.' Crystal went and stood close to the photograph. 'Who took it?'

Hanson looked at her. 'Do you know, that's a question I hadn't thought to ask? I don't know. Why?'

'I was just wondering. He looks happy. Yet wherever he was when it was taken doesn't look that homely, does it?'

Hanson got up, went and stood next to her. 'I assumed someone in his family took it.' She pointed to the dark background. 'See that small, brighter patch with the wavy edges behind him?' Hanson traced her finger across the smooth surface. 'I can't make out what it is, can you?'

Crystal stood back, narrowed her eyes as she fixed on it. 'It could be a window, although, if it is it's a funny shape and very small. What you said just now. About people in photographs telling us something? Now that I really look at him, do you know what I think he's saying loud and clear? "I love you".' Seeing Hanson's surprise, she laughed. 'My mom says I'm a total romantic.'

Hanson grinned. 'Your mom isn't wrong.'

Crystal returned to her office and Hanson lifted the photograph off the flip chart. She found herself wanting to believe that Matthew had found love. She turned it over. There was nothing on the reverse side. She fetched her phone. Her call was picked up almost immediately by Corrigan. 'Hey, Red. How're you doing?'

'Fine, thanks. This afternoon I received a crash course in ecumenical matters, if that's the correct word.'

'Delaney.' She heard the smile in his voice. 'How'd you get on with him?'

'OK, I think. He didn't recognise the names, you know, Chivers, Albright or Callum but he was helpful. He has two deacons we should maybe talk to.' She'd decided not to mention Delaney's views on psychology. They were his and not relevant to the case. 'I've got a question about the photograph we have of Matthew Flynn taken prior to his disappearance. Who supplied it to us?' She waited, hearing pages turn.

He was back. 'His father, Brad Flynn.'

'Did he say anything about it?'

'Only that it was the latest one he had. They hadn't got another of Matthew taken near the time he disappeared. I got the impression that he had to search for it.'

'Did he say where it was taken?'

'Nope.'

Hanson thought of the photographs she regularly took of Maisie to celebrate some large or small event, or just casually, because she needed to capture her daughter's face. She couldn't imagine that need changing much in the next what, five years? She sighed, reminding herself that not all parents maintained an emotional closeness with their children. Her own mother arrived inside her head. *Prime example.*

Corrigan was speaking. 'I'm heading out to the house where Matthew Flynn was living when he disappeared. Hold on, Red. Watts wants a word.'

Watts's voice sounded in her ear. 'How'd it go with the God-botherer?'

She eye-rolled. 'He told me how St Bartholomew's is organised. It's run as a kind of cooperative using business principles. Very modern.'

'Sounds as good a way as any to get money into the collection plate.'

She closed her eyes. Watts's unerring cynicism could be wearing. 'I just told Corrigan that Delaney has two deacons working with him. We'll want to talk to them sometime. How did your interview go with Spencer Albright?'

'Never happened.'

'Oh? Why not?'

'We can't find him. Corrigan reckons he's "on the lam".'

'What will you do?'

'I've got a few contacts keeping their eyes open for him, people who know him and his usual haunts. Once we track him down we'll have him in and he can tell us what he knows of St Bartholomew's and any visits he might have made to it, vandalism or theft-wise.'

Corrigan rang the bell of the three-floor terraced house and waited. He rang a second time, then a third. Stepping back from the door he looked up at the windows. All closed. Some with blinds fully down. He took out his phone. In seconds his mobile-to-mobile call rang somewhere inside. Face set, he pounded the door. 'Police, Mr Graham! Open up!'

Hurried feet sounded on stairs followed by more approaching the door. It was opened by a slim, bearded man in his early twenties in ratty-looking joggers and sweatshirt. He looked distracted. Corrigan walked inside without waiting for an invitation, breathing in cologne. He flipped identification, gazing around at what was visible of the ground floor. 'Lieutenant Corrigan. I phoned you this morning to say I was coming. Is there a problem here?'

Graham looked up at the tall officer and gave a bright smile. 'No, of course not. I was working in my study upstairs.'

Corrigan followed him to the back of the house, passing a large sitting room furnished in Mom-and-Pop-meets-Ikea. Graham led him into a well-equipped kitchen. 'Coffee?' he asked, pointing to a large stainless steel espresso machine.

'No, thanks. Like I said on the phone, I want to talk to you about Matthew Flynn.'

Graham waved him to a seat at the table, took one himself. 'What do you want to know?' he asked, legs moving in little bounces.

His index finger across his upper lip, Corrigan regarded him for several seconds. Graham looked away, then back, his hand busy at his facial hair, legs still bouncing.

'Let's start with what's in your head right now,' said Corrigan.

'Well, Matthew, obviously. I heard it on the news and it's very sad but I can't tell you much although obviously I hope—'

'How long have you lived here?'

'I came here about a year before Matthew arrived when I started at Aston University. Matthew was offered a place there the following year but he didn't take it up.'

'So why was he living here?'

Graham looked confused. 'Sorry?' He got no help from Corrigan. 'Well, his parents own this place. I suppose he wanted to move out of their house.'

'Why would he want that?'

Graham shrugged. 'The usual reason, I suppose. Freedom to do what he wanted.'

Corrigan slow-nodded. 'OK, Mr Graham. Matthew Flynn was your housemate for a while. Tell me what you learned about him during that time.'

Graham's hand was still worrying his beard. 'He was pretty decent, Matthew. Nice. Unsophisticated.' He frowned. 'Don't get the wrong idea. He was sharp, clever . . .' He fell silent.

'What else?' prompted Corrigan.

'That's about it.' He saw Corrigan's face register what looked like disbelief. 'I'm sorry but that's all I can think of. We were three guys. You know how it is. In and out. Got our own friends.'

'So, tell me about Matthew Flynn's friends.'

Graham pushed his hand through his hair. 'I never met any of them.'

Corrigan stood, face raised in the direction of the upper floor. 'Where's your housemate?'

Graham was on his feet. 'He had to go out.'

'When I rang you said you'd both be here.'

'He said he'd forgotten he had a late lecture—'

'Same place as you?'

Graham nodded. 'He's on a different course to me.'

Corrigan's eyes drifted slowly around the kitchen. 'Nice house. There's a lot of students in this city. How'd you get so lucky to find it?'

Graham's eyes slid away. 'An agent was handling it. We took a look, thought it was great and signed a rental agreement.'

'And the family said you could stay here after Matthew disappeared?' Graham didn't respond. 'That sounds very charitable, given the sad circumstances of Matthew going like he did.'

Graham's head came up. 'Like I said, we have an agreement.'

'Yeah, well I guess that makes all the difference.' Corrigan walked slowly towards the door, dissatisfaction evident on his face. 'I still want to talk to your housemate. You say he's not here?'

'He isn't.'

Corrigan slow-nodded again. There were no grounds on which he could initiate a search. 'What's his name?'

'Zach.' Corrigan waited some more. 'Zach Addison.'

'I guess I'll go find him, maybe catch him coming out of that lecture you mentioned, yeah?'

Graham nodded, his eyes sliding again.

Corrigan was now outside, deep-breathing sharp, cold air. He gazed up at the tall, narrow house. He had no intention of seeking out Addison. He got into the Volvo thinking of scruffy student clothes and strong cologne, one unasked question in his head: who's heavily into marijuana here?

Halfway through proofreading one of the draft articles she'd brought home, Hanson stopped, something relating to Matthew Flynn's remains nudging the inside of her head: the tiny fragments of something which Chong had vacuumed off his clothes during his post-mortem. So far as she knew, they hadn't yet been identified. She recalled Watts's view that it was likely evidence of Matthew continuing to use drugs since his caution for possession at the age of fifteen. Drug use placed individuals at all kinds of personal risk. If that applied to Matthew, they had to know. She pulled her work diary closer. One aspect of Matthew Flynn's young life which she wanted to get a grip on was what had happened to him following his caution. She had phoned Mrs Flynn recently and didn't relish doing so again at this particular time. And anyway, according to her two colleagues, neither parent appeared to have regarded their fifteen-year-old son's drug possession as a serious matter. There had been no indication that they remotely connected drug use to his disappearance.

What Hanson wanted was solid, unequivocal information. She knew that the disposal of such cautions varied but as a minor Matthew may have been referred to a youth offending team for support and possibly a social worker. She flipped pages, checked likely phone numbers and found two. She would contact both first thing Monday.

ELEVEN

Hanson's first call to Youth Offending had drawn a blank. There was no record of any referral in the name of Matthew Flynn. She ended the call and scrolled down her contact list. *Time to get more specific.* In the early morning relative quiet of headquarters she dialled a direct number and waited for her Social Services contact to respond.

'Ruth Grayson. How can I help?' Hanson grinned into the phone. 'Hello, Ruth Grayson. This is Kate Hanson and I'm pretty sure you'll find a way.'

A peal of delighted laughter sounded in her ear. 'Kate! How are you?'

'Fine, fine. Ruth, I need information if you've got it. I need to know what happened to a fifteen-year-old male at the time he was given a youth caution for drug possession around five years ago. There's nothing on the police database. Could you check it out if I give you his name and date of birth?' Hanson supplied Matthew Flynn's details. 'I was thinking that due to his young age he might have been referred to Youth Offending but they say not. You're my next hope. Actually, Ruth, you're my only hope. Is it possible he was given social work support?' She pictured Grayson, long-time worker in substance misuse. What she didn't know about available services wasn't worth knowing. Her response wasn't optimistic.

'Not too likely, actually, even for minors but I'll check and get back to you with anything I find.' Ending the call, Hanson joined in the conversation continuing around her.

'What's this I hear about marijuana?'

Corrigan pointed at data on the board. She saw a name underlined. William Graham. 'One of the guys who shared a house with Matthew Flynn. He didn't sound too keen to see me when I phoned him, slow to open the door when I got there and even less keen to tell me anything once I got inside. But it was an interesting visit on a number of levels. One being that the kitchen is fitted out with some pretty expensive stuff, for example a large espresso machine which I know from when I was fitting out my place would have cost over a grand.'

Hanson's brows shot upwards. 'I can't see three students buying something like that. Hang on, though. That house belongs to the Flynn family. Maybe Diana Flynn wanted Matthew to have some home comforts and thought nothing too good for her youngest son?'

'Possible,' said Corrigan. 'Except that I checked. That particular model is new. Only arrived on the market six months ago. Matthew never got to use it.'

Seeing Watts's wide grin she said, 'I think I'm starting to see a link between a pricey, state-of-the-art espresso machine and marijuana.'

'Knew you would,' said Corrigan. 'Picture this, Red. I beat on the door of the house. Like I said, Graham is real slow to respond. When he does, he's dressed in scruffy, in-for-the-day athletics gear, yet giving off a knock-down aroma of Hugo Boss. Before I get in there I'm kind of suspicious. When I leave I definitely am. That house smelled of weed.'

She could see there was more. 'So, what did you do?'

'Left Graham relieved but edgy. I've got two upstairs guys staking out the house. They've been there all night. When I spoke to them thirty minutes ago they were waiting for more officers.' The phone rang and he reached for it. 'Corrigan.' He nodded. 'Great. You filmed it? See you when you get here.' He put down the phone, his blue eyes on Watts then Hanson. 'Confirmation that the student house has a big sideline in horticulture. The third floor is full of hydroponic equipment, lights and a hundred-plus marijuana plants.' He pushed the chair to recline, stretched his arms and put his hands behind his head. 'Will Graham and his sidekick Zach Addison are on their way here.'

Hanson stared. Zach. The name Terri Brennan had mentioned. Somebody who was no friend of Matthew's. 'I know that name!' She looked at her watch and jumped up. 'Damn! I have to go but I'll be back at around two thirty.'

Watts's face was creased into a broad grin as he watched

her head for the door. 'What did I tell you, doc? This whole case is about drugs.'

'Several times, according to my recollection.'

Hanson hurried into her university room with five minutes to spare before the scheduled meeting with her research students. Dropping her belongings on the armchair she was halfway to her desk when she heard Crystal's voice. 'Kate?' She looked up as Crystal appeared. 'You've got a visitor.'

Hanson continued gathering files together. 'My research group is due here. Tell whoever it is to come back later.' Getting no response she looked up again.

'I think you need to have a brief word,' said Crystal, indicating her room.

Eyes on Crystal, Hanson walked to the door and stopped dead on seeing the small figure sitting there, nimble fingers tapping her phone. Maisie. 'What's happened? What's wrong? Are you feeling ill?' She went to her, glanced at the phone, recognising the 'Fashionable 13-Year-Old Girl' game.

Maisie's fingers paused. She avoided her mother's eyes. 'I think I might be getting a headache. I just need to be somewhere quiet.' Sitting on Crystal's desk, Hanson looked directly into her daughter's face, pushing back the riot of thick curls to lay her hand on her forehead. It felt cool.

As Crystal came in Maisie shook off the hand. 'Get off, Mom! I *said* I'm OK.'

Hanson searched the heart-shaped face, picking up sounds of her research students arriving inside her room, one of the voices Julian's. She went to the door, closed it and came back. 'I've got a meeting for the next hour. Stay here with Crystal and don't pester her and she might make you a hot drink.' She watched Maisie brighten. *Obviously not seriously off-colour.* 'As soon as my meeting finishes I'll take you home. What about your second lecture?'

Maisie shrugged, her eyes skimming Hanson's and away. 'Same lecturer as this morning. I already told her I was ill.'

Hanson gazed down at her daughter. 'Crystal, is it OK with you if Maisie stays in here?'

Crystal grinned at Maisie. 'Of course it is. I've got some biscuits in my drawer.'

'*Cool*,' said Maisie. Seeing her mother's frown she lost the smile. 'I'm starting to sort of, feel slightly better now.'

Hanson came into the house, Maisie trailing her. 'I know you're not unwell. I also know there's something going on. If you won't talk to me I can't sort it out, but count on it, Maisie, I'll find out what it is.' Ignoring the tut-and-pout as Maisie stomped the stairs, Hanson went into the kitchen.

Charlie looked up from the *Independent* crossword. 'Hello! I wasn't expecting you home just yet.'

'Neither was I. Maisie came to my office this afternoon.' She saw his quick concern. 'She's fine but she's up to something and I'm needed at headquarters. Can I leave her with you?' Getting a quick nod she headed into the hall. 'I'll be back as soon as I can.'

Fifteen minutes later she was inside UCU. 'How's it going?'

'Better than we hoped,' said Corrigan.

Watts's wide face was stretched into a pleased grin. Hanson rolled her eyes. *Just like the Cheshire cat.* 'You missed the interview with Graham. He sang like a canary,' he said.

'A well-worn but efficient idiom,' she snapped.

The cat-grin disappeared. 'What's got your goat now?'

'Nothing. Carry on, preferably without more animals.'

'According to Graham they were approached over twelve months ago by some bloke they didn't know who told them they could make a few grand by having the plants at the house and managing them. It was put to them as a no-risk set-up. Everything was supplied, brought to the house. When the crop was ready, it was taken away, again by people they didn't know. According to Graham, that is.'

'Twelve months?' queried Hanson. 'That means Matthew Flynn had to have been involved. Or at least aware.'

'Seems like it,' said Watts.

She looked across at Corrigan. 'Do you think Matthew was a willing participant?'

He raised both hands. 'He was living there. We go with what we're told until we learn otherwise.'

'But it's so contrary to what we know about him. Look.' She pointed at the words on the board.

Watts eyed them. 'Like Corrigan just said, it's what we've been told, doc, which might not be the whole picture.'

'But Terri Brennan *knew* Matthew.'

'Graham and Addison knew him. Probably better than she did.'

Head propped on one hand, Hanson's gaze was still on the board when Corrigan lifted the phone at its first ring. 'We're on our way,' he said.

They headed for the door, Corrigan turning to her. 'Zach Addison is ready for interview. Come and observe what I'm guessing will be a sanitized version of *My Life as a Marijuana Grower*.'

She watched her colleagues walk into the interview room and take seats opposite a twenty-something male and his white-haired solicitor. Zach Addison was good looking with the kind of inbred self-assurance she guessed had its roots in a back-ground of serious money. She listened as Corrigan established Addison's history. It confirmed her suspicion: money made by his banker father, reduced somewhat at the time of the economic downturn but still a family of significant means. Hanson's eyes narrowed as she listened. Whatever 'reduced' meant in terms of a banker's family, Addison's self-assurance was now looking more like a sense of entitlement.

Watts took up the questioning. 'Tell us who set you up in the marijuana business.'

Addison eyes passed slowly over Watts's face and creased suit. When he spoke, his voice was clipped, the accent metro-politan. 'Sorry. Could you repeat the question? I'm not quite clear what you said.'

Hanson felt heat rise in her chest. Watts repeated it.

'No idea,' said Addison. 'I never met anyone connected with it.'

'Our information is that you and Graham were approached with a proposition that could net you a thousand pounds a month and that following an agreement by you the equipment and plants were delivered to the house. What do you say?'

'If Graham told you that, he's a liar. He and Matthew Flynn sorted it all out. Graham had to have Flynn on side because the house belonged to his family. That stuff was already on the third floor before I knew anything about it.'

Watts gazed at him with deep dislike. 'Yeah, we get it. It was nothing to do with you.'

Addison's solicitor frowned. Corrigan took up the questioning. 'Where and when did that first approach happen?'

Addison raised his shoulders. 'For the tape!' snapped Watts.

'I just told you, I don't know.'

'Why did Matthew Flynn agree to be involved?' asked Corrigan.

The solicitor intervened, looking irritated. 'My client has already told you that he had no direct involvement in this "proposal". He cannot provide information about an arrangement to which he was not a party.'

Addison nodded, his voice smooth. 'I think you'll find that whereas I have no prior dealings with the law, Flynn already had a record for drugs.'

'You didn't dissociate yourself from what was on offer,' said Corrigan.

Addison shrugged. 'Like you said earlier, Matthew's family owned the house. It was Graham's idea. Once Matthew knew and he was cool with it, what could I do?'

'You could have found somewhere else to live!' snapped Watts.

'Why would I? It was a nice house. Comfortable. Convenient. I decided to ignore what was going on.'

'You expect us to believe you never benefitted financially from the stuff on the third floor?' asked Watts, his voice heavy with disbelief.

'I'm telling you, I didn't.'

'In which case it won't worry you that we'll be requesting your financial records.' Addison looked away.

Corrigan changed course. 'Like you said, the house belongs to Matthew Flynn's family. His parents would have visited to check on how Matthew was doing and that the house was being taken care of?' No response from Addison. 'Or was it only Mrs Flynn who made the house calls?'

Hanson saw wariness in Addison's face. His mouth remained firmly closed.

'It didn't concern you that she might go upstairs?' asked Corrigan. 'Discover what was going on up there?'

'That stuff was on the third floor. Graham used one small room up there as a study. Hardly more than a cupboard. The rest of it was unfurnished. She had no reason to go up there.'

Something in his tone, the first indication of emotion in Addison's voice, snagged Hanson's attention. Corrigan had certainly touched a tender spot. Her eyes fixed on Addison's face, the straight nose, the strong jawline around which she could see tension in the muscles beneath the skin. *He's dropped the dismissive, patronising attitude. He's not exactly nervous but he's busy thinking. About what?*

Corrigan continued. 'From what we know Mrs Flynn is a nice lady. Did she want the house to be comfortable for tenants? Did she care enough to provide high-end kitchen appliances?'

Addison's face set. He looked away. 'Her son lived there. Why wouldn't she?'

'Was she willing to provide comfort for tenants elsewhere in that house?'

Hanson knew where Corrigan's questions were leading. Addison's face tightened. 'No, and I don't like the inference you're making there.'

'What inference might that be?'

Addison's solicitor intervened, his voice weary. 'If we could move on, keeping to the facts of why my client has been arrested, please?'

'That's what I'm doing right now,' said Corrigan, his eyes fixed on Addison. 'Are you saying that Diana Flynn never went anywhere but the ground floor of that house?'

Addison's eyes shifted from Corrigan to Watts. 'Yes.' He looked up as both officers stood.

'You're looking worried, Mr Addison,' observed Corrigan. 'How about we take a short break while you consider your situation here?'

They returned to UCU. Hanson went straight to the board, read through all of the information they had on the Flynn family then looked at Corrigan. 'You think there was something going on between Addison and Diana Flynn?'

'I think it's very likely, although whether he'll admit it today isn't a sure thing,' said Corrigan.

Hanson walked to the window, gazed out. 'I'm struggling with the idea of Matthew Flynn being involved in that drugs set up.'

Watts shrugged. 'Maybe he wasn't the blue-eyed type that woman who worked with him said he was. Addison is right about him having form.'

Hanson wasn't about to let it go. 'One caution when he was a teenager? That doesn't make him some kind of drug baron five years later.'

'It's a tough judgement to make right now,' said Corrigan. 'We need to know more about him.'

Hanson left the window. 'What about Diana Flynn? We don't know much about her. I want to talk to her.' Watts and Corrigan exchanged glances. 'When do you plan to release this latest news about the marijuana?' she asked.

'Not until after the interviews are done and Graham and Addison have been charged,' said Watts. 'That house is in an area full of rental properties, a floating population and the raid was low key. Even if there has been local media interest there's probably nothing the Flynn family would have picked up on. It'll be a couple of days at least before they know what's happened and Graham and Addison won't be in a position to tell them.' She eyed him. 'OK, doc. Go and see her but don't let the cat out of the bag.'

'As if.' She headed for the door. 'I'll phone her later and arrange something.'

Hearing music playing upstairs, Hanson went into her study and started a search through her notes for the Flynn family's mobile numbers. She dialled one of them and waited. Her call was picked up. 'Hello?' said a female voice.

'Mrs Flynn? This is Kate Hanson. I'm part of the invest-igation into what happened to your son, Matthew. I want to say how sorry I am about that.' She left a pause. Diana Flynn didn't respond. 'I'd appreciate meeting you, say tomorrow if at all possible?'

'Why? Have the police got some news?'

Hanson closed her eyes against the hope in the voice. This was a bad time to talk to her. *Has to be done.* 'The investigation is ongoing and likely to be for some time. I need to talk to you.' She wrote down Diana Flynn's reluctant suggestion of a meeting at a hotel coffee shop in the city centre the following day. As the call ended she picked up movement on the upstairs landing. She came into the hall as Maisie leapt down the last three stairs. On seeing her, Maisie's facial expression changed to a pout.

'Maisie, we need to talk about today.'

'There's nothing to talk about.' She scowled. 'Nothing happened.'

'I've got no reason to believe that anything has,' said Hanson, frowning at her. 'But you've never come to my office unexpectedly before so, why today?'

'Why are you always like this?' she demanded. 'Like, totally suspicious and looking for problems. Why can't you be like other mothers and just accept what I'm saying without going on? It's *really* annoying.'

They came into the kitchen. Charlie gave Hanson a quizzical look and pointed to the lasagne she'd put in the oven earlier. She nodded and he opened the oven door. 'I doubt the existence of the mothers you describe, Maisie, and you haven't actually told me anything about today. I'm getting the idea that something did happen and I want to know what it was. Now.' She waited. Nothing. Placing her hands on her daughter's shoulders she turned her round. 'Look, Maisie, if there's any kind of problem with the maths lectures, if you're unhappy about anything, I can sort that out . . .'

Maisie wriggled free. 'You always think you can sort everything out, Mom, but you . . . There isn't anything.'

Watching Maisie sit at the table, elbows on it, her face closed, Hanson let the issue go. Whatever was on her daughter's mind – and Hanson was sure now that it had something to do with the maths lectures at the university – right now there was little she could do if Maisie wouldn't talk.

TWELVE

Driving into the city centre, Hanson was conducting a debate inside her head. It concerned Diana Flynn and what she herself was about to do. Which was to question a woman who, only days earlier had been informed that her missing son was never coming home. Hanson knew that she might be about to add to that suffering by asking her some potentially awkward questions about her private life. Hanson turned into the car park, the debate continuing: *If I don't raise this issue with her now, get her talking, very soon she and the family will be aware of the rental house being a cannabis factory and the arrests of Graham and Addison and we could be dealing with wall-to-wall silence from her and others in the family about anything which was occurring at that house as a bid to protect the memory of Matthew. Zach Addison could well be facing a prison sentence and Diana Flynn might possibly have her own reasons for not wanting to divulge anything about him.* Despite Watts's expressed confidence about the findings at the house being kept under wraps, she wondered if Diana Flynn might already be aware of the development.

She came into the hotel foyer and followed signs for its coffee shop. She was relieved to see that it was less than half full, Diana Flynn seated in a quiet corner. Hanson gave her a quick appraisal. Her blonde hair immaculate, she was wearing a cream sweater which Hanson guessed was cashmere, a long fitted skirt, the open edges at its front showing well-shaped legs in black tights and boots. Diana Flynn was managing her self-presentation but her drawn face indicated the effort required to hold herself together now that she knew what had happened to Matthew.

'Thank you for agreeing to meet with me, Mrs—'

'What's this about?' The blue eyes on Hanson were tired and distant. 'What do you want?'

Hanson sat, looking at her directly. 'I need information about the house in Erdington where Matthew was living at the time he disappeared.'

'We already told you,' she said wearily. 'He shared it with two other students.'

'A house which belonged to you and Mr Flynn?'

She sighed. 'Yes.'

Hanson kept her tone relaxed. 'But Matthew wasn't a student at that time?'

'No. We anticipated he would be by the time he started living there.'

Hanson took her time before launching into her next question, thinking how best to proceed, guessing that a direct reference to what she wanted to know wasn't going to be well received. 'Did he know those two students beforehand?'

Diana Flynn gave her a cool look. 'No. Matthew was living at home prior to his move there.'

Hanson chose her words. 'I need to talk to you about Matthew's caution for drugs.'

Diana Flynn's mouth became a thin line. 'That was a long time ago. Neither his father nor I regarded it as a problem, either then or later. He never gave us any anxiety before that or afterwards. My husband has boundless energy. He works hard, long hours. I brought up both boys and I'm proud of them . . .' She swallowed. 'I was proud of Matthew. He needed me in a way Dom never did.'

'He was sensitive?' asked Hanson, mindful of what Terri Brennan had said about Matthew.

'Yes. He was.'

'To your and your husband's knowledge, did Matthew have any involvement in drugs after receiving that caution?'

Hanson watched a pale red wave wash over Diana Flynn's neck. She stared at Hanson, her voice low but vehement. 'Of course he didn't! What he did at fifteen was a stupid, naïve action on his part when he was too young to appreciate the risks, the consequences. He would *never* have done anything like that again because he knew about those risks.'

Hanson slow-nodded. 'How did he know? Was he given professional support after the caution?'

Diana Flynn looked away. 'I don't know what you mean. My

husband dealt with the caution. We put it behind us. Forgot
about it. We're a strong family. That was all Matthew needed.
We supported him one hundred percent.'

Hanson gazed at her. 'Tell me about his two housemates.'

There was a lengthy pause. Again, Diana Flynn's eyes moved
from Hanson's. 'What about them?'

'Did you know them prior to their leasing the house?'

'No. We had the house registered with a letting agent. They
were the two best applicants at the time.'

'How, best?'

Diana Flynn looked impatient. 'The agent checked them out.
They'd both successfully completed their first year of study
and their financial status was such that they could afford the
monthly rent plus the tenancy deposit. Look, I'm tired, I've
still got a lot of shopping to do—'

'And you'd never met either of them before that?'

Diana Flynn gave her a cold look. 'I already answered
that. No.'

'But you met with both of them subsequently?'

Diana Flynn's eyes were anywhere but on Hanson. 'Of course
I did. I called in occasionally to see how Matthew was. I also
dropped by sometimes just to check that the house was being
properly looked after.'

'I thought agents did that.'

She gave Hanson a level look. 'There's nothing better than
doing those sorts of checks yourself.'

'Were they, are they, still satisfactory tenants?' asked Hanson.

'They wouldn't still be living at the house if they weren't.'

Hanson nodded. *Looks like she doesn't know about the
marijuana.* 'Some tenants can be unwelcoming of landlords
dropping by.'

The blue eyes narrowed on Hanson. 'They were fine with it.'
Diana Flynn lifted her coffee cup to her lips.

'What's William Graham like?' asked Hanson.

'Nice. Polite. What's he got to do with what happened to
my son?'

'Maybe nothing. Tell me about Zach Addison.'

The wariness was full on now, cup still raised. 'I don't know
what you mean.'

'There was no falling out between Mr Graham or Mr Addison and your son?'

'Of course not. They got on well.'

'You sound very certain, Mrs Flynn. Did you get to know Mr Graham and Mr Addison well?' Diana Flynn's face was now rigid, watchful. She didn't reply. 'We understand that you took flowers to the house occasionally. A nice gesture but unusual between property owner and tenants.' There was a heavy silence, filled by Hanson. 'Did Matthew ever question your visits to the house?'

Diana Flynn's coffee cup met its saucer with an audible click, causing two or three other customers to look across at their table. She glared at Hanson. 'I've got nothing more to say to you, except that if you repeat your accusation, I assure you, you'll regret it.'

'What accusation have I made, Mrs Flynn?' asked Hanson. She watched her signal to a waiter. If she was going to get anything from this woman she needed to be explicit. And quick. 'Mrs Flynn, I regret having to be direct but if there was or is anything between you and Zach Addison you need to tell me.' The waiter appeared. Diana Flynn was getting ready to leave, her hands shaking as she reached for her bag. 'My bill please. *Now.*'

'Certainly, Mrs Flynn. I trust everything was satisfactory as always?' She gave a curt nod and he went away. There was a short, tense silence until the waiter brought the bill and turned to go.

'*Wait,*' she said, searching her purse, taking out a ten-pound note and giving it to him. 'Don't bother about change.' She dropped her purse into her bag and stood, giving Hanson a challenging look. 'Do you know why I'm in town? I'll tell you, shall I? I have to find something to wear to my son's funeral.' Her lips trembled. She got control. 'Don't contact me again and stay away from my family.' Without a backward look she walked away from the table.

Hanson watched her go. She hadn't expected Diana Flynn to admit to anything but her behavioural and verbal responses told her all she needed to know: Diana Flynn and Addison had probably been involved in an intimate relationship at around the time Matthew disappeared. She frowned, chin supported on one hand. *What might that mean in respect of his murder? Possibly nothing. Yet it might provide some leverage for her colleagues when they resumed their interviews of Graham and Addison.*

Leaving the city centre she made a brief detour to the university. Coming into her room she went straight to the flip chart and stood, hands on hips, eyes moving over positive descriptors of Matthew Flynn. She read Terri Brennan's comment about how he had dealt with the difficult coffee shop customer. Honest, kindly Matthew who possibly wasn't too good at judging situations which might be volatile and possibly dangerous to him. Hanson added notes, recalling the waiter addressing Mrs Flynn by name, her hasty exit from the hotel coffee shop. It was very possible that Zach Addison's stance in interview might change once he realised that they knew about his relationship with Diana Flynn. She had no idea what it might add to their investigation of Matthew's death, if anything, but they needed all the information it was possible to get.

THIRTEEN

H anson walked into UCU the following morning to find her colleagues deep in discussion. 'I say we should be a presence,' said Watts. 'And you can explain the technicalities of it.'

'There probably won't be any,' said Corrigan. 'Just a straight service but seven o'clock fits with my schedule. Armed Response finishes at six thirty. I'll meet you there.'

She looked from him to Watts. 'You two have a date?'

'One of Delaney's deacons phoned,' said Watts. 'We've got an official invite to the re-consecration service at St Bartholomew's tonight.'

'Seems Delaney already had one planned in respect of the

vandalism,' said Corrigan. 'Matthew Flynn's body being found within the church building seems to have incentivised him. Come with us, Red.'

Watts nodded. 'The three of us should be there.'

'I'll think about it. I'm not sure how welcome I might be.' She told them of Delaney's comments about her profession.

Corrigan didn't look surprised. 'Like I said, he's on the traditional side.'

'Come on, doc. You could do with an outing.'

Is this what my social life's come to? 'OK. By the way, I've asked a Social Services contact to check out any information available on Matthew Flynn following his caution. If he was given support at the time we need to know who provided it. It could give us useful information about him and his life back then, plus any associates.'

'And the likelihood of his sticking with the drugs,' said Watts.

She walked to the board and pointed. 'Kind Matthew, honest Matthew. I can't believe he was part of that marijuana scheme.' She glanced at Corrigan. 'Do we know if the Flynn family has been invited to the service? If so, that's another reason I might not be welcome. I met with Diana Flynn yesterday and followed up the theory about her and Addison. I'm certain they were having a relationship.' She returned to the table. 'I've been thinking about that. We already have an indication that Matthew may have been a little naïve, not too skilled at dealing with challenging personal situations. How might he have reacted if he learned that his mother was having sex with one of his housemates?'

Watts exchanged a look with Corrigan. 'How certain are you about this relationship?' he asked her.

'Certain enough, short of actual proof.'

'Works for me,' said Corrigan. 'We'll ask Addison directly.'

She looked from him to Watts. 'When?'

Watts pointed at the clock. 'Five minutes from now. If we're going to charge him we have to get a move on.'

She looked up at the Smartboard and the depiction of Matthew Flynn's throat injury. 'My concern is what might have happened at that house if Matthew found out about his mother and Addison and challenged him. Matthew might have threatened to tell his father about it and about the marijuana. Such threats could have been enough to invite a violent response from Addison, possibly Graham, too. That whole rented house needs to be forensically examined.' She saw Watts reach for the phone. 'Tell the SOCOs they're looking for massive blood loss.'

Addison was sitting next to his solicitor, his face resigned. 'Look, charge me, if that's what you're going to do.'

Watching through glass, Hanson saw a look pass between Watts and Corrigan. 'There's something else we'd like to ask you about,' said Watts. 'How was your relationship with Matthew Flynn?'

Addison's heavy brows met. 'There was hardly a relationship. I met him for the first time late last summer when he moved into the house. By October he was gone. Disappeared.'

Watts studied him. 'Long enough for a falling out.'

Addison looked at his solicitor then back. 'We got on OK.'

'Did Matthew Flynn know about you and his mother?'

Addison stared at him, started to speak then closed his mouth. His solicitor raised a hand. 'A minute, please.' They waited as he leant forward to murmur low words into Addison's ear. Whatever was said resulted in some shoulder-shrugging from Addison and glared looks for Watts and Corrigan. The solicitor straightened and Addison folded his arms.

'That's got nothing to do with why I'm here so, no comment.'

'Was there ever an altercation between you and Matthew Flynn?' asked Corrigan.

'I don't know what you're talking about.' He got a warning look from his solicitor. 'No comment.'

'You don't need to know, Mr Addison,' said Corrigan. 'Just answer the question. Was there ever any kind of physical altercation between you and Matthew Flynn?'

Addison studied the floor. Watts proceeded to charge him with organising the growth of cannabis plants sufficient to produce significant quantities for commercial use. As Addison was escorted away from the interview room followed by his solicitor, Hanson came inside.

'You're going to charge Graham too?'

'Yeah. The SOCOs are on their way to the house. Maybe

we'll be charging one or both with murder by the time they've finished.'

Hanson was aware of the heat as soon as they entered the church that evening. Unbuttoning her heavy tweed overcoat she picked up the low sounds of organ music. In front of them was a sea of heads, most members of the congregation conversing in hushed voices, their faces animated. The atmosphere felt heavy with anticipation. She looked for the Flynn family but didn't see them. Her gaze was drawn to the far end of the church and the huge stained glass window. Lights mounted on huge metal rings suspended by chains from high crossbeams turned the window's reds, yellows and blues to jewels. Lilies in tall vases stood at multiple places around the church. She looked at those nearest to her, pulsing out their heavy scent, fleshy, spotted petals furled back like trumpet-blares, stamens exposed.

She and her colleagues made their way further inside, scanning the crammed pews for available seats. Amid the low murmurings of the congregation, plus a few finger-points in their direction, Hanson saw a space and went to it, Watts following. Taking a seat she looked round for Corrigan. He was still standing, his head bowed. She looked away, feeling like an intruder, trying to recall the last time she'd attended a service of any kind. A long time ago. Her eyes moved over the church's interior. It was undeniably beautiful. She straightened to get a view of the altar. It was covered in white cloth deeply bordered with lace, the tall brass candleholders bearing slender, lit candles placed at either end, between them multiple items of brassware, light glinting off crucifixes and other more intricate designs.

She looked up as Corrigan joined them. The murmurings of the congregation stopped. A door to one side opened and the congregation rose as one. A robed priest appeared holding a small brass object suspended by a chain. In the loaded silence Father Delaney came into view, his massive form clothed in red. He faced the altar and knelt. Hanson watched as the brass object was swung. Smoke billowed from it and rose upwards. Delaney also rose, turned to face the wrapt and silent congregation and lowered his hands. Everyone sat. Delaney's voice flowed over them.

'Oh, Lord accept this smoke as a symbol of our prayers rising to thee. May it purify all it touches.' Surprised at the clarity of his voice, Hanson gave him a close look, saw the tiny microphone attached to his robe. Voices around them rose in an assent to his words. The heavy scent of lilies and the smoke were now inside her nose. Amid the bowed heads she watched and listened to Delaney. 'This, your house has been tainted by those who seek only to despoil with the symbolism of evil. There has been damage to its fabric and the destruction of a young life which you with your all-seeing eyes know, oh Lord. We resist evil in *all* its forms, whether criminal or spiritual. Hear our prayers for a young life drawn cruelly to an end.' Delaney's arms rose along with his voice. 'We *beseech* you, oh Lord! Take hold of the dragon, the serpent which is the devil and Satan,' he intoned. '*Cast* him into the bottomless pit! *Drive* him from wherever unclean spirits hide.'

Hanson stared, her mouth slightly open. She looked at the people nearby murmuring responses. Watts's lips were pressed together. Corrigan's face was closed. Delaney's voice rose again. 'Cast out all *satanic* powers, all evil doers, all the legions of the *wicked*! We live in godless times. The worried and the frightened seek salvation in the falsehood of activities they believe calm the spirit and ease the soul but we who are gathered here know the undeniable Truth! Christ himself cast out demons and he guides me now.' He lowered his arms. 'Let us pray to the Madonna to help us.' After a minute of silence his voice climbed still further. 'Oh, Lord, the devil has been at work here!' The congregation murmured assent. 'This assembly knows the true God, which is also here. We reject consumerism and the reliance on the individual, the psyche.' Hanson's eyes widened. His voice was thunderous now. 'Oh, Satan! Lucifer! Beelzebub! Whatever name you choose, hear *this*. We do not doubt your existence.' He flung his arms wide. Background sounds from the organ now swelled. 'You are present yet in hiding. I say to you in the name of the Lord, be *gone*!'

The congregation erupted, repeating his words. Hanson stared at Delaney's reddened face, the lights and their reflection off the brasses making her eyes burn, the smell of lilies and smoke filling her head. Hanson had been shallow breathing for several minutes. Her forehead felt damp. She had to be away from this. She stood, squeezed past Corrigan, went to the door, passing several people holding collection plates and out.

She stood on the grass, gulping cold night air, gazing at gravestones. The church door opened and her two colleagues emerged. She breathed deeply, pulling more cold air into her chest.

'You all right, doc?' asked Watts.

'Fine now.' She pressed the back of her hand to her forehead. It was clammy. 'Just a bad case of sensory overload.' She looked up at them. 'What did you make of that?'

Corrigan looked at the church. 'It's still going on. I said he was a traditionalist but I never saw anything so over the top.'

'I don't go for that fire-and-brimstone stuff, myself,' sniffed Watts. 'But they're lapping it up in there.'

'It's more exorcism than anything,' said Corrigan. 'I didn't see the Flynn family.'

Hanson shook her head. 'Just as well, given the tone, the drama.'

They walked away from the church in silence. When they got to their vehicles Hanson called to them. 'Come back to my house and say hello to Charlie. Have something warming.'

Across the city, white-suited figures entered the Erdington house carrying their forensic equipment and cases. Reaching the top of the house they put on eye protectors and face masks and moved in silence and minimal lighting, actions smoothly orchestrated as one officer sprayed a section of each room's floor and wall whilst another recorded it on video and yet another took photographs. They were on a quest for blood. A lot of blood. Once an area was sprayed a forensic light source was activated and all other light extinguished. The light source was drawn slowly, methodically over the sprayed area. The process was painstakingly repeated in each room on each floor.

After two hours of careful examination, they packed their cases and left the house to darkness and silence.

Charlie reached into a high cupboard for small glasses which he handed to Hanson to put on the tray next to a bottle of brandy. 'How did it go at the church?'

'A good night out for anybody who likes a religious rant,' said Watts.

Hanson looked at the kitchen clock then at Charlie. 'It's only nine o'clock. Did Maisie say why she wanted to go to bed so early? Did she seem unwell?'

'She didn't say, so I didn't ask, but she did look tired.' Hanson carried the tray to the table, listening to her colleagues describe their experience at St Bartholomew's. 'An *exorcism*?' Charlie's eyebrows rose. 'Does that kind of thing still happen?'

'Apparently it does and it was an experience, I can tell you.' Hanson poured brandy and offered glasses. 'You know *The Crucible*. It was like that, with Father Delaney finger-jabbing the congregation, roaring and railing at the "evil within".'

Watts took a glass. 'Say what you like, they were all enjoying it.'

'Is that what usually happens in a re-consecration?' she asked Corrigan.

'I never went to one and I never saw that kind of fervour in any church I attended, back home or here. But as Watts says, it seemed to work for Delaney's parishioners.'

Watts sipped brandy. 'It would have upset the Flynn family, you can bet on it.'

Hanson nodded. *And Diana Flynn has had enough upset. Caused by me.* A thought occurred to her. If Brad Flynn was unaware of his wife's affair with Addison, would Diana Flynn tell him about it, now that she was aware that the police knew? She recalled what her colleagues had told her about Brad Flynn: entrepreneur, controller, a man with a large ego. *No. Diana won't tell him.* She sighed at the assumption she'd made. *For all we know, he might already have known.*

'The family doesn't have a connection to that church?' asked Charlie.

Corrigan shook his head. 'None at all.'

'So why was this victim's body left there?'

Hanson and her colleagues exchanged glances. 'We don't know,' said Watts. His phone buzzed. He brought it out of his pocket. 'Yeah? What did you get?' He listened, all eyes turned on him. 'Thanks.' He ended the call. 'Forensics. They've tested the whole of the Erdington house.' Hanson and Corrigan waited.

'No blood in the quantities we were expecting. In fact, no blood full stop.'

Hanson was at the door, seeing her colleagues out. 'What have you got planned for tomorrow?'

'Once Corrigan's finished with Armed Response, he's searching databases, everything we've got for information on Spencer Albright and keeping me updated on anything he finds while I'm out checking the places Albright's known to frequent. We need to find him. He knows that church. He'd been there before Chivers even knew about it. For all we know, he could have decided to make himself scarce because he knows something about Matthew Flynn's body being left in that crypt.'

'Still no news on the bits of trace evidence Chong vacuumed from Matthew Flynn's clothes?' asked Hanson.

'I would have let you know if there was, doc. Chong's got a lot on but tomorrow morning I'll risk getting chewed up by asking her.'

'How about you, Red?' asked Corrigan. 'Got any plans?'

'Yes. I want an answer to Charlie's question: why was Matthew's body at St Bartholomews?'

Hanson switched off her bedside light, her head occupied with events of the evening. She pictured the scene in her kitchen, Charlie on one side of the table, Corrigan on the other, both tall, both dark, with that similar air of earnest consideration. *I never realised before how alike they are.* She sat up, pounded her pillow, lay back. *Pick the bones out of that, Sigmund.*

FOURTEEN

It was late afternoon, cold and crisp, when Hanson arrived at the church, the colour of its stone façade warmed a little by a meagre, low sun. She looked up at it, memories of the previous evening diminished by daylight. Her eyes drifted up to gargoyles mounted high above her, heads horned, crooked and voracious mouths stretched, their eyes hooded. Words drifted into her head which she'd heard but now poorly recalled. Something about eyes being where demons hide.

A muted groan sent her whirling. A sixty-something man in heavy jacket and scarf was toiling some distance away at a patch of bare earth encircled by a brick border, brown paper sacks on either side of him. He squinted up at her as she approached. 'Can I help you?'

'I'm hoping to see Father Delaney.' He got slowly to his feet. 'No, please. I can see you're hard at work.' He stood with a grimace, rubbing at his knees. She upped her age estimate a decade. *Maybe more?*

'I'm never too busy to talk to a church visitor. Father Delaney usually has choir practice around about now, after school hours, but I haven't seen him.' He pointed to the sacks. 'Come the spring and the work will have been worth it. *Narcissus pseudonarcissus* and *Tulipa gesneriana*. Daffodil bulbs in that one, tulips in the other. Something else for the local children to walk over. Chilly, isn't it?'

She nodded. 'How long have you been the gardener here?'

He laughed. 'St Bartholomew's doesn't employ one. We do it all: an army of parishioner-volunteers helps maintain the church, inside and out.'

She recalled Corrigan giving similar information. Despite her reservations about the re-consecration service, Hanson had to acknowledge that Delaney inspired devotion in his elderly church attenders.

'I saw you here last night,' he continued. 'Did you enjoy the service?'

Hanson chose her words. 'It was certainly dramatic.'

'Indeed, it was. That's Father Delaney. He's been a godsend to this church.' He frowned, offered her his hand, saw the soil on it and withdrew it. 'Sorry. My name's Alfred.'

'Hello, Alfred. I'm Kate.' She watched his gaze move slowly over the freshly dug bed.

'He asks a lot of us but no more than he demands of himself and his deacons.'

She was aware now that she had been misled by Alfred's

vigour. He had to be in his eighties. 'Do many of the congregation give freely of their time?'

'Yes, particularly the members of the committee. We're very
willing to do so because of Father Delaney.'

'Why is he a "godsend", exactly?' she asked.

'Because he's brought new life, new blood to St Bartholomew's.
When he first came this was a failing church with an elderly,
ever-decreasing congregation. That was twenty or more years
ago.' He smiled at her. 'I was comparatively young then. Our
congregation was very small and, sad to say, disengaged. Last
night is an example of how that's changed. A church so full in
these times is a rarity. Father Delaney has brought commitment,
energy and vitality back to us. In return we support and reward
the church.' He paused. 'No one individual is more important
than the church itself, of course.' He pointed to the sacks of
bulbs. 'I'm sorry to cut our conversation short but I must get
on. I want to finish here in daylight. Why don't you check at
the house and see if he's there?'

He went slowly onto his knees as Hanson headed for Church
House, noticing a small blue car parked outside. Surely too
small to accommodate Delaney's bulk? She couldn't recall it
being there when she'd come to talk to him previously. She
went up the steps, onto the wide porch and rang the bell, then
rang it again. She picked up movement beyond the lace curtain.
It came closer. The front door was opened by a middle-aged
woman wearing a salmon-pink jumper and patterned leggings.
'What do you want?'

'I'd like to see—' Hanson's words were stopped by a high-
pitched screech from within the house.

'Wait here,' the woman snapped. She hurried away, down
the shadowy corridor beyond the hallway, hips massive and
dimpled within the leggings. When she didn't reappear Hanson
stepped inside and headed in the same direction. She found her
in a large, basic kitchen opening the valve of a hefty, old-
fashioned pressure cooker.

'Hello . . .?'

The woman spun and glared. 'I told you to wait.'

Hanson nodded. 'I know, but when you didn't return I thought
I'd come inside in case something was wrong.'

The woman shoved the pressure cooker to the back of the stove. 'Nothing's wrong. Father Delaney's dinner is in this old thing which has to be watched.' She looked Hanson up and down. 'Now you're in, what do you want?' She asked again, the accent sounding local to Hanson's ears.

'I'd like a brief word with Father Delaney.'

A satisfied expression crossed the woman's face. 'You can't. He's not here.'

When nothing further was forthcoming Hanson asked, 'You work here?'

The woman's lips curled downwards. 'I don't come here for the fun of it. I'm his housekeeper.'

'When will he be back?'

'Depends.'

The sound of something heavy hitting the upper floor drifted downwards to the kitchen. Hanson glanced upwards then at the housekeeper. Seeing no response to the sound she said, 'Do you want to attend to that?'

The housekeeper's eyes didn't move from Hanson's face. 'No need. My niece is up there. She's a bit caggie-handed. She'll sort it.'

'You were saying that Father Delaney's return depended on something?' prompted Hanson.

'Was I?' She lifted the pressure cooker's lid, jabbed at the contents with a wooden spoon. Hanson's eyes drifted over chunks of dark-looking meat and a couple of fat garlic bulbs. The lid slammed down. 'I'll see you out.'

Hanson glanced towards the window where several plants in small pots sat on the sill, only one familiar to her: mint. She looked beyond to the extensive rear garden. 'Do you work on the garden too?'

The housekeeper was now in the dark passageway, on her way to the front door. 'I keep this place ticking over. I've got no time for anything else. Come on.'

Hanson followed. 'Does the church committee take responsibility for it?'

The housekeeper turned, her face expressionless. 'Yes, but I'm the one who says what they put in. I know my plants and herbs. You ask a lot of questions.'

Hanson stepped onto the porch, reaching out a quick hand

to the already-closing door, thinking of what Alfred had said about Delaney's current whereabouts. 'You haven't told me where Father Delaney is. I need to see him.'

'He's over at the church taking choir practice. There's still half an hour left and he doesn't like being interrupted.'

Hanson frowned. 'I didn't hear anything when I was outside the church a few minutes ago.'

The housekeeper gave her an up-down look. 'Why would you? It's only a few kids and he's got a lot of stuff to tell 'em about the service they're singing at in a few days' time.'

Hanson was about to ask if she could wait for Delaney, imagined this woman's pleased refusal and decided against it. The small, hard eyes were on her. She nodded at Hanson's hair. 'That your natural colour?' Startled at the bluntness, Hanson stared at the woman, seeing for the first time the hairs on either side of her upper lip. Before Hanson could formulate a response the eyes gave her another once-over, settling on the olive-green parka.

'I'm after a new winter coat. Bet that set you back a bob or two.' Hanson turned and started down the steps, the house-keeper's words coming after her. 'Don't forget what I said! You *wait* till he's finished. He doesn't like being disturbed at choir practice.'

Alfred was nowhere in sight as Hanson followed the path between the headstones and on towards the church. She was within a couple of metres of it, irritated still by the housekeeper's crassness, when she picked up the sweet sound of young voices raised in unison. Reaching the door she pushed it open and went inside, moving slowly along a narrow side-aisle. The lilies from the previous evening were still in their vases, the air heavy with their scent, the candles, unlit, still in their tall holders, the brasses standing at attention. Father Delaney was facing three rows of fresh-faced boys in the choir stall, music in his left hand, the other energetically emphasising tempo as they sang, their voices soaring to the vaulted ceiling, their mouths wide. He brought his hands slowly downwards and to a quick halt. The singing stopped as one voice.

'Well done. Well done,' he enthused. 'That will do for today.' The boys clambered down from the stall and Hanson noted that several of them still had that pure, genderless beauty of the pre-adolescent male. Delaney called to one of them. 'Hugo, dear boy, come here. I have the music for your solo.' Hanson watched as the boy came to him and the vast priest pointed out details on the sheet music, his face benign as he smiled down at him. 'Here, do you see? You'll need to focus on your breathing at this point to reach that note.' Seeing the boy's keen attention, Hanson smiled to herself. The smile faded as she watched Delaney's huge, plump hand move from the music and arrived on the boy's soft-looking blond curls, his eyes fixed on the boy's head. Disconcerted, she heard Delaney speak again, his voice low. 'Yes, Hugo. I think you'll manage it nicely if you practice and we have two or three more rehearsals here.'

Hanson stepped forward. 'Father Delaney?' Her voice sounded loud, harsh to her own ears.

Delaney turned, gave her a calm glance, a nod, then back to the boy. 'Run along, Hugo, and don't forget, next practice is early Sunday morning.' Hugo joined his fellow choristers as they rushed for the main door in a jostle of feet and were gone.

Delaney returned the music to its stand. 'What can I do for you, Professor Hanson?' His plump-cheeked, unlined face was now turned to her, eyes made small by the fleshy pockets above and beneath.

She scrambled for the reason which had brought her to him. 'I was here last night. For the re-consecration service.'

'Yes. I saw you.'

'I understood the service was to purify the church following the vandalism and also the concealment of Matthew Flynn's body, but I didn't see anyone from his family.'

'No.' He gathered up sheets of music. 'They were invited as a courtesy but they must have decided against attending. They would have been very welcome, of course, but I don't know the family. The service was as much for St Bartholomew's congregation which has been upset by recent events.'

'So, the Flynn family has no connection to this church?'

'None at all.'

'Can you think of any reason why their son's body would have been concealed in the crypt here?'

'I had wondered about that myself. No, I can't.' He gave her a genial nod. 'I've finished here. I need to turn off the lights and lock up.' She followed him. Outside the sky had clouded over. He turned to her. 'Is there anything else I can help you with?'

She couldn't leave the puzzle of Matthew Flynn's body being here. 'You'll understand that my police colleagues and I are curious as to why Matthew Flynn's body was brought here, to this place. Whoever did that appears to have had a key. Does that concern you, Father Delaney?'

'Of course it does but as I said to Lieutenant Corrigan, I had no idea as to the existence of such a key. In all the years of my ministry here I have not known the crypt to be opened. If such a key exists, it could have been stolen. It could be anywhere.' He looked down at her, his face benign, genuinely regretful. 'I wish I could help you, which is self-serving on my part of course. Whatever I'm able to do to speed up the police investigation to a conclusion is good for St Bartholomew's. Unfortunately, I can't help.' He turned to lock the heavy door. 'Our parishioners know about the remains being here, of course and it's extremely upsetting for them. I've listened to their comments but heard nothing which suggests that any of them have knowledge of this young man. Which isn't surprising in itself, of course, given their years.' He gave her an appraising look. 'How did you know where to find me?'

'I went to Church House. Your housekeeper told me.'

He smiled. 'Ah. You've met the fearsome Gorridge. Did she issue directives and overstep social boundaries?' His eyes twinkled. 'Don't be put off by Eunice or take her manner personally. She's indiscriminate in the way she deals with people but she has a good heart.'

Ahead of them Alfred was back, planting bulbs. Hanson saw Delaney's attention move from him to her car and back. 'That's Alfred Best, one of our congregation stalwarts. Alfred?' he called. Alfred got slowly to his feet. 'Would you get out the hose and give Professor Hanson's car a quick wash, there's a good chap? I hear council workers were out early this morning, gritting and salting the roads.'

Hanson looked at Alfred. 'Oh, no please—'

Delaney was walking away. 'So nice to meet you again,

Professor Hanson. I regret I couldn't help but please come again if you have any further questions.'

She watched him move smoothly away to Church House, surprisingly light on his feet for such a heavy man, then looked to where Alfred was dragging a heavy garden hose in the direction of her car. She went after him. 'Alfred, *wait*. It isn't necessary.'

'It's no trouble.' He manipulated the head of the hose and water shot out of it and all over her car. He trained it on the wheels then the lower bodywork. After a few minutes he turned off the hose and looked up at a turbulent sky. 'If you'll excuse me, I still have more bulbs to plant and I can't do it once darkness falls.'

Hanson came into UCU feeling dispirited. Watts looked up from the big work table. 'You look like your tail's dragging, doc.'

The door opened again and Corrigan followed her inside. 'Hi, Red. You look—'

'You're taking a risk if you say I look done in and fed up.' Pushing her hair off her face she stared moodily at the notes on the board. She was overstretched at the university and her head was crammed with impressions gathered over the last few days they'd been on this case. She was unsure of where she was going with any of them, if anywhere and Maisie had been intermittently in her head since her unexpected arrival at her university room a couple of days ago. Hanson still didn't know what that was about and Maisie wasn't talking.

Something else was bothering her. She sat on the table, pressing her hands against her eyes, the scene she'd witnessed in the church this afternoon still in her head. *OK. Delaney placed his hand on a boy's head. Not the best idea for any professional in these times but on its own not something to leap to a massive assumption about either.* She frowned. *What was my immediate response? Surprise? Unease? Enough on which to base suspicion?* Letting her hands drop she said, 'I'm tired and I feel I'm getting nowhere. The only up-side today is that I had my car washed by a kindly octogenerian.'

Watts winked at Corrigan. 'That's new boyfriends for you, doc. They'll do anything to get on your good side.'

Opening her mouth to make a snappy reply, she felt the

frustrations and confusions inside her head stop their clamour. She burst into laughter, unable to stop, knowing that her colleagues were enjoying the spectacle. Corrigan grinned at her as she fingered away mascara.

'Feel better, now your corset's loosened?' asked Watts.

'Yes, thanks.' She looked at them. 'We don't know what this case is about, do we?' Seeing Watts's mouth open she shook her head. 'Think about it. First, it's about drugs then, it's about money, and now we know about the relationship between Diana Flynn and Zach Addison, maybe it's about sex? Yet, none of it is making any sense to me or giving me a psychological direction, an investigative angle, a coherent explanation as to why somebody decided that at twenty years old Matthew Flynn had to die and in the horrendous way he did.'

Watts stood. 'We were saying more or less the same before you arrived. Corrigan and me are prioritising Albright. We've chased down various sightings of him but none have been any use so far. He's in none of his usual haunts.'

She watched him go to the refreshment centre in the corner then looked to Corrigan. 'Any ideas for a way forward?'

He was looking thoughtful. 'What if Matthew Flynn's murder has some historical, rather than current relevance?'

'At twenty, how much history did he have?'

She followed Corrigan's eyes to the board. 'What about his school?' he asked.

'Matthew Flynn was still school-age when he was cautioned for drug possession.' She walked to it and pointed. 'Did you put this information up?'

'Julian the data-hound tracked it down.'

She read it. 'Claremont Independent School for Boys'. She tapped an icon. A photograph of a central Victorian façade with modern wings on either side appeared, plus location and other details. 'I'm going there,' she said.

Watts came to the table, three mugs clutched in his big hand. 'For what, exactly?'

She was on her way through the door. 'Background. I'm not sure. But if I don't, I'll not know anything there is to know, will I?'

He shook his head. 'Can't argue with that.'

* * *

Hanson had phoned and spoken to the head of school who had agreed for her to see Angus Robbe, form tutor and head of year to fifteen-year-old Matthew Flynn, that same early evening. She was now inside a heavily panelled room, sitting across from an austere looking man who was evidently not too happy at finding himself in this situation. She was waiting for his response to her question about how the drug offence had come to light, watching as he chose his words. 'Five years is a long time in this profession. Pupils, staff, come and go, but as far as I recall, it was the PE master who found them.' He lapsed into silence.

She studied him. 'Mr Robbe, I was under the impression that Matthew Flynn was at some kind of party when he accepted the drugs he was charged with possessing. Are you saying the party was *here*? On school premises?'

Robbe gave a reluctant nod. He leant towards her, his face earnest. 'It caused a furore here, I can tell you. Claremont had had nothing like it in all its history.' He pursed his lips. 'And nothing since.'

'Tell me about the party.'

He shrugged. 'Some of the pupils were having an end-of-academic-year get-together in the sixth form hub.'

She frowned. 'Matthew Flynn wasn't a sixth former.'

'No, but he and a couple of his friends wangled invitations.' He sent her one of his few direct looks so far. 'You know what the young are like. Things got a bit out of hand.'

'There was supervision?' she asked.

'Of course, but . . . not constant. It was a very busy time for all the staff here.'

'Were you involved in the celebration or its supervision?'

He gave a vehement headshake. 'Not at all, I'm glad to say.' He leant on the desk, giving her a conspiratorial look, his voice low. She recognised in him someone who liked to gossip. 'It caused the most *almighty* shake-up as you can probably imagine. A school like this can do without incidents of that kind: illicit substances, police! Heads didn't exactly roll but . . .' He hesitated. Hanson widened her eyes at him. He lowered his voice further. 'All I'll say is that certain staff who were viewed as "neglecting their duties" that night did not return for the next academic year.' He sat back, arms folded, pushing down the corners of his mouth.

'The school wanted to show parents and pupils alike that it didn't and wouldn't tolerate such a fiasco in future.'

'What happened to those staff members?' nudged Hanson.

Robbe shrugged. 'They left. They knew they had no future here and their references were good enough to get other teaching jobs.'

Hanson looked down at her listed questions. 'Tell me whatever you recall of Matthew Flynn.'

He gave her a scandalised look. 'I was *shocked* that he was involved. I *really* was. He was such a nice boy: pleasant, courteous, intelligent. No high-flyer, you understand. I'd say more of a slogger. We had Dominic his brother here a few years before, you know.' He sat back, waiting for Hanson's response.

She nodded encouragement. '*Really*? What can you tell me about him?'

Robbe was enjoying himself. 'There was quite an age gap between the two. It was Dominic who was the high flyer in that family. He was also an arrogant, self-serving lout.' He caught Hanson's look of surprise. 'I've had some good years here and I have a loyalty to the place but I have no problem speaking my mind on certain issues. I'm only part-time since I retired. Latin teachers aren't that easy to come by these days so they asked me back. Plus, Mr Flynn is no longer involved with the school. When he was, you didn't want to cross him.'

'*Really*?' repeated Hanson.

He glanced at the door then leant towards her. 'You'll have noticed the school's two new wings as you came in?' She nodded. 'Flynn contributed his own money to the cost of building them.' He saw her surprise. 'So did others, of course.' He fussily pulled at his shirt cuffs beneath the tweed jacket. 'Most of the pupils who come here are from money. The difference between them and Flynn was that Flynn thought his money entitled him to make demands.'

'Demands,' echoed Hanson.

Robbe nodded, his voice barely audible. 'He would doubtless deny it but once it was clear that Matthew wasn't as smart as his brother, Mr Flynn requested that I, shall we say, "improve" on his son's grades. When I refused his attitude was challenging to say the least.'

'How?'

Robbe considered the question. 'Would you believe, verbally angry and physically threatening? That's exactly how it came across to me.'

Hanson was at a loss. 'Why was it so important for Matthew to do well at Latin?'

Robbe rolled his eyes. 'No, no,' he said testily. 'I've always taught English and Maths here, in addition to Latin. There was never sufficient take-up of Latin for a full-time post.' Whilst Hanson was absorbing this, Robbe stood. 'As a part-timer I'm usually gone by now.'

She nodded, reaching for her bag. 'What was Mr Flynn's response to Matthew's involvement with drugs?'

'Ha! Not bothered in the slightest. The school offered to find private counselling for the boy. The police had suggested something of the sort because of Matthew's relatively young age and that he might need help to be more self-assertive. Flynn rejected that outright. He also took the same stance to what the school was offering, saying he already had something in mind.'

'Which was?' asked Hanson.

Robbe shrugged. 'He didn't give any details. Between you and me he probably did nothing.'

Hanson was back at the university and unsettled. Earlier she'd thought of ringing Ruth Grayson at Social Services, then reconsidered. If a busy person agrees to do you a favour by chasing up information, the last thing you should do is put pressure on her. Her phone rang and she dug it out of her bag. It was Watts.

'How did you get on at Matthew Flynn's school?' he asked, without preamble as usual.

'I know more about Brad Flynn than we did: a man who likes to get his own way and isn't too bothered how he achieves it. A bit of a fixer, by all accounts.' She told him about Flynn's contribution to the funding of the school building project. 'The teacher I spoke to was clear that Flynn felt that that gave him the right to demand his son's grades be inflated.'

Watts's response was succinct. '*Git.*'

'He also said that the police advised that Matthew undertake some kind of offence-related work to help him resist peer pressure around drugs. The school also offered help. Flynn refused both, saying he had a better idea, but what that was and if it was true, I don't have a clue. Are you still there?'

'I'm sitting outside your building. Fancy a quick trip to Birmingham Prison?'

Watts waited at the first internal door for Hanson to be cleared by the officer inside the glassed-in reception, watched as he quasi-saluted her. Hanson was no more a stranger to this place than was Watts. She'd told him of a time she'd come here on a snowy January day suffering from flu because a judge had directed that she see one of its remand prisoners. The officer on duty had refused her permission to take medication inside with her. He'd relented on the medication then refused permission for her to take water onto the wing so she could take it when required. He watched her now, here on her own terms, belongings locked inside the Range Rover, carrying nothing but a notebook and pencil and asking for nothing. They walked on to the internal automated door. It slid open and they entered the holding area.

'What's your thinking?' she asked.

He kept his eyes on the officers high above them behind glass, their mouths moving. 'Diana Flynn and Zach Addison had a thing going between them. If Matthew Flynn cottoned on to it, he might have challenged Addison somewhere other than the rented house and got more than he bargained for.'

'I've had second thoughts about Matthew initiating aggression towards Addison,' she said. 'Addison is much bigger built.'

'Remember what you told us? That Matthew Flynn might not always have judged social situations too well?'

'True,' she conceded. 'But his other personal qualities don't fit with him initiating aggression.'

Watts gave her a direct look. 'Like we talked about before, finding out that Addison was bedding his mother might have set him off.'

She glanced up at him. 'We need to know about Zach Addison's capacity for violence.'

Watts's eyes were now on the still chatting officers. 'Come on!' he muttered.

As if his voice had carried, one of the prison officers reached out a casual hand to a control panel and the door in front of them slid open. Watts and Hanson continued on to where an officer was waiting.

'Follow me, please,' she said.

They did, along walkways and up a flight of stairs. After a couple of minutes she left them inside a smallish office, equipped with little more than a table, four chairs and an empty bookcase. Hanson gave it a critical glance. 'I've spent quite a few hours in here since I qualified. This is the room visiting psychologists and psychiatrists use to see prisoners.'

Watts looked around. 'Thought it had an iffy feel to it.'

She gave him a sideways glance. 'What's the format when he arrives?'

'I do the intros then you feel free to carry on. Addison's agreed to talk to us because he thinks it might be in his best interests if he does.'

'And is it?'

'Haven't decided. He doesn't know about the forensic search of the house, by the way.'

They turned as the door opened and Addison came into the room, the escort officer still at the door, her hand grasping the handle. 'Ten minutes.' She withdrew and the door closed on her. Addison gave Hanson a quick, searching look, his eyes settling on Watts.

'Mr Addison, this is Professor Hanson who's working with us on the Matthew Flynn case. She's got some questions for you. Questions which might help us get to why Matthew Flynn was killed.' Addison looked at her.

She'd decided to be direct. 'I want to talk to you about the sexual relationship between you and Matthew's mother, Diana Flynn.' In the silence she half-anticipated a 'No comment' response.

'There wasn't one,' he said.

Hanson held his gaze. At least he was talking. 'Two minutes gone already, Mr Addison. If that's how you intend to respond we might as well finish this meeting now.' She was on her feet.

Addison sent Watts a confused glance. 'You heard the professor. What's it going to be?'

Addison looked down at the table. It was evident from the shadows under his eyes, his unshaven, sullen face that he was not happy with his current accommodation. 'OK. What if there was? It wasn't a big deal.'

Hanson sat, eyes focused on his face. 'It might have been a "big deal" for her son.'

Addison looked from her to Watts and shook his head. 'Whatever was between me and Diana was nothing to do with Matthew.'

'Oh yeah?' said Watts. 'That how you see it? He's young, he's just got a bit of independence from home, albeit shared with you and Graham and wham!' His broad hand hit the table top. 'Next thing he knows, his own mother and one of his housemates are playing patta-cake together.' Addison said nothing.

Hanson continued. 'There was some kind of aggravation, a row between you and Matthew.'

'No. There wasn't.'

She studied him. 'Mr Flynn is very wealthy. Powerful. Did Matthew threaten to tell his father what he'd found out about you and his mother?'

Addison's face reddened. 'I didn't kill Matthew!'

She gazed into his eyes. 'Then tell us who did.'

'How the hell should I know?' He pressed his lips together, then: 'I had no reason to kill him. There was never any indication, any sign that he knew about Diana and me.'

Hanson's eyes stayed on his face. 'That's what you say.' She paused. 'We know that when Diana Flynn came to the house she brought flowers and that it annoyed Matthew.' She leant towards Addison. 'Annoyed because he guessed that his mother was bringing them for *you*.'

Addison sighed, ran a hand through his hair. 'You're dead wrong. OK, OK, you're partly right. Diana would make out that the flowers were for Matthew but it annoyed him because it was *flowers*. His old man used to make crafty digs about him.'

Hanson frowned. 'What kind of "digs"?'

Addison shrugged. 'You know. About him not having a girlfriend.'

She glanced at Watts, then back to Addison. 'You must have gotten to know Matthew a little during the short time you and he shared the house. Was there any foundation for those "digs" as far as you were concerned?'

Addison shrugged. 'I never got that impression of him.'

'Do you know if he had a girlfriend?'

He shook his head. 'Not during the time I knew him.'

'Did he ever mention someone called Honey?'

'Honey?' He frowned. 'No, never. And I'm telling you: Matthew didn't know about me and Diana.'

They reached Watts's vehicle parked several metres away from the prison entrance. He gazed across the road at its red-brick bulk. 'OK, doc. Let's hear it. Is he telling us the truth?'

'I think he is. Whatever was going on or going wrong in Matthew Flynn's life when he, Graham and Addison shared that house, I doubt that his mother's relationship with Addison had any relevance. I don't believe he knew.' They got into the Range Rover.

'One good theory gone west,' said Watts. 'Wonder if Brad Flynn knew what his wife was up to?'

Hanson fastened her seatbelt. 'If he did, what possible bearing might that have on his son being killed in the dreadful way that he was?'

'Just talking to myself, doc. I haven't got a clue.'

FIFTEEN

Hanson brought the morning meeting with her research students to a close. 'Good work everybody for sticking to the submissions programme we agreed. Julian? Your closing date is the most pressing. Just six more days. Do you think you'll manage it?'

'A day in the computer lab plus a night and another day writing it up should do it.'

'OK. Let me know if you need anything.'

Watching them cram books and notes into their backpacks she reached for her phone now buzzing its way across her desk and checked the caller's name. *Oh, please, please.* 'Hi, Ruth.'

'Got something for you, Kate.' Hanson grabbed a pen. 'Bless you. Tell me.'

'A reference to a Matthew Flynn with the same birth date you gave me attending a drug support group.'

'Ruth, you're a lifesaver. Who ran it?'

'It's still ongoing. All I know is that it has no connection with Social Services nor the Probation Service. It's called One Day.'

'Where is it?' She wrote down the address, a possibility sliding into her head. 'Ruth, you wouldn't happen to have a list of attendees of this One Day at the time Matthew Flynn was there?'

'Yes, I do. Ten of them. Full names in alphabetical order with their dates of birth. Want a copy?'

'Please. If you have the list there, is there a Callum on it, by any chance?' There was a short silence. 'Now, how did you know that? Yes, there is. Callum Foley.' She gave Foley's date of birth.

Hanson smiled into the phone. 'A lucky guess. Thanks, Ruth. I'm really grateful to you.'

She ended the call, rang UCU and got Corrigan. 'Hi, it's me.'

'Hi, me.'

'I know who Callum is. The friend who went with Matthew Flynn to the tattoo parlour. His full name is Callum Foley.' She gave the date of birth and repeated what she'd been told about the drug support group and its location.

'Watts will sure as hell like this,' said Corrigan. 'He's been looking for anything that plays up the drug connection, particularly one which connects Matthew Flynn with this Callum guy.'

'When is he back?' She heard a voice in the background.

'He just came in.'

'Tell him I think all three of us should take a look at this group. Let him know the details. How about I meet you there this afternoon?' She waited.

Corrigan was back in seconds. 'Forty-five minutes suit you, Red?'

Ending the call, Hanson went to the flip chart, her eyes tracking the growing list of facts and impressions she'd added over recent days, including Addison's now admitted relationship with Matthew Flynn's mother. From what she knew of Brad Flynn from her colleagues' brief contact with him, plus a single source at their son's school, the consistent indications were that he was controlling, determined, probably ruthless in pursuit of what he wanted. Did that mean he would be equally ruthless in his response to events in his personal life? She frowned at the written information. If Flynn were to find out about his wife's relationship with Addison it all pointed to his response being swift and aggressive. Trusting that Diana Flynn would have the good sense never to divulge it to him, Hanson added the basic facts they had about the drug support group, checked her watch and headed out.

The address Ruth had given Hanson was an old, one-time library building facing onto a busy high street a couple of miles from headquarters. Corrigan had checked Callum Foley's details on the police national computer: petty theft, drug offences. Walking through the main entrance with her colleagues Hanson knew from a glance at Watts's face that he was hell-bent on wringing every bit of information from this lead. They came into a spacious central room where a spiky-haired woman with red, swaying earrings was seated at an inquiry desk. Watts reached inside his coat.

'We're here for One Day,' he said.

She smiled up at him, face serene. 'Aren't we all? We do a mindfulness course which I can recommend.'

Face set, Watts showed his identification. 'The drug group. Where is it?'

Eyes widening at his change of tone, she pointed to a door ahead of them. 'It's in a separate building across the yard.' Watts turned and they started towards it. Red-Earrings was on her feet. 'No, stop! You have to wait here. The group still has another five minutes.'

Watts turned to her. 'Phone through now to whoever's in charge over there and say that West Midlands Police want a word.'

She glanced at her watch and picked up the phone, her eyes on them. 'Jeremy? There are police officers here to see you.' She nodded. 'OK.' She replaced the phone. 'He's coming. You can sit over there.'

'We'll stand.'

He paced as Corrigan followed Hanson to a wall display of local art. At the sound of a door opening they turned. A tall man in his mid-thirties in black jeans and a black polo neck sweater was coming inside. He walked towards them and Hanson got an immediate shock of recognition. Judging by her colleagues' faces, so had they. It was the priest who had swung the incense burner at St Bartholomew's church. He glanced at the identification Watts was holding up. 'Detective Sergeant Watts. You were at our re-consecration service.' He nodded at Corrigan and Hanson. 'So were your colleagues. I'm Jeremy Fellowes, deacon at St Bartholomew's.'

'What's your connection to this One Day drugs set-up?' demanded Watts.

Fellowes gave him a calm smile. 'It's my responsibility. I organise and run it.'

Hanson pictured the board in UCU, the information put there by Corrigan of details gained from Father Delaney including Fellowes' name.

Watts's eyes narrowed. 'How come you and the church are involved in it?'

'St Bartholomew's Church takes its social and community responsibilities extremely seriously,' said Fellowes. 'It does a considerable amount of outreach work. It's my job as deacon to run the One Day drug support group.'

'We need to talk to you,' said Watts. 'Is there anywhere more private than this?'

Fellowes looked untroubled by the request. 'Of course. The group attendees have left now. They come and go via a door on the other side of the courtyard to avoid the scrutiny and judgement they inevitably anticipate due to their offences. If you'll follow me?'

They did, Hanson suppressing a clamour of questions inside her head, hoping that this positive-looking man was about to provide some answers. He led them inside a small building, across the main room, its chairs neatly stacked, to a much smaller one Fellowes indicated was his office. He turned to them. 'I hope your being here isn't about any of the attendees of our group?'

Watts sidestepped the question. 'You work at St Bartholomew's Church.'

Fellowes nodded. 'You know I do. I just confirmed it.'

Hanson saw Watts's face heat up. 'You also know we're investigating the remains found in the church's crypt.'

'Yes.' He looked at each of them. 'But I don't understand why you appear to be rather annoyed, Detective Sergeant—'

'Then I'll spell it out for you! *One,* you know the remains have been identified as those of Matthew Flynn. *Two,* we know that when he was fifteen he was given a caution for drug possession, following which he attended this group, and *three,* you and Father Delaney both know about one *and* two and neither he nor you said a word to us about it! If you need a fourth reason why I'm "annoyed", we had to find out from Social Services that Matthew Flynn came here!'

The deacon gazed back at him, unperturbed. 'Father Delaney has not discussed this matter with me. I suggest you go to him for an explanation as to why he did not mention it. I didn't do so because the name meant nothing to me.'

Watts's face was incendiary. 'How long have you been running this One Day?'

Fellowes thought about it. 'It would be about six years now.'

'Right! So, you do remember Matthew Flynn.'

'No.'

Watts stared at him, his colour deepening. Hanson intervened. 'As DS Watts has indicated we have reliable information that Matthew Flynn attended the group you run here.'

The deacon gave her a patient look. 'I don't doubt what you're saying but I run two groups per week here, with approximately ten attendees in each. That amounts to a lot of young people over the years.'

'Are they all adolescents?' she asked.

'The age range is from sixteen to nineteen.'

'Matthew Flynn was fifteen, sir,' said Corrigan.

'If he received his caution at fifteen, it's likely that by the time we were able to provide a place for him here he would have been approaching sixteen.'

Watts shot the deacon a disgruntled look. 'You keep records of whoever comes here?'

'Of course.'

'What information do you record?'

'Name, age, offence details, attendance at One Day, progress made—'

'Show us all the records you've got going back five years.'

The deacon stood, taking keys from his jeans pocket. They watched him go to a large metal cupboard in one corner of the room, unlock it, look along the contents of several shelves then select a box file. He brought it to them, placing it on a nearby table.

'One more thing,' said Watts, looking no happier than he had since the conversation began. 'Do you recognise the name Callum Foley?'

Hanson caught a glimpse of something in the deacon's eyes. 'Callum Foley . . . Now that name does sound familiar but I can't say why. Who is he?'

Watts jabbed a thick forefinger at the box file. 'If he was part of the same group as Matthew Flynn, his details will be in that?'

'Yes, but . . .'

Watts hefted the box file. 'Don't let us hold you up. After we've read through this lot, we'll have more questions.'

As Fellowes walked to the door Hanson followed him. 'Wait. I recall Father Delaney mentioning a second deacon. Does he have any involvement with the drug groups?'

He looked at her, his face suddenly unreadable. 'You're referring to Richard Burns. He's due back in a couple of days but he's had no involvement in One Day.'

Hanson nodded, her eyes on his. 'Thank you.' It had been the merest shadow behind Fellowes' otherwise candid face but Hanson made a mental note of it.

They each took paper records from the box file. Hanson read the neat, handwritten records, looking for something which might relate to their case, something which would cause a tightening inside her chest, that whizz-bang of neurones firing and coming together inside her head. She reached the last sheet, read it and sat back. Nothing. A quick glance at her two colleagues told a similar story.

'There's a few more here,' said Watts, passing them across the table. She took some, read more neatly written lines. The impression she now had of 'One Day' was of a well-run group with defined objectives and a programme of skill-building designed to help young attendees avoid drug-taking in the future. On the last but one sheet she found the first reference to Matthew Flynn. She checked the date: July, some five years previous. She ran her finger along the close-written line to the name of the organisation or individual responsible for his referral.

'Guess who referred Matthew to the One Day group.' Her colleagues looked up. 'His father. Brad Flynn.'

Watts took the sheet from her. 'The same Brad Flynn who didn't take his son's arrest and caution seriously and never mentioned St Bartholomew's or this group to us.'

'Apparently so. Matthew doesn't seem to have attended that often.'

'I've found Callum Foley,' said Corrigan, holding up a sheet. 'He attended just four of the twelve sessions on offer.' He read on. 'He dropped out, which, it says here "was not unexpected, given that he had formed a friendship with another group member, despite the usual advice to attendees not to do so".' He looked up. 'No award for guessing who that was.'

'Matthew Flynn,' said Hanson. 'Their limited attendance record, plus the intervening years, could explain why Fellowes didn't recall either of them.'

'Anything else?' asked Watts.

Corrigan turned a page. 'It says here both Flynn and Foley were last seen outside this building on a day they were due to attend a group meeting but they never came inside. This was in September of that year.'

'They obviously formed a friendship here and five years later we know that Callum Foley had an inverted crucifix tattoo and that he accompanied Matthew Flynn to get something similar done,' said Hanson.

'They must have hit it off from the start,' said Watts. 'Maybe the deacon can fill us in, once we remind him of what's in these records. I want to see Delaney as well. He's got some explaining to do.'

Hanson's phone buzzed. She reached for it. 'Hi Julian.'

'Kate, I'm at uni and I need some help.'

'I'll be back around four thirty.'

'I need to see you now.'

She traced an index finger over the fine line between her brows. It wasn't like Julian to demand her time. He was clearly in a real fix with his research paper. 'I'll be there in half an hour—'

'I'm in the computer lab.' He was gone.

She stood. 'I have to get back to the university.' She reached for her belongings as Watts returned most of the record sheets to the box file.

'I'm taking these sheets with me. Corrigan's got armed response in an hour but I'll have a quick word with Fellowes about what we've found and then I'm on my way to see Delaney. I'll also be talking to Brad Flynn, soon as. I want to know why both of them have been so cagey about Matthew Flynn's connection with St Bartholomew's Church.'

As Hanson and Corrigan left, Watts walked with measured steps to where Fellowes was in the process of cleaning a whiteboard in the main room. He straightened and turned, his eyes on the A4s in Watts's big hand. 'I'm taking these sheets back to headquarters.' Fellowes opened his mouth. Watts carried on. 'They show that Matthew Flynn was part of your group at the request of his father, Brad Flynn.'

'I don't know anything about that . . .'

'They also show that both Flynn and Callum Foley attended four sessions here.'

Fellowes nodded. 'Which is probably why my recall of them isn't good.'

Watts studied him. 'Or you want to protect your church by denying any knowledge.'

For the first time Fellowes' face lost some of its serenity. 'Detective Sergeant, I can assure you that I have no reason to do that.'

'How do you get on with Delaney?'

'What do you mean?' Fellowes saw that Watts wasn't going to leave without some kind of answer. 'We are colleagues. "Getting on" in the way you probably mean is not relevant. We are a family in Christ. We accept each other, respect the church and serve the Lord in our individual ways.'

Watts turned on his heel. 'You don't say.'

Not waiting for the arthritic lift, Hanson took the stairs to the top floor of the psychology building, hoping that Julian's research problem could be sorted by quick adjustments followed by equally quick computer checking. Opening the door she stopped dead. Maisie was sitting at one of the tables, face stormy.

Julian came to her. 'It's OK, Kate. Something happened up here earlier and—'

'What happened?' she demanded, going to Maisie, various possibilities flooding her head, none of them pleasant. She knew the computer lab from her own days here as a PhD graduate student: a haven of quiet during the day, a potentially disturbing place of odd sounds once the building grew deserted and winter daylight started to fade. Maisie folded her arms on the table and lowered her head onto them. Heart pounding, Hanson recalled her many admonishments to Maisie to use the lab only in the company of other students. But if she had come here alone today the card-swiping mechanism on the door would have offered protection from anyone with no right to be here. She sat next to her, lowering her voice. 'Maisie? What's happened?'

Maisie raised her head, face flushed. 'There was a fight.'

Hanson stared at her. 'A *what*?' She took a quick glance around the room for signs of disorder she might have missed. There were none. She looked up at Julian who was sitting on the edge of a nearby table, arms folded, then back to Maisie. 'That kind of behaviour is not tolerated anywhere on this campus. Tell me the names of the parties involved in this fight and I'll notify the vice chancellor.'

Maisie didn't respond but Julian did. 'One was Anthony Barclay from your stats group.'

Hanson pictured Barclay: short, compact, cocksure and

invariably offhand. *No surprise there.* 'I'll report him.' She fumed. 'Who else?' Seconds ticked by. 'Maisie?'

'Me.'

Hanson stared at her, unable to comprehend the single word. 'This isn't making any sense. How does this fight you mentioned fit in?'

Again it was Julian who filled the silence. 'Barclay's a real piece of work, Kate. Maisie's told me about him. He's been taking her work off her.'

His words brought sudden clarity to the concerns Hanson had had about Maisie over the last few days. She turned to her. 'Is this what happened the other day?' Maisie looked away. 'Why on earth didn't you *tell* me?'

Maisie's brows lowered further. 'I can sort things out myself.'

'No, Maisie. You can't.' She stared at her. 'What happened here exactly?' Maisie rested her chin on her arms, face closed. Hanson looked up at Julian. 'What else do you know?'

He shrugged. 'Not much. I came up here to work. I got to the door and heard voices. I recognised Maisie's. I heard a shout and Barclay came limping out and disappeared down the stairs.'

Maisie sat up looking pleased. 'I did it.'

'Did what?' asked Hanson.

'Kicked him.'

Hanson stared at her, horrified, the full reality of what she'd been told now dawning. 'You *what*? I can't believe . . . Maisie, that's assault!'

Maisie gave her a mutinous look. 'I don't care! When we were working on our last assignment he asked for my work so he could copy it into his. I kept saying no. He came up here—'

'He followed you?'

'Dunno, but he tried to take my stuff. So I kicked him.'

Hanson sat and looked at her, a question now in her head which had to be asked. 'Did he touch you in any way? Because if he did—'

'Course not. When he refused to give my stuff back, I kicked him in the leg, got it off him and he rushed out and Julian arrived.'

Hanson ran her hands through her hair. 'I have to think about this.' In truth, she already had. No one would know of

this incident. Unless Barclay had already spoken of it? If he
had she'd think again. She looked down at Maisie. 'I don't
agree with what you did. You should have told me about his
pressuring you and I'd have taken care of it.'

'You'd have gone nuts and reported him.'

'And you wouldn't have assaulted him and put yourself in
the wrong!' She closed her eyes, breathed. 'OK. Like I said,
we say nothing about this for now. Leave it with me. Thanks
for ringing me, Julian.' She turned to Maisie. 'Get your things.
I'm taking you home.'

Hot-faced, Maisie pushed creased-looking papers into her
bag.

Inside his study at Church House Father Delaney looked askance
at Watts. 'Detective Sergeant, I assure you that it never occurred
to me for one moment that this boy Flynn was in any way
connected to the One Day drug support group we run. If it had,
I would have told you. I simply didn't know.' Watts looked
him in the eye. 'According to information we've got, Matthew
Flynn was referred to your group by his father, Brad Flynn. I
assume you've heard of him?'

'Yes, of course. He's often in the local news for his business
exploits and so forth but I had no communication from or with
him.' Delaney gave a vigorous headshake, cheeks and jowls
quivering. 'I must take issue with what you just said, Detective
Sergeant. The One Day group is not *mine*. I do not have and
never have had direct involvement in it.'

Watts's eyes were still fixed on Delaney's face. 'Once you knew
the identity of the remains in the crypt, how come you didn't link
him to the drug support work being done by your church?'

Delaney stared at him. 'Why would I do so? I've just told
you, I have no direct involvement in the drug groups the church
runs. Never have. They're Jeremy Fellowes' responsibility. I
have the utmost regard for Jeremy's work here. He's very
responsible. Please talk to him. You're welcome to talk to both
my deacons. Actually, Richard Burns isn't available right
now but he will be in a couple of days. Ask them whatever
questions you like. They will tell you about the high level of
involvement St Bartholomew's has had with numerous

community initiatives over the years to the present time. It's impossible to remember all of the names of those the church supports and as I said, I have no direct role in the drug-related services we provide.'

'We spoke to Fellowes earlier this afternoon. He did recall Matthew Flynn after we found references to him in the records.'

Delaney looked impatient. 'That's exactly what I'm saying to you, Detective Sergeant. One can't reasonably be expected to recall a name from years back without some context.'

Watts studied the plump face. 'That "context" jogged Fellowes' memory for another name.'

Delaney waited, huge arms in their wide sleeves folded over his girth. 'Oh?'

Watts was busy thinking. About how adept Hanson was at picking up defensiveness. But she was also the first to acknowledge that body language wasn't all it was cracked up to be when it came to making judgements about somebody's honesty. Still. Delaney wasn't going anywhere. There would be other opportunities for them to talk to him and for Hanson to be a part of it. 'Does the name, Callum Foley ring a bell?'

Delaney looked at him. 'Excuse me?'

'Callum Foley,' he enunciated. 'Another lad who went to the drug support group at the same time as Matthew Flynn. Looks like they were good mates.'

Delaney gave him a direct look, raising his massive shoulders. 'What can I say except to repeat what I've just said? I have never had any involvement in the drug support work. I had no way of linking it to the boy found dead in the crypt and I certainly have no recollection of this other name.' He paused. 'Wait. Your colleague, Professor Hanson mentioned a single name like that a few days ago. I didn't know that one, either.'

'As the priest in charge here don't you keep an eye on initiatives like One Day?'

'I trust my deacons. My role here is to lead this church and ensure it goes from strength to—'

'We can't locate Callum Foley.'

Delaney looked at him. 'I wish I could be of assistance but I've never heard of a Callum Foley.'

Watts slow-nodded, recalling a brief exchange between Hanson and himself a short while ago: you could only drag information out of somebody if there was something to drag. He got to his feet. 'Our investigation is widening. I'm sure you'll understand when I say that we'll be back here to see you again.'

Delaney also stood. 'Of course, Detective Sergeant. You and your colleagues are welcome here at any time.'

Hanson looked across the kitchen to where Maisie was listlessly prodding pasta with her fork. She had tried the sympathetic approach, moved to reasonableness and five minutes ago she'd arrived at direct-and-fractious which had also got her precisely nowhere. She took a deep breath. 'All I want to know is why you didn't say you were finding three lectures a week difficult?' Silence. She ran a hand through her hair. 'It's not like I didn't suspect you might be having difficulties, Maisie. You're only thirteen and you're sharing a lecture room with eighteen—, nineteen-year-olds. You know I wasn't in favour of the increase to three days. I thought it might be difficult but your father said to let you have a chance—'

Maisie jumped up, face furious. 'Don't you dare blame Daddy! You're always the same, Mom. You think you know everything and you're on top of everything and know best and nobody else has a clue. That's what Daddy says and he's right!'

Hanson watched, open-mouthed as Maisie stormed from the kitchen, listened as her feet pounded the stairs, followed by a door slam, wondering in some idling compartment of her mind whether it had lengthened the hairline crack in the plaster above it. She folded her arms around herself. *On top of everything? Me? If only.*

'Is it safe to come in?' She looked up at Charlie's tentative face, giving him a weary grin.

'Yes. The fallout is all mine.'

He smiled. 'How about some tea? Brandy?'

'Both?' She shook her head. 'Tea would be good.' She watched him cross the kitchen. 'Maisie has always been spirited but lately we seem to clash more and more.'

He filled the kettle. 'Probably because lately she's thirteen. Try not to get overwhelmed by it and don't doubt yourself.'

Since their reconciliation there had been a tacit agreement between them that the past they had shared should stay exactly where it was. She watched him assemble cups. She needed to ask the question. 'What was I like at thirteen, Charlie? Was I awful?'

He looked at her and shook his head. 'The *worst*.' She laughed. He brought cups to the table and sat opposite her. 'You were as feisty and opinionated as Maisie. Like most thirteen-year-olds, in fact.'

She stared out of the window into darkness. 'I don't know what I'm doing, Charlie. Not here, not at headquarters and I'm falling behind at work. Which isn't unusual when I'm part of an investigation but . . .' She rested her head on her hand. 'I'm tired of playing catch-up in my own life.'

'Would it be easier if you just had home and the university?'

She gave it some thought. Possibly. But that would mean no police colleagues. No Corrigan. Plus, her work with the force had been a strong factor in her promotion. It validated the work she did at the university. If she ended her association with headquarters it would be like pressing her own professional self-destruct button. And no Corrigan. *Oh, shut up.*

'Family is a given, Charlie, and I can't give either of the other two up.' She stood. 'It's only half-nine but I'm going to bed.'

'Good idea. It will all look different tomorrow.'

She went out of the kitchen and upstairs, taking her doubts with her.

SIXTEEN

Coming into the Saturday morning calm of the psychology building, Hanson was resolute in what she needed: catch-up time. A normal day's work. Over the next three hours she checked and emailed four of the most urgent research papers to their respective journal editors. She looked at the hard copies stacked neatly in the out-tray on her desk ready for posting. Job done. She was now on the phone, listening to Corrigan's voice.

'Callum Foley has dropped off the radar. He's had no involvement with any official body of the kind a young guy with no
job and no money would need. We thought he might be living
rough so we checked the official homeless services here and in
London. Their data's not reliable because of the nature of the
client group but it was worth a try. We got zip. He could be
just about anywhere.'

'What about his family?' She listened as Corrigan spoke
away from the phone. 'Hang on there, Red.'

Watts came onto the line. 'Doc, we've tried making contact
with Foley's mother but the phone is dead and she's not
answering her door to a uniform. Could you go and see if you
have better luck?'

Hanson wrote down the details. 'OK. I'm onto it.'

'Very upbeat,' he said. 'I like it.'

She smiled into the phone. 'Try it yourself sometime.'

'Too much of a realist, doc. I had a word with Fellowes after
you left yesterday. It's possible he didn't remember Flynn or
this Foley. I went to see Delaney. He told me he himself had
no dealings with the drug group at all, which is why he didn't
see a link to Matthew Flynn. He says he doesn't know Brad
Flynn and he didn't recognise the name Callum Foley.'

Searching for a bell and not finding one, Hanson thumped the
flaking paintwork on the door. A second thump dislodged more
flakes. 'Mrs Foley? Can you open the door, please?' She paused,
waiting. 'Mrs Foley . . .?' The door opened a few centimetres,
part of a blotched face visible in the narrow space.

'If you're not from the Social or the surgery you can *piss* off.'

Hanson placed both hands against dirty wood. 'Please, Mrs
Foley, I need to talk to you.' The minimal resistance on the
other side stopped. She pushed at it as the woman she'd come
here to see shuffled away.

Stepping inside, Hanson went from crisp late-autumn air into
a miasma she could almost taste. The over-ripe, sour smells of
stale alcohol, cigarettes and acrid body odour dropped on her
like unwashed wool. Shallow-breathing and only when she had
to, she walked inside the room Mrs Foley had disappeared into
to find her slumped on a greasy-looking sofa pulled up to a

blasting gas fire, surrounded by a detritus of take-away food containers and junk mail, her head and neck sunk into her shoulders. The heat and the rancid smell of the place made Hanson's senses reel. She swallowed.

'I need to talk to you about your son Callum.' She looked into veined eyes in the seamed, blotchy face, guessing that Foley was still several years short of her fiftieth birthday.

'I've got nothing to say about him. I only see that bastard when he's after something.'

'When was the last time you saw him?'

Foley's wavering head turned in Hanson's general direction. 'You think I keep a bloody engagement diary on the go? If I did, there'd be sod-all in it.' She lit a cigarette, fingers trembling and pulled in smoke. 'It was months ago.'

Hanson was still standing, the carpet lifting whenever she moved her feet. 'Was it in the summer? Before that?' She watched as Foley drew in more smoke.

'Couldn't say.'

'You said Callum generally came when he wanted something. The last time he came here, what did he want?'

'He never said but I could see he was in trouble.' She laughed, quick and humourless. 'Ha! He was *always* in bloody trouble, but this time I knew it was something big.' Hanson saw her eyes narrow, the hand holding the cigarette making small jabbing movements. 'Oh, *yes*. Big trouble. I thought at the time, He's upset somebody, the stupid bastard. I told him to hop it. I didn't want trouble following him to my door.'

Hanson frowned. 'What was it that made you so sure he was in trouble?'

Foley glanced up at her and away. 'All edgy, he was. I'd never seen him like that.' There was a pause. Hanson waited. 'I did wonder at the time if he was back on the stuff.' She pointed across the room to a low sideboard. 'When he thought I wasn't looking, he went through that, all quiet like, but I saw him. Probably looking for whatever he could take and flog. Ha! That'd be the day.' She gave Hanson an unsteady, up-down look. 'You got kids?' Hanson said nothing. Foley shrugged, pulled in more smoke. 'Take it from me, don't bother. All they do is take-take-take then bugger off.'

Hanson pointed to the sideboard. 'Mrs Foley, is it OK if I take a look inside?'

Foley squirmed, looked up at Hanson, her eyes narrowing. 'Why?' Getting no response, she shrugged, fell back against the sofa, face crumpling. 'He never gave me anything in his whole miserable life except trouble.'

Ignoring the maudlin sobs, Hanson went to the sideboard and opened its two wide doors. Inside was a jumble of items including empty cider bottles and one of whisky, almost empty. She didn't want to have physical contact with anything in this house but she had no choice. Reaching inside she removed the bottles and placed them on the sticky carpet, reached again and pulled out a mix of papers, mostly bills and yet more junk mail. Hanson began examining every item. She was stopped by something unexpected.

'Mrs Foley? Mrs *Foley.*'

Foley looked up through half-closed eyes. 'Yeah?'

Hanson was holding up a photograph. 'Is this your son, Callum?'

The eyes took time to focus. 'Yeah. That's him. *Tosser.*'

Hanson longed to be outside, away from bitterness and hopelessness. 'May I borrow it?'

'Do what you like. It's no use to me.'

Resuming her search, Hanson was near the bottom of the pile when an envelope got her attention. The only one she'd found. Through its window she could see money. She lifted it out by one corner, pulled the torn edges apart and gazed down at a single fifty-pound note. Replacing all she'd removed from the sideboard except for the envelope and the photograph, Hanson went to Foley. 'I need to take this envelope with me, Mrs Foley.'

Foley struggled upright, eyes narrowing on it. 'Hey! I can see money in that! Give it here.'

Hanson put the envelope inside her bag. Foley looked at her, enraged. 'Who do you think you are? That's mine! It's in my house and possession is nine . . . summat of the law . . .'

'This is police business. I'm taking it.'

Foley was on her feet, swaying. 'I've got expenses. You know how much gas costs these days? *And cider*, thought Hanson.

She opened her wallet, took out a twenty-pound note, under

no illusions about how it would be spent. 'I'll leave you this in exchange for the envelope.'

Foley pointed a finger. 'You taking me for a mug? Twenty quid for fifty! I'll have the law on you . . .'

'I'll make sure that your son's photograph is returned to you.'

Snatching the twenty pounds, Foley began waving her arms. 'Don't *bother*. G'on! Bang the door shut on your way out, you snotty cow and leave me in peace . . .'

Hanson was inside her car, its windows fully open, waiting for her call to be picked up. 'PM suite. Chong speaking. Hi, Hanson.'

'If you've got a minute I need you to read out the serial numbers of the fifty-pound notes found inside Matthew Flynn's boot.'

'Hang on.' She was back promptly. 'OK, the numbers are . . .'

Listening, Hanson gazed at the number on the note lying in her lap. Thanking Chong, she cut the call. Two missing young men, one known to be dead, the whereabouts of the other unknown. It didn't look good for Callum Foley. She started the engine.

Hanson got out of her car, quietly closing its door. She'd been drawn here. Matthew Flynn and Callum Foley had known each other in life. Both were known to have used drugs. And both had been sent to the One Day drug support group run by this place. She looked from the church to the spacious grounds, headstones leaning like random teeth. The whole place was deserted and deathly quiet except for the low hum of traffic some distance away. They didn't know where Matthew Flynn was killed or when but this had been his resting place. She went to the church door. It was shut tight. She looked towards Church House. There was no car outside. It had a shut-in look. Whoever had interred Matthew here had got inside the crypt without causing damage. Matthew's body could have been left in other places arguably easier than this to access. They now knew that Matthew and Callum Foley were friends. They had no idea where Foley was. None of it made any sense but experience was telling Hanson that there was meaning and relevance somewhere in what they had. She shivered as sudden cloud blocked the weak November sun, darkening the immediate area. No. It didn't look good for Callum.

With a last glance at Church House as the sun reappeared, she stopped, shielding her eyes from thin rays which disappeared as quickly as they'd arrived but enough to show something moving at one of the upstairs windows. She was sure of it. She started walking, eyes fixed on it, brows drawn together. *Surely . . . ?* Cloud moved, the sun came again, turning the glass into an impenetrable, reflective square. She stopped, letting her arm drop. Whatever she thought she'd seen was gone. A trick of the light. Turning, she headed for her car, wanting to share what she'd found at the Foley house with her colleagues. She had the door open when she heard a low, familiar voice.

'Hello again.'

Looking up she saw a lone figure sitting on a bench nearby. It was the elderly gardener who had washed her car under Father Delaney's direction. She went to him. 'Hello, Alfred.' He waved his hand to her, dabbing at his eyes. She sat beside him. 'Is anything wrong?'

'This cold weather makes my eyes water.' He smiled at her. 'How are you?'

'Fine, thanks.'

He pointed at the uncultivated land stretching ahead in gentle undulations towards the distant road below them. 'I was thinking how lucky we are to have space like this in a Birmingham suburb. I often come here, you know. It helps me get things into proportion. Worries and so forth. They pile up, don't they?' She nodded. 'But just a few minutes sitting here, thinking and I usually sort them out.' He looked at her. 'I have sorted them and I know what I have to do.'

Hanson wondered what worries he had. 'I'm glad to hear it,' she said. There was a short, companionable silence as they both gazed out on space and trees, a few still giving up their remaining leaves to sudden gusts. Hanson stood. 'I'd better get back to work.'

Alfred nodded. 'I have to leave, too. I was just wondering what I could take to my wife.' Seeing Hanson's uncertainty he said, 'She's in a care home just over there.' He pointed in the general direction of the university. 'I thought of flowers because she still loves them but they're so expensive at this time of the year.'

'What about a chocolate treat?' suggested Hanson.

He shook his head. 'I've been told not to by staff. If she gets a chance she eats it all and then she's ill. If they take it away and give her a little bit every day she gets upset. Cries like a child.' He shook his head and got slowly to his feet.

'I'm really sorry,' said Hanson, unable to think of anything else to say. There wasn't anything.

'No need,' he said. 'She's safe there. I see her every day. The staff say she doesn't know me but I know there's still something there.' He nodded. 'And if there isn't, I still get to see her. Be with her. Remember what it was like once.' He looked at his watch. 'Better make tracks or I'll miss my bus.'

Hanson also checked the time, glanced up at the darkening sky. 'I'll take you, Alfred. It's probably on my way.'

'You're very kind, but no. I use the time on the bus to think of things to tell Evelyn. Things I know she would be interested in. Just in case it means something. Today I'm taking some photographs from home to show her. She might remember who the people are. If she doesn't, I'll tell her about them. I know she likes me to do that, although of course she forgets what I say almost straight away.' He began walking away from her, then turned. 'Will I see you again?'

Hanson nodded. 'My colleagues and I still have a lot to do here.'

Alfred gave her a faint smile and a nod as he turned away. 'Good luck. Don't give up.'

She watched him go, knowing that in the space of a couple of hours she had seen the worst in maternal bitterness and the best in enduring devotion. She returned to her car with one last glance at Church House. *What's happened to Callum Foley? Where is he?* She thought it all too likely that he was dead. If he was alive, the places he might be were endless. Truth was, he could be just about anywhere. She felt a sudden wave of helplessness. They couldn't search everywhere. It cost too much. The chief was already reining them in.

Starting the engine, Alfred's last words still inside her head, she scrabbled inside her bag for her phone, searched her contact list, pressed and waited. If she was right about Foley, they needed help to focus a search. And she knew just the person who might help them.

'Hi, Jake. I'll be at the university in ten minutes. Silly question, but have you got some time to spare?'

Having phoned ahead to check that her colleagues would be there, Hanson walked into UCU, followed by a tall, rangy man in his early thirties, a bulging leather satchel hanging from one shoulder. As he entered he scanned the room, his eyes finally settling on the Smartboard.

'Have a seat, Jake. This is Detective Sergeant Bernard Watts who is the officer in charge of the investigation and this is Lieutenant Joseph Corrigan who is headquarters' firearms trainer and also part of the Unsolved Crime Unit.' She looked at her colleagues. 'This is Dr Jake Petrie. He's a geoscientist from the university. He'll explain shortly why I've asked him to come here, but first . . .' She reached into her bag and took out the envelope. 'I've seen Callum Foley's mother. She couldn't recall when she last saw him but he left an envelope at her house.' She pointed to the postmark. 'It isn't proof but it suggests that Callum made that visit to his mother's home at around the time Matthew Flynn was last seen alive at the tattoo parlour.' She opened the envelope and took out the fifty-pound note by its corner. 'This serial number fits the sequence of those found in Matthew Flynn's boot.'

Her two colleagues leant forward to look at it. 'Good work, doc.'

'It's yet more proof of a connection between Matthew and Callum Foley. They appear to have been friends but beyond that we don't know. Foley's mother isn't able to provide any reliable information but she says he's in big trouble and Corrigan's search didn't turn up any official indication that he's still participating in the usual aspects of life. I think Callum Foley is probably dead. We need to start searching for his body.'

Watts shook his head. 'You know our situation, doc. We've got no starting point for a search and no money for guesswork.'

'I know, but I've thought of a way.' She grinned at Jake, 'And we can take as a starting point the location in which Matthew Flynn was found.'

Watts shook his head. 'I hear what you're saying but if he is somewhere there, it's a big area of open land. The chief won't sanction it.'

'What if it's a different kind of search? Light on personnel and with a little flair and ingenuity.' She looked encouragingly at Petrie. 'OK, Jake. Pitch to them what you have and how it could help us.'

Jake looked at Watts and Corrigan, his face animated. 'Geoscience has a lot to offer criminal investigations such as yours, particularly in the location of illicit burials. What I'm talking about isn't merely theoretical. My team has already developed several techniques: remote sensing, electrical resistivity, ground-penetrating radar. What I'm offering is the latest technique using them all.' Hanson glanced around the table. Corrigan looked to be already in.

Watts's face told a different story. '"Team" sounds expensive,' he said. 'We've got no finances.'

'I'm offering my assistance gratis.'

'Show them, Jake,' prompted Hanson.

'As Kate said, what I have doesn't require a lot of manpower.' He delved into the crammed satchel and brought out a large black and white photograph. He held it up to them. 'This is Oscar.' Watts's brows merged and lowered. 'It's my prototype and I'll provide it and my expertise free for any search you want.'

'Hot *dog*,' murmured Corrigan, his eyes on the photograph. 'A drone.'

Watts peered at it. 'I've read about these things. They're the future for all kinds of stuff, right?'

Jake nodded. 'They're already here but Oscar's the first for the kind of work I'm interested in.'

'How many body searches have you used it on?' asked Corrigan.

Petrie looked him in the eye. 'None involving human remains but we've had success with pig carcasses. Like I said, this is a prototype.' He looked around the table. 'But, it's all you need, plus me and my computer software to interpret its findings.' He grinned. 'We're quick and we're zero cost. If Oscar comes up with a result I get a research paper out of it.'

'What do you think?' asked Hanson. She watched the exchange of looks between Watts and Corrigan.

'We say yes but it's urgent,' said Watts.

Jake lifted his satchel. 'Brilliant. Come up with a specific date and let me know.'

Music with a repetitive beat was filtering down from the first floor. Maisie and Chelsey were upstairs eating Chinese food. Hanson checked the table beneath which a hopeful Mugger was crouched, awaiting windfalls.

'Fork?' she asked Watts. He nodded. 'Ta. Chopsticks and me don't get on.' Fetching one, she joined her colleagues and Charlie at the table. They ate in relative silence for a couple of minutes, broken by Charlie.

'How's the case?'

'Looks like it's starting to move,' said Corrigan. 'We can link Matthew Flynn to a similar-age teen named Callum Foley via money Flynn had hidden on his person when he died. About five years back, both these young guys received support in relation to drug offences. That support was provided by St Bartholomew's Church. We know what happened to Flynn: he ended up interred in the church crypt and nobody would have been the wiser for years, except for a break-in.'

'Sounds like progress,' said Charlie. 'How about the other boy, this – Foley?'

'We don't know where he is. We've checked the usual sources and come up empty. Thanks to Kate, we know he visited his mother and left money hidden at her house. That's the other link to Flynn.'

'Sounds complex.'

Hanson had been following the exchange. 'Father Delaney who is in charge at St Bartholomew's knew about Matthew Flynn's murder but he didn't tell us about his church's role in supporting Flynn around his drug use. He claims he didn't know.'

Charlie looked up at her. 'If he didn't, somebody else must. I'd be interested in whoever was directly involved in running that support group.'

'We've spoken to him,' said Corrigan. 'He admitted that both Flynn and Foley attended the group but that he hadn't mentioned it before because he didn't remember them.' Corrigan looked at Hanson. 'Watts and I think Father Delaney needs another visit and we'll be speaking to Richard Burns, his other deacon.'

Hanson nodded, debating with herself whether it was time to tell them what she'd seen at the choir rehearsal. She looked up to find Watts's eyes on her.

'Got something on your mind, doc?'

She had to tell them. They needed to know. 'Yes, I have. I saw something at the church. But I don't want a possibly harmless gesture to become an issue.'

'Tell us about it,' said Watts.

Hanson described her visit to Church House, being told by the housekeeper that Delaney was at choir practice and going to the church. 'I stood inside listening to the choir. As the practice finished Delaney called one of the boys to him to give him some music and advice and . . . he placed his hand on the boy's head.'

'That it?' asked Watts, staring at her.

She nodded. 'In itself it's nothing, I know but . . . his action had an impact on me. I found it a bit disturbing.'

'Did Delaney know you were there?' asked Corrigan.

'I'm not sure. Possibly.'

Watts looked doubtful. 'If he knew you were watching him and he was up to no good, he wouldn't have put a hand on this kid, surely?'

She didn't want to get into this. It was one more uncertainty in a case already riddled with them but she had to tell them what she knew from cases she'd worked on in the past. That it was not unknown for those with a sexual interest in children to inappropriately touch them whilst under supervision.

Charlie looked shocked when he heard this. 'What? Why?'

'Because they're sexually deviant. Because they consider themselves cleverer than everyone else. Because they get a kick out of showing their true selves to experts and other professionals in situations where there's natural, close, playful contact between adults and their children. Delaney didn't appear surprised when he saw me but I don't know if he knew I was there. Maybe I overreacted to an innocent gesture but if that's what it was I would have expected Delaney to be more astute, more aware of his behaviour, more cautious.' She stood and began gathering plates. Picking up the sound of Watts's phone, she and Corrigan carried plates across the kitchen to where Charlie was stacking the dishwasher.

'When was this? Yeah. Yeah. Where is it?' He met their eyes. 'Right. Ten minutes.' He cut the call. 'That was headquarters. There's been an incident at a care home. One deceased. They're treating it as a suicide.'

Hanson stared at him, hardly aware of Charlie taking plates from her hands. *How many care homes are there in this city?* 'Why are they informing UCU about a suicide?'

'Because the dead man was a member of St Bartholomew's. Alfred Best.' He stood, jostling the table, upending a small sea salt grinder. She watched him reach for a few granules and throw them over his left shoulder. 'One way to blind the devil, doc.'

Directly ahead, intermittent blue lights were reflecting off wet tarmac. Three patrol cars with Battenburg markings and hi-visibility chevrons were parked, plus a low black station wagon with tinted windows, all facing a modern four-storey building.

They got out of Watts's vehicle and walked the building's wide driveway. Hanson felt disconnected. This was where Alfred was coming this afternoon. She looked upwards at rows of large, modern, sash windows. Somewhere inside was his wife. The reason he was here at all.

'Must cost a ransom to keep somebody here,' said Watts, raising a hand to Gus Stirling, one of the 'upstairs' officers emerging from inside and walking steadily towards them.

'Sad business,' said Gus, his voice low. 'The chief told us of the deceased's connection to St Bartholomew's so I thought you should know. He's at the rear of the building.'

They followed him into the building's main entrance, through to the back and out into a spacious courtyard, yellow light from wall-mounted fixtures illuminating what would be flowerbeds in spring, wooden benches and a central water feature surrounded by wet grass and yet more wet, black tarmac. A pale, loose-weave blanket had been dropped over something lying there, parts of it showing dark stains. Hanson stared at it with that same detachment she'd had since they'd been told what had happened.

'We've been here a while, waiting to be told how he died,' said Gus, pointing to a white-suited figure. 'Dr Chong arrived five minutes before you did.'

With a terse nod Watts headed for the pathologist, Corrigan and Hanson following. As they reached her, Chong lifted a corner of the blanket and looked up at them. Hanson stared straight ahead at nothing in particular. 'All I've done so far is ID him with the help of the worker in charge of the evening shift here.' Watts and Corrigan looked down at what was visible. 'I've not met him. Have you, Corrigan?' Corrigan shook his head.

Hanson looked down, nodded then away. 'Alfred Best. I saw him this afternoon,' she said, barely recognising her own voice.

Chong pointed upwards at the building. 'Fourth floor. Five windows in from the left. The one that's open. He came out of there.'

'What time did it happen?' asked Corrigan.

'According to a worker who was caring for a resident in the next room but one, she heard a loud bang followed by a cry and checked her watch. It was nine thirty.'

'Want to see his wife's room?' asked Gus.

A spacious lift took them to the fourth floor. There was no need for them to locate the room. Two officers were guarding the doorway. A man and a woman in white, fitted uniforms and soft-soled shoes, were also there, the man leaning against the wall, staring at the floor, the woman quietly crying. They entered the spacious, comfortable room, cold due to the open window, and stood close to the door. Hanson glanced at the wide, hospital-style bed. Empty.

A SOCO came to them, pointing to the window. 'We've lifted prints off the frame and taken casts of the scuffmarks on the sill but it looks straightforward enough. All the indicators point to suicide. Deceased was eighty-one years old, not a big man, but active. Getting out of that window wouldn't have presented him with a problem.'

Hanson was thinking of spring bulbs. What had Alfred said when she saw him last? That they would look lovely in the spring.

'I'd like copies of all the results as soon as you've got 'em,' said Watts. He turned to Gus who was standing close to the door. 'You've talked to the woman in the next but one room? The one who heard the noise?'

'Yeah. She'd gone to draw the curtains in that room which also has a blind to help the resident sleep so she was at the window for some seconds.' He consulted his notes. 'According to her, she heard a loud bang or thump which she thinks came from this room. A male colleague with her opened the door and looked out but saw nothing. She reached up to pull down the blind and saw what she described as a dark shape falling to the ground.'

Hanson's attention was on the window, its shape, its size, its height from the floor. It wouldn't have presented Alfred with any problem to push up that window, climb onto the ledge and let gravity take him. She closed her eyes.

'OK,' said Watts. 'Put us down for copy statements, Gus.'

'Already done.' They left the room and took the lift to the ground in silence.

SEVENTEEN

Charlie placed a large bowl of oatmeal on the table in front of Maisie. 'Here you go. I'll keep you company while you eat.'

Hanson came into the kitchen, dressed for work. 'Do as Grandpa says. When you've finished I'll give you a lift into school.' She checked that her phone was in her bag, conscious of Charlie's eyes on her. When she'd arrived home in Sunday's early hours she'd told him about the suicide. About Alfred Best. She'd cried. A quiet day of trying to catch up on her sleep and her university work had followed. And here was another Monday morning bringing tasks she needed to get on with, things she had to do.

Maisie lifted her spoon and poked the oatmeal. 'Not hungry.'

'You will be midmorning if you don't eat it.' She was thinking about her daughter's current situation at the university. It had been in her head intermittently during the previous day and night, keeping thoughts of Alfred at bay. She had made a decision. 'I've decided, Maisie. I'm going to change your maths lectures at the university to two days a week, as it was last year.' She watched her daughter's eyes widen, saw equal measures of relief and anxiety.

'What about Daddy? He's really proud of me doing the extra day.'

Hanson saw the deep pink bottom lip tremble. She put her arm around the small shoulders. 'You'll still be doing two days. Your father is an adult.' *More or less.* 'You don't need to worry about him. He'll agree with me that what you feel happy doing, what feels right for you is what matters.'

Maisie shrugged. 'I dunno. Most of the students are OK. They call me Brainiac, but I don't mind. Bernie Watts calls me Brainbox and that's OK, too. It's just, after what happened at lectures and in the computer lab . . . I thought I could handle it but now . . . I'm not sure I can.'

Hanson placed her hand under Maisie's chin, raised the small face to hers. 'I'll have a word with Daddy. It'll be fine.'

Within ten minutes the oatmeal had disappeared and Maisie was yelling from the front door. '*Mom.* Come on!'

Hanson grabbed her coat, bag and briefcase. Charlie followed her down the hall and out. 'Good girl,' he said quietly.

She turned to him. 'Who, me? Or Maisie?'

'Both.'

After dropping Maisie at her school Hanson drove onto the campus and went straight to her room. Getting her phone out, she selected a contact and checked her watch. *He should be in his office by now.* 'Morning, Kevin. We need to talk—'

'Sorry, Kate. Not today.'

She frowned at the brusqueness. 'Yes, today. Now.' She waited out the brief pause, suspecting he'd gone somewhere quiet at his law chambers.

'Right.' He sighed. 'I'm due in court in half an hour and then I'm on a train to London. What's so damned urgent?'

'Our daughter.' She told him what had happened to Maisie

in the computer lab. About the pressure being exerted on her by an undergraduate to give him her work, culminating in Maisie kicking him.

He laughed. 'Good for her! You should be pleased she can assert herself.'

Hanson closed her eyes. 'That's not assertiveness and you're missing the point! I think Maisie was already struggling with the extra day of lectures. Put yourself in her place: she's with undergrads significantly older than she is, she's also probably much better at maths than most of them—'

'Atta-girl!'

'And I want the arrangement to go back to what it was last year: two lectures per week.'

'Oh, come on, Kate! A few hard knocks is what life's about and Maisie needs to know it. You're overprotective. Except when it comes to your own job, that is.'

She closed her eyes again. She wouldn't bite. Wouldn't ask him what he meant. 'The incident has made Maisie unsure of herself. She needs to get her confidence back. The student in question doesn't attend her lectures on the other two days so I'm letting you know what's going to happen.' She cut the call as Crystal came in carrying post.

'Morning, Kate. Did you see the message on your desk?' Hanson picked up the pink slip and read it. She was wanted at headquarters. By the chief. Grabbing her coat and bag she headed for the door.

Julian was in UCU when Hanson arrived. 'Watts and Corrigan are already up there,' he said.

Throwing her coat onto the table she headed down the corridor and upstairs, pausing at the chief's door to get her breathing under control, knocked and pushed open the door. One glance told her that whatever this was about it was causing a lot of tension. Corrigan's face was unreadable. Both the chief and Watts looked heated.

The chief looked up at her. 'Glad you're here. Maybe *you* can explain why you three saw it as part of your remit to attend a suicide scene last night?'

Playing quick catch-up, Hanson responded. 'That suicide is

somebody with a link to St Bartholomew's Church which has become a focus of our investigation of the murder of Matthew Flynn and the disappearance of another young—'

'Hear that?' the chief barked, pointing at her, glowering at her colleagues. *'That's* exactly what I'm talking about. The inability of the Unsolved Crime Unit, you three, to stick to what you're told to do.' He looked from one to the other of them, his jowls mottled. 'That isn't the only reason I wanted to see you. This morning I've had two complaints about UCU.' They exchanged quick glances, watched as he picked up a memo pad. 'The first one was from Father Delaney who was measured in his tone but said that he feels his church is becoming the target of a police witch hunt and that he fears more vandalism in future because of it.'

Hanson shook her head. 'That's ridiculous. We're conducting a murder investigation which—'

'He also said that several of his parishioners and others in the area have contacted the church website to express upset at police focus on the church and its members.'

She looked at him in disbelief. The chief pointed his forefinger at her. 'The other complaint is about *you*.' She waited, open-mouthed. 'The complainant is here, he's angry and he's demanded a meeting with all three of you. I agreed because if I didn't he'd probably go to the newspapers. I've insisted that in that meeting I do the talking, paraphrasing what has upset him to keep things civil.' He picked up the desk phone, hit a button and waited. 'Show them in.'

They sat in uncomfortable silence, Hanson's head scrambling over what this was about, the chief forcing his face into a semblance of calm reasonableness. There was a peremptory knock on the door. It was opened by a uniformed officer. Brad Flynn walked inside followed by Dominic Flynn, neither of them looking at anyone. The chief nodded to them. 'Have seats, please.' Once they were seated he spoke, his voice a steady monotone, his eyes on Hanson. 'Mr Flynn believes that you exerted undue pressure on his wife by demanding to see her at a time she was emotionally vulnerable. Mr Flynn also says that the nature of the questions you asked her has put strain on their relationship and exposed them to social media scrutiny and comment.' Brad Flynn did not look at her. Dominic Flynn was staring out of the window. The chief continued. 'The essence of Mr Flynn's complaint is that you released information about his wife having an association with a Zach Addison which has resulted in a flood of derogatory comments about her to their social media accounts.'

'I did not,' said Hanson, matching the chief's monotone, her face expressionless. Inside, she was furious. She gazed across at Brad Flynn who kept his eyes averted. Dominic Flynn was looking uncomfortable, his arms folded, his gaze on the floor, the expression on his face suggesting that he could think of several places he'd rather be right now.

The chief turned to Brad Flynn. 'Professor Hanson has heard your complaint and she's denied it. Leave the matter with me, Mr Flynn. I'll investigate it fully and get back to you on any action this force proposes to take.' The chief turned his attention to Dominic Flynn. 'Is there anything specific you'd like to say or add?'

Dominic looked at his watch then out of the window. 'No. Nothing.'

Brad Flynn stood, nodded to the chief and headed for the door, Dominic following him. The door closed and the chief turned to Hanson. 'Dominic Flynn looked like he was here under protest but you've made an enemy in his father.'

'We know Brad Flynn likes to control situations,' said Hanson. 'I've got serious doubts that his wife told him anything. I think he somehow found out about her affair and he wants to try some damage limitation of his reputation and his ego by switching the focus onto me. Make me look bad at my job.'

Looking marginally more relaxed, the chief gave a thin smile. 'This whole mess is looking better by the minute. You're saying you didn't speak to his wife?'

'Yes, I did.'

The smile disappeared. 'But you didn't accuse her of having an affair, like Flynn is saying?'

'I didn't "accuse". I raised it indirectly . . .'

'Oh, for . . .' The chief was back to irate. 'Delaney. Brad Flynn. Two separate individuals who want you three off this case and I'm the one who has to smooth them down.'

'We don't bow to that kind of pressure,' said Watts.

Hanson watched the chief's rage climb. 'You don't have to! It's *me* that has to do the bowing, the smoothing, the negotiating.' He rummaged in a drawer of his desk. 'Only nine thirty and my head's splitting. Just . . . *go*. Keep your contacts with Delaney and Flynn to a minimum unless you've got a specific reason to justify it to me first!'

They came into UCU. Hanson broke the silence. 'It was my idea to focus on the church.'

'We agreed. Our leads were pointing to it,' said Corrigan.

Watts sat heavily, eyes on Hanson. 'I know we've discussed it but that time you saw Delaney with the kid from the choir, do you think he realised you'd seen what he did?'

Hanson raised her shoulders. 'I try to keep a professional face, whatever I see or hear, but . . . I just don't know. Why?'

'Because a complaint by Delaney could be his way of diverting attention from himself. I'm not so bothered about Flynn. You were right about his wife and Zach Addison. What's upsetting Flynn is that it's out there for all to see.' He loosened his tie. 'I don't hold with all this Twittering and Twattering but it looks like it's something he and his wife go in for. In which case, somebody ought to tell both of them: if they don't like the comebacks they shouldn't be on it.'

There was a short silence. 'So, what do we do now?' asked Hanson.

'Get onto this mate of yours. The one with the drone. Tell him we're ready when he is.'

'What about the chief?' She watched him go to the board and point at various items of information.

'What he doesn't know can't hurt him. Matthew Flynn's remains were left inside the church's locked crypt. He'd attended a drug group run by the church. So did Callum Foley. Spencer Albright has form for church theft and before he dropped off the planet he told Chivers that St Bartholomew's security was poor.' He came back to the table. 'We need to find both Foley and Albright. We need to know whether they're dead. I want that drone.'

*   *   *

Hanson was inside the Geoscience department, looking down at the black metal contraption, each of its outstretched 'arms' surmounted by propellers. 'Small, isn't it?' she offered, looking at what was probably UCU's only hope.

Jake gazed down at it, a father exhibiting his first-born. 'Also light and very easily controlled.' He pointed out features. 'That's the camera. There's a couple of other bits and bobs, the ground-reading technology which communicates results direct to this.' He went to the small laptop sitting on the workbench, opened it up. 'Have a look.' He pointed. 'I've checked out this map of the land around the church. We're in luck. There are only the two buildings: the church itself and this place.' He pointed to what Hanson knew to be Church House. 'We don't need to fly over either of them, which means we don't have any trespass violations to worry about.'

Hanson nodded. *Unless Father Delaney or members of his committee see it operating.*

He pointed to a small area on the map some distance from the extensive piece of land on which the church, the churchyard and Delaney's house were situated. 'We'll start there. It's separate from the church and given we're talking clandestine burial it looks like a good place, screened by trees from anybody who might be coming and going to the church.'

'We're ready to go with it, Jake. How are you fixed?'

'Ready when you are. Any time in the next two days is good for me.'

'Hang on.' She got out her phone, tapped it, spoke and turned back to Jake. 'DS Watts says this evening.'

Jake grinned. 'Cool.'

They came onto the land Jake had selected for the drone's task, Hanson's eyes on the church and Church House some distance to the right of where they were, both in darkness. She scanned the area for signs of Delaney or anyone else associated with the church. There was no one. The whole place was deserted. Jake strode ahead of them carrying his equipment, a graduate student in tow, Hanson and her colleagues following, getting occasional glimpses of the leaning stones of the churchyard. They were here to locate an illicit burial if one existed, one which might yield the remains of either Callum Foley or Spencer Albright. *Maybe both, if we're lucky.* She bit her lip. Jake set down the equipment and his student unpacked it and set it up with practiced ease.

He looked around. 'This area is nice and open for Oscar to roam. Do his thing.'

They watched as he got busy with the laptop, Corrigan looking beguiled by the technology, Watts suspicious. Jake gazed upwards at gathering cloud, frowned at a quick fierce gust making nearby tree limbs wave, scattering crisp leaves around their feet.

'That wind could be a problem if it sticks around. Oscar likes calm conditions.'

Over the next few minutes the wind died. Hanson's attention remained on the trees and undergrowth, uneasy now. She wanted Jake to complete his survey quickly so they could leave. Hearing sudden enthusiasm in her colleagues' voices she looked to where the drone was sitting, several of its propellers now spinning, Jake's attention fixed on the laptop. At a single key-tap command they watched the spindly, black, mosquito-like object rise into the air, emitting a low buzzing sound, dipping slightly to one side then the other. Faces raised, they watched it climb, hover and suddenly accelerate towards the edge of the open area of land and begin moving steadily along its perimeter. Intrigued, Hanson stared at it then went to where Jake was standing with the laptop, his student pointing to the screen, their eyes fixed on it. Hanson looked upwards, searching for the drone. She couldn't see it. A quick movement among the screen of trees separating them from the church and Delaney's house sent tension surging through her. She glanced at her colleagues, fully occupied with the drone's activities and back, scanning the trees. They hadn't seen it but she had. Someone was here. Someone on the move. There it was again! A quick flash of white among the branches. Too small for Delaney. Hanson broke into a run, heading for the tree cover. She had to talk to whoever it was. Explain what they were doing and why.

'Wait!' It ran like the wind then stopped, still obscured by trees. Hanson also stopped, uncertain. It turned quickly and ran noiselessly away, leaving her staring helplessly after it. *That was no obese priest, no elderly parishioner.*

She returned to her colleagues who were still gathered around
the apparatus. Corrigan looked up at her. 'That you who shouted,
Red?'

'Yes. I thought I saw something. Someone.'

Watts frowned. 'And?'

'It ran.'

'Blimey. Let's hope it was nobody connected with the church.
We don't need more trouble.'

'How long will it take to survey the area?' she asked Jake.

Watts looked across at him. 'The Doc's of an impatient
disposition but we'll all feel easier once it's finished and we're
away from here.'

'I'd say around fifteen more minutes, then it's back to Geoscience
with the data, examine the results and try interpreting them.'

Watts's brows met. 'Try? Let's get something straight
here: we need this and soon.' Hanson sent him a look. 'I'm not
the only one in UCU who's impatient.'

Jake's eyes were on the screen. 'This survey is experimental
for me and my department so I want to get it right. When we
get back, we'll work on it until we think we've got a conclusive
picture of what lies beneath, if anything.'

Seeing Watts's doubtful look, Hanson recalled her own early
weeks as part of UCU, and his jibes about "ivory-tower
academics". 'They want to try working in the real world for a
change!' he'd railed.

After several more minutes the drone appeared above them
and lowered itself elegantly to the ground. Taking leave of
Jake and his student, with his promise to get back to them as
soon as he could, they returned to UCU.

'I did see something, you know,' said Hanson.

'Let's hope it wasn't Delaney or his deacons on the prowl.'

'It wasn't. It was quick-moving. Wraithlike.'

Watts looked at her, clearly edgy. 'Let's hope your mate Jake
gets back to us with a result before the chief catches on to what
we've been up to.'

Hanson was overcome by tiredness. 'I'm going home.' She
stopped as she reached the door. 'I just remembered. Those tiny
bits of vegetation that Chong collected from Matthew Flynn's
clothing. Has she said anything about them?'

Watts shook his head. 'Only that they were too small and not enough to identify but she confirmed what she said originally: vegetable matter of some kind, which tells me—'

She gave him a weary look. 'Yes, drugs. We *know*.'

'I'm definitely being railroaded here,' murmured Hanson a couple of hours later as she threw down a card, her mind on bed and sleep.

Maisie rolled her eyes. 'That's because you're not keeping the rules in your head, Mom. You're not concentrating.' She turned to Charlie. 'What have you got, Grandpa?' Charlie laid down his cards with the air of a magician at a final reveal.

'Wow,' breathed Maisie. She looked at him. 'You were wasted in the law. You should have been a cardsharp.'

Hanson began gathering the cards, listening to Charlie's laugh. 'Time you were in bed, Maisie.'

Against the usual backdrop of protests, she glanced at Maisie and Charlie. Her family. All that really mattered was that they were healthy and happy. And safe. Earlier in the day she'd informed the vice chancellor that she wanted to reduce Maisie's attendance at maths lectures to the original two days. She hadn't given a reason. She'd also told Kevin of the change. He hadn't been impressed. She gave a mental shrug. The decision wasn't set in stone. If Maisie decided at some point in the future that she was ready to increase her lectures they'd talk about it.

Four hours of disturbed sleep and Hanson was being pursued by something faceless, white, grasping arms extended. She was dragged to full consciousness by her phone on the bedside table.

4.00 a.m. and rain was falling out of blackness, bowing branches, turning their few remaining leaves glossy. Watts gulped hot tea from a plastic cup, watching Petrie working beneath a hastily erected cover, cagoule shiny, rain dripping from its hood as he talked to Chong and the SOCOs, pointing out features from the data he'd printed off, his face animated. Watts took another gulp of tea, wondering if this particular academic ever slept. If he did, it had to be in the daytime. Probably had a sideline as a vampire. He was savouring the action as SOCOs carrying portable lights and a folded gazebo canopy, another two with shovels, dispersed to a small area a few metres away at the edge of the clearing and stood. A thumbs-up from Petrie and the gazebo rose, the lights came on and the shovels drove downwards. Watching rectangles of sodden grass being sliced from their moorings and dropped to one side, Watts ruminated on the hours he'd spent waiting, watching, as experts dug into earth or disappeared beneath water to lift out whatever was there, then stepped back to allow for other, different expertise. He glanced over at Chong now, close to the excavation, pointing and talking, Petrie alongside her, his hand movements cautioning. It would be Chong's turn soon. She would allow Watts a brief look at whatever was there, after which she would take charge of it if it was human, and he'd wait some more for the post-mortem results. Over thirty or so years, it added up to a lot of waiting.

He turned as Hanson approached in response to his call, face intent, damp springs of hair escaping from her hood. She arrived at his side, scanning their surroundings. Given her attention to detail and her reluctance to let anything go, he wouldn't have been surprised if she was still looking for whoever she said she'd seen here earlier.

'What do we know?' she asked.

'Nothing beyond the drone identifying what looks to be an illicit burial according to your mate, Petrie, who can't be sure right now if it's human. Or a large dog. Or a small horse.'

She looked across at the excavation in progress then up at him. 'Is that your sarcastic streak talking?'

He grinned, drank tea. 'Petrie is cautious but he's also your confident type. He's saying it could be human.'

She waited. 'And you're sufficiently confident to blow the secrecy of what we've done by bringing Chong and the SOCOs out here?'

He didn't reply. Her words had brought the scene with the chief the previous day into his head.

'What are you thinking?' she asked.

'I'm asking myself what sort of job it is where you hope you're digging somebody up.'

She shivered. He poured more tea. 'Here, grab hold. Excuse the mug.'

She took it from him, placed her hands around it and drank. 'Where's Corrigan?' she asked.

'He's busy.' He glanced at her in profile, getting nothing but he guessed she was thinking plenty, wondering what Corrigan was busy doing. He gave a mental shrug. Nothing to do with him how the two of them organised their lives. Or didn't. They couldn't seem to get it together. Right now, apart from Armed Response, Corrigan was busy doing one of the other things that he did well. 'He's at headquarters, going through the paperwork Gus's team removed from Alfred Best's property.'

'Oh.'

He glanced at her again, wondering whether Delaney's complaint to the chief was aimed at deflecting attention from what Hanson had seen inside the church. Watts had never known her show what she was thinking to people involved in their cases. A closed book, was what she normally was. One of the things about her which had taken him a while to get used to. He straightened, eyes narrowing on the excavation. Chong was on her knees beneath the plastic awning, a wide swathe of raw earth now visible, the SOCOs and their shovels at rest.

'Look lively, doc.' He murmured. 'I think we're in business.'

They walked the few metres of soaked grass, went under the gazebo and stood looking down at the indistinct shape around which Chong was carefully loosening damp, red-brown earth. They watched her work steadily, an outline slowly emerging. One side of a head. One shoulder. The beginnings of an upper arm?

'What are you hoping for, Watts?' asked Chong without moving her attention from her task.

'That we've got either Spencer Albright or Callum Foley.'

She continued the deft scraping. 'Care to tell me something about them?'

'Both young, say eighteen to twenty-four. Albright was last seen around six weeks ago. It's a can't-say for Foley.'

Eyes on the remains she said, 'I've got male, possibly youthful. Beyond that, you'll have to wait.'

'Ta for that,' he said, moving away, Hanson following.

'What do you think?' she asked, voice low and urgent. 'Foley or Albright?'

'Slacken the suspenders. We'll know soon enough.'

EIGHTEEN

Hanson arrived in UCU the following afternoon to find Corrigan on the phone surrounded by papers in orderly piles. Watts was going through one of them.

'Any more news?' she asked of their early-hours visit to what had turned out to be a grave.

He turned pages. 'Not yet.'

She walked to the window, looked across the parking area to the smart little terraced houses on the other side of the road. 'I've been thinking.'

'Dangerous times, Corrigan. Brace yourself.'

She turned to them. 'About Alfred Best. He told me he had problems. Whatever they were, he was still very upbeat that afternoon, just hours before he died. He told me about his wife being in a care home. I assumed that was the source of the problems he mentioned.'

'And?'

'It was the way he spoke about her and his efforts to give her some quality of life. He was so positive. He saw it as a challenge, not a source of despair.'

Corrigan's eyes were on her, phone still to his ear. 'What's bothering you, Red?'

'His death being regarded as a suicide. It makes no sense, given what I saw of him just hours before.' She looked down at the table. 'Alfred's papers?'

'Yep.' He spoke into the phone. 'Yeah, I'm still here.'

Watts glanced across at him then back to Hanson. 'Corrigan was here late last night reading through the info that Upstairs collected from Best's house and we've got copies of statements from workers at the care home. Have a look.'

She took the statements and sat on the table to read them,

picking up Corrigan's low responses to whoever was at the other end of his call. Part-way through the third statement, that of a care assistant who had greeted Alfred on his arrival, she stopped. 'This isn't right.'

Watts looked up. 'What isn't?'

'This statement made by the member of staff who saw Alfred on his arrival. Listen: "I know Mr Alfred Best. His wife has been a resident in the home where I work for almost two years. He arrived at about six o'clock in the evening. He looked very dejected and hardly spoke when I said hello to him. I took the lift with him to his wife's room. As we stepped from the lift he became agitated, asking how his wife was, if she was upset. I reassured him that Mrs Best was fine but he remained agitated. I asked if he wanted me to accompany him into his wife's room but he said no. He went inside and immediately closed the door on me. Again, this was unusual because Mr Best was always very polite. A short time later I heard shouts and another assistant came to tell me that Mr Best had fallen from one of the fourth-floor windows and was lying on the ground at the rear of the building".' Hanson shook her head. 'That's what I was saying. It doesn't make sense.'

Watts took the statement she was holding out to him and skimmed it. 'What's wrong with it?'

'Everything. It doesn't fit with how he was that afternoon. I just told you what an upbeat and cheerful person he was. He'd made plans for that visit to his wife. He was taking some photographs to show her. He was looking forward to it. As I left he was about to get the bus there.'

Watts frowned. 'Yeah? So?'

'What happened to make him go from that to appearing so low in mood to a member of staff barely an hour later?' she demanded. 'How could his mood, his demeanour, have changed so radically to what the care worker says here?' She pointed at lines in the statement. 'She's describing him as agitated, possibly depressed and abrupt. Forget the how. I want to know *why*.'

'Maybe he had some bad news after you saw him. Or, he started thinking about how long his wife had been in that home and how many years more he'd have to visit her there and started getting depressed, feeling he'd had enough—'

'No, no.' Hanson shook her head. 'He wasn't like that.'

'You didn't know him, doc. You'd only seen him a couple of times.'

She took the statement from him, skimmed it again. 'I'm telling you, this isn't right. I'm not doubting the care assistant's recall but I can't believe he changed so drastically in such a short time, sufficient to make him step out of a fourth-floor window.'

She placed the statement on the table, getting a quick rush of doubt. Watts was right. She didn't know Alfred. She stared down at the statement. What she did know was the suicide research: prior to that final act of self-destruction, extremely depressed people were often reported as appearing lighter in mood than those who knew them had witnessed in a consider-able while. It was to do with their anticipation of an end to the exhaustion of being depressed. No. What she'd seen of Alfred that afternoon, what she'd read in this statement was the wrong way round. It didn't fit.

Watts's voice broke into her thoughts. 'So something happened between the time you saw him and the time he arrived at the care home. Maybe he had a phone call. Bad news.'

'Did he have a phone on him?'

Watts took his phone from his pocket, tapped it, while Hanson focused on the Smartboard's information, wondering again where she was going with all of this. She re-tuned to Watts's voice. 'Chong says no phone.'

She looked up, seeing Corrigan end his call. He and Watts exchange glances. 'He'll get back to us,' said Corrigan. He looked across at Hanson. 'An historical line of inquiry I'm following up with a pal. Might be nothing.' He pointed to the stacked paperwork on the table. 'Got some interesting informa-tion here on Alfred Best's life and financial situation.' She went and stood next to him, eyes on the papers as he pointed to them. 'These here are his bank and other financial records. Alfred Best was a wealthy guy.'

'Really? That's good, given that his wife's care was probably expensive.'

Corrigan pointed to other papers. 'Back in the 70s Alfred started his own real estate business which earned him a lot of money until around 2006 when he sold it.'

'Why did he sell it?'

'According to his financial adviser at the time, he wanted to retire, spend more time with his wife. They had no children. The money he got from the sale of the company, plus properties he owned which he sold at around the same time, netted a cool £1.5 million.'

Hanson's eyes rounded. She looked down at the papers on the table then at Corrigan. 'You said Alfred "was" wealthy.' She looked down at the papers. 'Are all these saying that he wasn't when he died?'

Corrigan reached for various A4s and put them in order in front of her. 'Take a look at these.' He pointed to regular items on bank statements going back several years. 'For a long time he was withdrawing a heap of money every couple of months.'

'For his wife's care?'

Corrigan shook his head. 'That was debited from his account direct to the home.'

'So . . . what was he doing with so much money each month?' She traced her finger down each of the sheets. 'The withdrawals he made weren't for set amounts.' She looked up. 'Maybe there was someone in Alfred's life to whom he owed a debt or felt responsible for?'

Watts came to look down at the records. 'There's another interpretation. What do you think of him being blackmailed?'

'*Blackmailed*?' She looked from him to Corrigan. 'This is an eighty-something-year-old man we're talking about. A man whose life revolved around his wife and his church.'

'Blackmail can be about something in the long-ago, doc. Old stuff coming home to roost, you know? There's a lot of that happening these days.'

Historical child abuse allegations against several famous personalities surged into Hanson's head. *Surely not Alfred?* As the thoughts crystalized she recalled men she had evaluated professionally in terms of their sexual risk: older men, one or two in their seventies, many of them married, some successful, many of them likeable, all of them admitting years-old offences. Preoccupied, she heard the phone ring, half-listened as Corrigan took the call, his tone grabbing her attention.

'Thanks a lot, Walt! I thought it was worth checking out.

Yeah, you too. See ya, buddy.' He ended the call. Hanson saw Watts's raised eyebrows, Corrigan's nod. He looked at her. 'We know Delaney was in Boston twenty years back and it got me thinking. It was a long shot but I called one of the guys I worked with on the Boston force. He's gone through all the records looking for Delaney's name.' He stood and walked towards the board. 'He found it.'

Hanson stared at him open-mouthed. 'Are you saying that Delaney has a *police* record in America?'

'No. But his name is mentioned. He left Boston in around 1991 and came back to the UK. Six months after he left the US, an allegation by a minor was made against him.'

'Meaning, exactly?'

'A person under eighteen.'

'What happened to the allegation?'

Corrigan gave her a direct look. 'We're talking over two decades ago, yeah? We're all a lot savvier now at investigating sexual crime but back then the minor who made the complaint was deemed to be unreliable.'

'So the allegation of this minor, this boy, wasn't considered strong?'

'Kind of, Red. Except that the complainant was an almost-eighteen-year-old female.'

Hanson's head was a desert. '*Female*?' She shook her head. 'This is like knitting smoke. What else do you know?'

Corrigan read from notes he'd made. 'The female complained to friends about Delaney constantly watching her when she was inside or around his church. Seems she told her folks about it. The crunch came when she alleged she saw him staring into her bedroom window at the ground-floor apartment she shared with another female. She reported him, it was investigated and on the basis of it being at most a non-contact issue, given that the police weren't too convinced about what she was saying, they logged it and that was it.'

'So, this female alleged he was a voyeur.'

Watts looked at her. 'Remind us what the research has to say about that?'

She raised her shoulders. 'It's mixed. Those who engage in watching, spying on others, particularly when they're engaged in say undressing as this young woman might have been if she was in her bedroom, are a diverse group. The behaviour is now considered more widespread than originally thought. One theory is that for the committed voyeur, watching becomes the primary sexual act. Like you said, Corrigan, not so much was known about the investigation of sexual crime back then. Voyeurism is now an offence.' They looked at each other. 'What are you going to do about Delaney?'

'Not much we can do,' said Corrigan. 'There's no outstanding charge against him in the US so we can't arrest him.'

Hanson thought about what she'd just been told. They had no way of evaluating the young woman's years-old allegation. And what relevance could it have to their case or an eighty-year-old's suicide? Feeling chilled, something moving inside her head which she couldn't get hold of, she pointed at the papers on the table. 'What about all of this? Alfred's death?'

Watts looked down at it. 'We'll keep it for a couple of days, do some checks. See what we can learn about his life. If we don't find anything of interest we give it back to Upstairs, plus what Corrigan's got from the financial records and leave them to pursue it.' He looked across at her. 'For some reason Best was out of money, he was worried about how he's going to finance his wife's care. He felt guilty about her and decided suicide is his way out. It works for me.'

Hanson stared up at the board. 'Maybe.'

In the gathering shadow of her university room, head thumping from lack of sleep, Hanson read the email on her screen. It was from Jake Petrie: 'Hi, Kate. I'm writing up Oscar's performance in UCU's investigation. I'd appreciate your letting me know the outcome of your case so I can reference it in a future article.' *Another academic preparing research papers.* She sent him a quick, affirmative response. Whatever the 'outcome' for UCU, Jake's drone had succeeded: it had found human remains quickly and with minimal cost. Jake was on his way to the professional recognition he deserved.

She leant on the desk, her eyes on the flip chart and the stark black words there, plus the two photographs: Matthew. Callum. Still no news from Chong. Where the hell was UCU going with this? *Probably to hell.* She went to the flip chart, removed the photographs, placed them on her desk then tore off the sheet of notes, letting it fall to the floor, her eyes on the pristine sheet beneath. Taking the black marker she drew a large circle and wrote Matthew Flynn's name inside it. Matthew, twenty years old, throat hacked out for a reason she and her UCU colleagues still did not understand. Until they did, they would not know by whom. Matthew had a caution for a drug offence, hid money inside his boot, went with Callum Foley, another drug group attendee, to get a tattoo put on his neck. An inverted crucifix. Callum Foley had a similar one. She wrote Foley's name inside the circle. The drug support group was run by St Bartholomew's Church. It couldn't be established for certain, but from what UCU knew, both young men seemed to have disappeared at around the same time. Before Foley did so, he took an envelope containing a fifty-pound note and concealed it at his mother's house. That note bore a serial number that fitted the sequence of those in Matthew Flynn's boot. She stood back.

What else? Matthew appeared to be somewhat distant from his family. She added more names. Prior to his disappearance he had shared a house with two students, William Graham and Zach Addison. Both of them were operating a cannabis farm within that house. For all UCU knew, Matthew was involved in that. *More drugs. More money.* Addison was in a sexual relationship with Matthew's mother. *More sex.* Hanson added lines radiating from the circle, wrote names, thoughts tumbling into her head then onto the flip chart. *Where's the sense?*

She stepped back, looked at the two names within the circle, sure now, regardless of who Chong was working on, that Foley was as dead as Matthew. And where did Spencer Albright who was suspected of having stolen from St Bartholomew's fit into all of this? Was he responsible for the vandalism? Were they his remains they'd seen and which were now lying in the PM suite? She added a word: pentagram.

She surveyed all she'd written. So many names. Brad Flynn, wealthy businessman and fixer. Son Dominic following in his steps. *Had Matthew felt excluded or rejected?* Diana Flynn having sex with Zach Addison in the house where her son lived. Father Delaney, his plump hand on blond curls, leaving Hanson uncertain of his motive. And now they'd found a long-ago allegation against him by a female two decades ago and six thousand miles away. What about the deacons at the church? She added their names. One of them they hadn't yet met. Was he still on retreat? Had he returned? She leant her forehead against a cool white space on the paper, straightened, added Alfred's name, one of an army of elderly parishioners who supported the church and who was now dead, possibly by his own hand, leaving a wife who didn't know anyone any more and more debt than money. She started as her phone rang, anxiety peaking when she saw her caller's name.

'Charlie? Is everything OK?'

His calm voice came into her ear. 'Fine. Why wouldn't it be? I thought I'd take my daughter and granddaughter out to dinner tonight. What do you think?'

'That's a lovely idea. Thank you.' The silence between them lengthened.

'What is it, Kate?'

She didn't want to burden him. He'd been ill. The words came, anyway. 'It's this case. I'm – lost, Charlie.'

'That sounds to me like tiredness talking. An evening out is what you need. A chance to step back. A break will give you the energy to take a look at where you are and see exactly what you've got.'

Her conversation with Charlie ended as her desk phone rang. It was Watts. 'We'll have info on the remains found by the drone in around half an hour.'

Fetching her coat and bag she took a last look at the flip chart. Maybe Charlie is right. *Maybe the answer or its direction is somewhere here but I'm too tired to see it.* She hesitated. Something important was missing. She went back to her desk, reached for the photographs of Matthew Flynn and Callum Foley and placed them on the rim of the flip chart stand.

She ran a finger lightly over both. They were the reason for all of this.

Hanson went directly to the pathology suite where her two colleagues were waiting. 'What's happening?' she asked, thrusting her arms into a blue coverall.

Watts shrugged. 'Nothing so far—' They turned as Igor wheeled a trolley supporting a grey body bag towards them, aligned the trolley with the steel examination table and applied the brake. The door opened and Chong came inside with a nod to them.

'Prompt and keen as expected.' She and Igor took hold of the body bag and transferred it to the examination table in one practiced movement. Its weight didn't seem to give them a problem. 'Masks on, if you've got any sense.' She unzipped the bag and folded back its sides.

The sweetish, cloying, unmistakable aroma rolled out. The smell of the dead. A smell like no other. Hanson pressed her mask to her nose and mouth, eyes drifting over now recognisable aspects of what was lying in front of them, what they'd seen at the burial site augmented by detail. The head appeared intact, the face still an unidentifiable series of small hills and valleys. The torso and limbs were stained dark by the rich earth in which the body had lain for many months, much of the flesh gone. Hanson's eyes settled on a darkened area directly below the chin.

'DNA confirmation,' said Chong. 'Callum Foley, aged twenty years nine months when he was last seen approximately one year ago. Inverted crucifix tattoo on right side of neck reminiscent of that noted on Matthew Flynn's remains.' They waited as she pushed an X-ray plate into a lightbox, switched it on. She returned to the table, activated a water spray and brought it towards the upper body. 'Watch,' she said. The fine mist struck the area of the lower face and neck. Rivulets ran downwards, carrying soil debris with it to the examination table. They stared in silence at the wreckage left behind. 'His murderer didn't see fit to cover him with anything except the impacted earth, which there seems to be no end to on his remains. I removed much of it when I started work on him and took that.' She pointed at the X-ray. 'That is Foley's throat and the gaping hole in it.'

'A re-run of Matthew Flynn's injury,' said Corrigan.

Chong nodded. 'I can't give you a better idea of what caused it than I did for Matthew Flynn: some kind of implement with sharp aspects on all sides. No other injuries. No blood that wasn't his.' She reached for a shallow, stainless steel bowl. They stared down at its contents: a small, clear plastic bag, a dark seam of something gathered along its lower edge. 'Come closer, children. You'll want to know about this.'

They closed in on the examination table, the smell very pressing now, their focus on Chong as she carefully upended the plastic bag and shook out its contents. Tiny shreds and bits of unidentified matter poured into the small bowl. She pointed to another near to Corrigan. He reached for it and passed it to her. She held both the labelled bowls towards them, raising one.

'Take a look. These are the tiny traces I gathered from Callum Foley's pockets and the seams of his clothing. This bowl holds what I vacuumed from Matthew Flynn's clothing which you've already seen.' She paused. They stared. 'It's all of the same origin.'

'Some type of drug?' asked Watts.

'Sorry to wreck your theory, but no. These are all the remains of plants. Take a closer look.' Using a thin metal tool, she moved the tiny particles around. 'Having collected around eighty percent more of it from Foley I've been able to identify it all. It's from a variety of different sources.' She moved the tool around the bowl. 'These seeds are Queen Anne's Lace, an attractive wild flower, aka "Devil's plague". These right here are oregano and these are St John's Wort. These bigger items here are from a plant known as Devil's Bit.'

Hanson pointed. 'Are those black things cloves?'

'That's exactly what they are,' said Chong. 'And this here is dried garlic.'

Watts frowned at it. 'So? What's the point of it? Why would Flynn and Foley have all of this on them?'

Chong eyed him. 'Bearing in mind that I'm merely the messenger here, all of it is supposedly capable of repelling evil.'

'You, what?' He narrowed his eyes on the bowls' contents, face set. 'That kind of thing is twaddle!'

She sighed, straightened. 'As I said, merely the messenger.'

Vexed, he took the tool she was offering him and prodded the tiny bits of vegetation. 'I thought garlic was associated with vampires?'

Chong nodded. 'There's a belief that it has a role in warding off evil.'

Watts huffed. 'Who believes that stuff? It's all mumbo-jumbo.'

'That's not the point,' said Hanson.

'So, what is?' he demanded.

She looked down at all that remained of Callum Foley. 'I'd say it's about whether he and Matthew believed it. Or how frightened he was.'

Hanson was back at the university, still preoccupied by what Chong had shown them. It looked as though both Matthew Flynn and Callum Foley were in a state of fear prior to their deaths. Going directly to the flip chart she picked up the sheet she had left lying on the floor and searched all of the information on it. Words there now claimed her attention: pentagram, inverted crucifix, torn throat. She added others given to them by Chong earlier, ending with Devil's Bit. Watts was right. Nobody capable of critical, rational thinking would believe this stuff. Her eyes moved over the lines, stopping at a single descriptor she'd written for Matthew Flynn: naïve.

Folding her arms, giving them a brisk rub she walked into the adjoining room. Crystal looked up from her screen, fingers halting. 'Kate?'

'Do you remember a case in Wiltshire I consulted on about three years ago, involving devil worship?'

'Still got the goose bumps to prove it,' said Crystal leaving her desk for the bank of nearby filing cabinets. Opening a drawer, walking her fingers across several files, she stopped and withdrew one. 'Found it.'

Hanson returned to her room with it. Ten minutes' immersion in the notes she had made at the time and the case was back in her head: it had involved what had been presented to her at the outset as a cult but in reality was a fraudulent set-up. She sped through the research articles she'd downloaded at the time, some supportive of the existence of demonic influences and attesting to the strange behavioural changes the phenomena was capable of causing, including suicide. *If Alfred's death was not a suicide, had he been as fearful for his life as Matthew and Callum appeared to have been?* She frowned. *I didn't see any fear.* She read the research data she'd gathered relating to those who associate themselves with devil worship: masochistic, self-deprecating, willing to abandon all personal responsibility in exchange for the security of a powerful leader. She skimmed through the rest of the data then pushed the file away. Alfred had been a member of St Bartholomew's, had given his free time to supporting and maintaining it. Alfred, a wealthy man during most of his life, brought to near-penury at its end. Both Matthew Flynn and Callum Foley had had brief indirect contact with the same church in their short lives. She stopped, hands clasped at her mouth. Was she seeing tenuous links where they didn't exist? Or making the wrong links? Was she seeing in the language, the dark imagery of this case a meaning which belonged only in Hollywood horror?

She gathered the articles together, replaced them in the file. She had to talk to Delaney again. Slamming a mental door on the chief's rage at Delaney's complaints about UCU, she knew it had to be soon.

I can do diplomacy to get the information I want: what was Alfred's role and place in the church? What is Delaney's stance towards Satanism? What has he to say about his own history in the USA, if he's willing to say anything at all?

Collecting her coat and bag, she was on her way.

NINETEEN

The laden tray thumped onto the low table in Father Delaney's study. He tracked the broad back and massive hips on their way to the door. 'Thank you, Mrs Gorridge. Very kind.' The door closed with a decisive click. In the fifteen or so minutes Hanson had been there Delaney had been entirely pleasant. He hadn't alluded to his complaint about UCU by either word or demeanour. Right now he was smiling at her. 'Gorridge is not happy. Which isn't a rare occurrence I will admit but today it has a specific cause. We had a meeting of the diocese here this morning. Gorridge dislikes the bishop and she's none too keen on providing refreshments for him. Or anyone else for that matter.'

'Why does she dislike the bishop?' asked Hanson in conversational mode, accepting tea.

'Because she finds him patronising and "holier-than-thou" as she puts it.' He laughed. 'Gorridge is totally irreligious.' Hanson eyed him, surprised. 'It's true,' he said. 'She works hard in this house but refuses to set foot inside the church, which is partly why we have to rely on parishioners to keep it up to scratch as regards dusting, flowers and so forth. Those duties are part of her employment contract but I don't insist. I know she needs the money the church pays her.'

'Isn't that unusual, her not being religious? I'd assumed there would be some expectation by the church that anyone employed by it would have some degree of faith.'

'I don't know about it being unusual. All I know is that she does a good job keeping this old place clean and dusted and providing meals.'

'She and her niece,' said Hanson.

Delaney nodded, his face suddenly serious. 'Yes. A sad story. Gorridge's sister died unexpectedly several years ago, leaving a child. Gorridge took responsibility for its upbringing, which she has done on very little money. I don't believe there was anyone else who would do it, but I don't know the details and I haven't dared ask.'

'Does she live locally?' asked Hanson.

'Primrose Way, just off the main road about a mile from here.' He heaved a sigh. 'My dealings are strictly with Gorridge but I understand the young person has problems. I imagine life would have been even more problematic without a family member like Gorridge stepping forward to do her Christian duty.' His eyes twinkled. 'Not that *she* would see it in those terms and I certainly wouldn't presume to say so directly to her.' There was a brief pause, during which Hanson found herself struggling to resist the unexpected warmth of this man whom she found so ambiguous. 'You seem preoccupied,' he said. 'Can I help?'

Hanson relaxed her face. *Obviously, I'm not as enigmatic as I thought.* She had decided during the journey here how she would introduce her visit. 'I want to say how much the Unsolved Crime Unit regrets any problems it may have inadvertently caused St Bartholomew's.' She ignored Watts's disapproving face zooming into her head; she couldn't recall him ever acknowledging regrets about anything he'd done as part of what he called The Job.

'My dear young woman, there's no need,' said Delaney. 'That was actually the bishop's doing. Done at his behest. He raised it as an issue some days ago and insisted that I relay his view to the Chief Superintendent. It was also the reason for his visit here this morning. He takes an inordinate interest in what he terms our "community alliance". He sees our role within the community as one which provides practical as well as spiritual support via our outreach work. He also expects me to be responsible for management of the church's reputation in the locality. He's extremely sensitive to stresses from outside our community which he regards as a potential threat to its reputation.' He looked across at Hanson. 'I don't happen to agree with him. This church stands on its reputation, but the bishop requires what we do to be, well, let me say, "stage managed" . . .' He paused. 'I acquiesce where it doesn't feel too contrary to my own values. He's extremely annoyed still about ongoing police interest here. He's also very critical of my decision not to report the vandalism when it happened.' He sighed. 'Although, of course, he would not have been happy if I had done so. Not an easy man to work with, as I'm sure you'll appreciate.'

'Does he approve of the way you run St Bartholomew's on business lines?'

Delaney gave an energetic nod. 'An excellent question which has two answers: yes and no. He views the business world as unethical but he knows he cannot deny the benefits he witnesses here. Neither can he deny the significant growth in our congregation over recent years, nor the money we save by working together to support the fabric of the church. He's also extremely approving of the funding we attract to run our various community initiatives.'

Hanson studied him. 'I hadn't associated the priesthood with a knowledge of business.'

He returned her look. 'Which is why many of our churches

are in a parlous state. Don't make the mistake of assuming that those who work within the church to serve the Lord are unworldly. Both of my deacons were professional men prior to joining the church. Jeremy Fellowes was a qualified counsellor and Richard Burns an accountant.' Seeing Hanson's surprise he smiled. 'And I learned from my time in the United States that business can be ethical and that its acumen has relevance for the church.' He paused, sipped tea. 'I've told you about our challenges here. You and your colleagues are also experiencing significant difficulties in your investigation?'

Their eyes met. She saw naked curiosity in his. She chose her words. 'The kinds of cases the Unsolved Crime Unit investigates are by definition difficult. We search for means, motive and opportunity, often months, sometimes years, after an event.'

It was Delaney who now looked uncertain. 'I think I understand "means" – it's about being able to commit the crime?'

'Yes. Physical strength or access to a weapon. Motive and opportunity can be hard to establish at a distance in time. When someone goes missing and is then found dead it can be very difficult to establish exactly when and why he or she died.'

Delaney shook his head, looking sympathetic. 'That poor boy, Matthew Flynn. And his family, of course. I asked Fellowes who runs the drug support groups to tell me all he knows. He's confirmed that Matthew Flynn briefly attended one group. He appears to know little else about him. I hope you find the answer to what happened to the boy soon. It is having a very negative impact on some of our older members.'

She gazed at the plump, troubled face. Headquarters had stifled news of the finding of Callum Foley's body for now. She'd waited for some indication that Delaney was aware of it but it hadn't come. Once he did know, Callum Foley's relative proximity to the church would have further negative impact on him and his congregation. His reference to the older members of his congregation brought Hanson to another line of inquiry. 'It seems that Alfred Best was a rather troubled man.'

Delaney's face changed. He pressed his palms together, brought his hands to his mouth. 'A dreadful state of affairs. As a church we oppose suicide, of course, because it is contrary to our love for the eternal Lord. Alfred was surely gravely disturbed to commit such a dreadful act. I feel responsible to a degree because I had no unawareness of his state of mind and deeply regretful that he felt unable to confide in me. It has made me think about the Flynn boy's death. I should have done more to encourage Mr and Mrs Flynn to attend our re-consecration service. It would have been an opportunity to talk with them, to sympathise and offer our support. It might have comforted them.'

She looked at him. Really looked at him. Beyond the vast girth, the fleshy face, was this genuine kindness and honesty about his own limitations she was seeing? Was he expressing sincere regret that he had not done whatever he could? She couldn't decide. Had his earlier remarks to her about psychology and her own lack of religious faith somehow coloured her view of him? Everyone had his or her own story. She didn't yet know his. It was time she did. 'You referred earlier to your work in America and its influence on you.'

'Yes.' His eyes were on hers. 'Meeting your colleague Lieutenant Corrigan took me back there: the Charles River, Cambridge, Harvard.' He smiled. 'Even the Combat Zone. A wonderful city.'

'You enjoyed your stay there.'

'I did. Very much.'

'Yet you came back?'

He nodded. 'My contract with the church there ended. I'd completed the time I agreed to serve.'

'Your stay there was entirely positive?'

He gave a gentle headshake. 'Is anything ever "entirely positive", Professor Hanson?' He fell silent, his eyes fixed on hers. 'I believe you are really asking me about an allegation made against me by a young woman there.'

She was completely thrown. She'd come prepared to raise the issue with him, never anticipating that he would do so. She hadn't expected this candour. *Work with people and they'll invariably surprise you.* 'Yes, I am.'

He gazed out of the window, his face bleak. 'I hadn't the slightest idea about it until I had been back here for several weeks. A church colleague in Boston rang to tell me. I was never contacted by the US authorities but I knew immediately who had made the allegation: a young woman who was a member of the congregation at the church in which I served. Anyone, any male whose work places him in close physical or emotional proximity to others, especially those who are vulnerable in some way, runs such a risk. I never knew the young woman directly but I'd taken her confession on a few occasions. I never divulged what she said at those times, of course, but I can tell you that she was a very disturbed young person.' He looked down at his hands. 'A very sad young woman. I didn't mention it to Lieutenant Corrigan because it was more than twenty years ago and not pertinent to his inquiries.' He looked up at her. 'I've told you now so that you and your police colleagues can see that I harbour no secret from years ago.'

In the following silence she re-ordered her thoughts, including the brief scene she had witnessed at the choir practice. Deciding not to raise such an equivocal issue with him, she went to the last question she'd brought here. 'What is the church's policy or attitude to the occult? To Satanism?'

He leant forward, forearms resting on his wide knees, his brow furrowed. 'What weighty issues we're discussing, Professor Hanson.' He paused. 'Attitudes within the church have radically changed over recent years. We've all heard of church leaders who profess not to believe in God. I'm guided by my own beliefs. I am a believer but that does not extend to a belief in evil personified.'

Hanson was confused. 'But what about the re-consecration service? It felt to me very much like a statement of belief in evil in the form of the devil.'

He regarded her, his face patient. 'If you look inside any church building you will be immediately aware of the importance most religions place on setting, on presentation. Within religious expression there's a strong element of theatre in its most basic form.' He raised his hands. 'Take this house, for example. The furniture, everything in it: Victorian theatre. I live with it because I'm required to. I don't live *by* it.' He stood and looked down at her, his round face kindly. 'You know, you're very welcome to visit the church whenever you need or wish to. Our church is for all.'

She stood. 'Has Richard Burns, your other deacon, returned from his retreat?'

'We're expecting him later this evening.' He accompanied her to the front door, Hanson still conflicted in her views of him. She'd come here anticipating that she would leave knowing what she thought of him yet she remained unsure. He opened the door for her and she noticed that some of the paint had been removed. He followed her eyes. 'Frank, another of our faithful helpers, has offered to paint the outside of the house for nothing more than lunch expenses.' He squinted up at the sky. 'I hope the weather holds for him in the next four days or so.' He stepped out onto the veranda with her. 'Are you still bringing your psychology to bear on the police investigation?'

'It's not "my" psychology, Father Delaney.'

He nodded, gazing in the direction of the church. 'I assume that you would deem anyone who claims to hear the divine voice of our Lord to be mentally unhinged.'

'I wouldn't base any opinion on just one aspect of a person's behaviour.' She turned towards the steps. 'Thank you for your time, Father Delaney.'

'You're welcome. If you need to speak to Richard Burns he'll be in the church tomorrow afternoon, carrying out a delayed inventory of our bibles and hymn books.'

Hanson eyed Maisie's face in the soft lighting of the restaurant. A devotee of the pizza restaurant and casual self-presentation, Maisie had gone to considerable effort with her appearance this evening and was sitting very straight, hair drawn back and restrained in decorative clips behind her head, no phone in evidence, clearly thrilled by the fine dining experience being provided by her grandpa. As was Hanson herself. She looked around the Brindleyplace restaurant. 'This was a really good idea, Charlie.'

'I thought we could all benefit from an evening out.'

She glanced at him, keeping it short, mindful of Maisie's proximity. 'You're OK?'

'Never better.'

Almost unnoticed, the waiter cleared the table and there

followed a short interval as Maisie's finger hovered over the dessert menu. She gave Hanson a quick glance. 'The fruit plate is healthy . . . but I like the sound of the three ice creams 'cos one is pistachio . . . Wait! The soufflé with chocolate ice cream inside it sounds yummy although I really like pistachio . . .'

Charlie leant towards her and the menu. 'Why don't you order the soufflé and ask the waiter if you can swap the choco-late ice cream for pistachio?' When the waiter returned Maisie ordered her dessert with aplomb, grinning at her grandfather as the waiter went away.

They came out of the restaurant half an hour later into cold, the darkness relieved by the bright windows of other restaurants and tiny white lights strung on leafless trees. Maisie was talking into her phone. Hanson saw her hold it up to her own face, the illuminated trees a backdrop. The ubiquitous selfie.

Charlie smiled at Hanson. 'Did you sort out your problem, earlier? The one that had you feeling lost?'

Her eyes swept the immediate area. *It's so good to be out here and not working.* 'Maybe, but there's still a lot to do.'

He placed his hand lightly on her arm. 'I'll miss that drive of yours and Maisie's energy when I go home.'

'Then don't go.'

'I can't stay, Kate. My life, my friends are in Worcester and you need your home back.'

They followed Maisie dancing ahead of them, all notions of sophistication gone.

TWENTY

Inside UCU early next morning Hanson recounted her visit to Delaney. 'I haven't made up my mind but I know one thing about him. He's a realist. I wouldn't be surprised if his own religious beliefs are limited to some degree.'

Watts looked quizzical. 'How's that work for a rev?'

'In recent years some ministers of the church have expressed doubts about some aspects of religion. Even God.'

'Sounds to me like an easy way for the likes of Delaney to talk themselves out of a job. What else was he on about?'

'He brought up the US allegation before I did.' Watts glanced at Corrigan. 'Did you hear that?'

Corrigan nodded, passing an email across the table towards her. 'Take a look at this. It concerns the eighteen-year-old woman who made the allegation against him.'

She took it, slowly read it. 'It says here she had difficulties with managing her moods, that she saw Delaney as a father figure to whom she was drawn when she was emotionally unstable but that following her making the allegation her condition stabilised and she withdrew it.' She looked up. 'He didn't give me much detail about the allegation, other than he didn't know her well, although he'd taken her confession a few times.' She passed the email back to Corrigan.

'What do you make of it, doc?' asked Watts.

'It's hard to know, given the lack of detail and the distance in time.'

Watts was unimpressed. 'Delaney with his hand on a choir boy's head, remember? I know where I stand on this sex angle.' For Watts the arrival of the email, had linked smoothly into other events in this case: the choirboy, Alfred Best's suicide, with what he probably considered a satisfying click. She could see he wanted to talk about it. 'I've been thinking about Alfred Best's money dwindling away. I raised the blackmail issue, remember? I still think it's possible he killed himself because he was out of money and worried about a dark secret coming out from years back.' Hanson's gaze was on him. 'I know you don't like it, doc, but give a thought to the number of historical sex crimes coming out in the last few years. While I'm on the subject, before you rule out Delaney you might think whether his way of coming across to you is just a clever tactic. Sex types are good at that.'

She glared at him. 'How would I get through a single day without you telling me the bloody obvious? And while we're discussing motive, I understood your motive-of-the-moment to be drugs.'

He busied himself with the papers in front of him. 'Still is. I'm not closing down any options. We don't know who killed either Matthew Flynn or Callum Foley or why but we've got no time to hang about. The clock's ticking because the chief's set it going. He wants answers and he's not about to give us more time because we've got yet another victim. He's not happy about that, by the way.'

Hanson was exasperated. 'So, what would he like us to do about Foley? Re-bury him? That might make it a tidier, less costly case!' She left the table and went to the board, her eyes moving over the information. 'I don't agree with you about Alfred.' She turned. 'And twelve months ago, when he was, what, eighty, do you think he would have been capable of murdering two strong, healthy males in their mid-teens? Because I don't.' Feeling her colleagues' eyes on her she moved her index finger over the board's smooth surface and pointed to the list of names. 'Delaney, Fellowes the deacon we met at One Day, Richard Burns the other deacon who is back now, by the way. Brad Flynn, Dominic Flynn. Zach Addison. They all had the opportunity to kill Matthew Flynn, Callum Foley and Alfred Best.' She looked at Watts. 'What's happened about Zach Addison?'

'You can strike him for Best's murder. He was still on remand.' Watts regarded her. 'Now you can give me one reason why Flynn would kill his own son.'

'I'm not suggesting he did. I'm identifying the parameters within which we're working here. The next is motive.'

'We've just discussed that,' said Watts. 'Sex and/or drugs.'

She turned back to the board. 'I just thought of another male. Spencer Albright. We don't know what's happened to him. He might have had reasons to "disappear". And don't forget Matthew's other housemate William Graham.' She added both names to the list as Corrigan stood.

'I've arranged to see the manager at Alfred Best's bank,' he said. 'He might know more about Best's financial arrangements than we've got so far.' Watts reached for the phone. 'I want another meeting with Addison at the prison. His solicitor is pushing for bail.' He looked at Hanson. 'Got any plans?'

'I want to talk to Richard Burns, the other deacon now he's back. Delaney said he would be at the church this afternoon. I'll go and see him there.' She watched Corrigan walk to the door, a quick thought coming into her head. 'Corrigan. What's the Combat Zone?'

He turned to her, surprised. 'An area of Boston, close to Faneuil Hall in the middle of the city.'

'What's it like?'

'Sleazy, back in the day. It was cleared in the late seventies, early eighties to make way for new civic buildings. Where'd this come from?'

She frowned at what was written in her notebook. 'Father Delaney mentioned it. But, according to what you just said, by the time he was working there it didn't exist anymore.'

Corrigan shrugged. 'Sounds like he might be playing mind games with you, Red.'

Alone in UCU, Hanson studied the listed names, still on a quest for motive. Sex. Secret sex. Illegal sex. Legitimate sex. Matthew Flynn had a girlfriend called Honey who appeared to have been such a well-kept secret that his own father continued to make jibes about Matthew's sexuality. Honey had been mentioned by only one person during the investigation, Terri Brennan. Was it possible Brennan was mistaken? Another possibility came into Hanson's head: had Matthew Flynn felt the need to invent a girlfriend?

She went to the board, tapped an icon. The screen was flooded with the photographs of both victims' bodies and the forensic artist's full colour representation of the damage to Matthew Flynn's neck. Hanson's eyes drifted over it all. If you do exist, who are you, Honey? What's your relevance to Matthew in life and in death, if any? Watts thought he knew the motive: 'Sex and/or drugs'. Where did fear come into it? So much fear that Matthew and Callum needed symbols, talismans to keep it at bay? Drugs was about money. Money hidden in a boot. Money Callum Foley hid at his mother's house. Money *from* what? *For* what?

The door opened and Gus came in, carrying a hefty file. 'Investigative info on the Best suicide. It seems pretty open and shut to us but Wattsie has asked for it.' He put it on the table. He was looking tired. 'When he's finished with it, tell him he can add Best's own papers and take it all to the basement.'

'How are you getting on with your reviews?' she asked.

He shook his head. 'I don't know how you investigate these cold cases and stay sane. You're welcome to them. We're working on the rapes and abductions and getting nowhere. It's the time element: witnesses have died, others have moved away and we can't locate them, there's alibis we can't check because people and even one or two places no longer exist. I tell you, it's all questions and no answers. Like I said, you're welcome.'

As Gus left Hanson fetched her coat, mulling over his words. She understood exactly what he was saying. What Gus didn't know was the pay-off from cold cases: that electrifying moment, that sudden realisation of finally, *finally* getting the answer when a years-old cold case offered up its solution and gave investigators that dual pay-off: knowledge and justice.

Hanson drove onto the open area and parked some distance away from a car already there. She glanced at her watch. It was barely twelve thirty. If Burns was already inside the church, she would talk to him then get back to the university. About to get out of her car she was startled by the sudden appearance of a man in paint–spattered overalls coming from the general direction of the church, a large paint tin in one hand. She watched him approach the other car, saw its lights flash and the boot lid flip open. Putting the paint tin inside, he stripped off overalls to reveal jeans and a sweatshirt and dropped them into the boot as Hanson approached.

'Excuse me, I need to talk to you. My name is Kate Hanson. I'm working with the police on the remains found here and the death of Alfred Best.'

'I've got nothing to say about that.' He turned, headed for his driver's door and got inside. She heard the engine start, watched as he made a quick exit, sending up a shower of gravel. *Burns can wait.* Rushing back to her car she got inside and followed him at a distance along the main road, down a narrow turn-off and into a pub carpark. She waited until he parked and disappeared inside the pub then slid into a parking space. She'd give him ten minutes, reasoning that even if he was no more pleased to see her than he had been just now, he would be reluctant to leave the lunch he'd ordered and paid for.

She came into the bar, headed for the table where he was sitting and sat opposite him. Lowering his knife and fork he cast a glance around the quiet lounge. 'I've told you, I don't want to talk to you. I've got nothing to say.'

'You were a friend of Alfred's.'

'No, I wasn't. He had fifteen, twenty years on me and I'm sorry he felt he had to do what he did but there's nothing I can tell you about him. Or that other thing that happened in the crypt.'

'But you knew Alfred?'

'So? There's a group of us who do what we can in and around the church. We all know each other but we're not friends. Whatever you want to know about Alfred, you're asking the wrong person.'

She gave him a direct look. 'You knew Alfred. You know what's happened to him. Come on, I need you to talk to me, Mr . . .?'

'Bennett. Frank Bennett.'

'OK, Frank, tell me about Alfred. He was financially well-off, wasn't he?'

He frowned at her, took a drink from his glass. 'If you say so. We never discussed that kind of thing.'

She waited. 'Tell me what kinds of things you and he did talk about.'

He put down his glass with a thump and lowered his voice. 'We weren't friends. We were both volunteer helpers at the church. I'm retired and I've got the time to do it. Alfred's wife wasn't well so I'm guessing the work he did around the church was a distraction for him. I felt sorry for him, if you must know.'

'Why, exactly?'

He rolled his eyes. '*Because* of his wife. Because he was lonely. He didn't have that many people to talk to. No wife he could share things with any more and no kids. I've still got my wife and we had five kids together and *they've* got kids. The hours I give to St Bartholomew's are a welcome break, I can tell you.'

'Alfred never mentioned the care home fees he was paying?'

He shifted uncomfortably. 'You just don't let up, do you? Yes, he mentioned them. It was a fortune and a big worry for him. I couldn't understand that. I got to thinking maybe he wasn't as well off as everybody thought. He never said as much to me. We didn't come from the same background, if you get me. Painting and decorating's been my trade for years but Alfred ran a proper business with premises. He was old school. He wouldn't have divulged his private details to me.'

She leant towards him. 'Father Delaney has told me that the church is organised as a business, that a committee gives time and skills to support it. I want the names of those parishioners who help support the church.'

'If you're so friendly with Delaney, you can ask him for the names.'

She changed tack. 'Was Alfred fairly typical of the church's retired members in terms of his financial situation . . .?'

He was on his feet. 'Like I said, ask Father Delaney.'

She watched him go, thinking about churches-as-businesses. Why not? People have given of their own money for centuries to build and support them in return for benefits at times of their own need. Except that nobody had helped Alfred. Glancing at her watch she hurried to her car. She'd get the names from Delaney. She drove out of the pub car park, thinking of the bland, smiling face, the twinkle in his eyes. Was Corrigan right about Delaney's comment about Boston's old red light district? That it was game-playing? She put the issue to rest and gave some thought to Richard Burns and the information she wanted from him. Following her meeting with him she'd go straight to the university and attack the work piling up there. She looked through the windscreen at a leaden sky, the afternoon so overcast it was almost dusk-like. Who was it who had mentioned wanting to be away from the church before darkness fell?

Alfred.

TWENTY-ONE

Under tumultuous cloud cover, the dark clad figure came into the church and stood in silence and shadow. A phone call had sent him here. Everything was getting out of control. He was out of his own control, he knew but there was too much at stake to stop now. Taking slow, deep breaths he started down the aisle. Reaching the altar he stared at the items on it. Reaching for a specific one, his attention was caught by a painting of the Virgin Mary and Child on a nearby wall, their faces pious, their eyes focused heavenwards. He knew about people and families. He knew about the church. All a sham. Phony. Fake. A lie, signifying nothing. He closed his eyes against the tightening inside his head. He felt like the boy with his finger in the dam, stopping water from dribbling out. His dam was falling into holes as fast as he could plug them. He tensed at a small sound from somewhere near the door he'd just come through. Turning, he saw it slowly open. He watched in disbelief as she came inside. Unbelievable luck. Or was it all part of an Almighty's plan? On a silent laugh he faded further into shadow, hefting the object in his hand, tapping it against his other, three short words replacing the pressure inside his head. *Seize the day.*

Hanson came inside the unlocked church, closed the door and listened. Nothing but silence. If she'd missed Deacon Burns she would have to come back another day. She needed answers and he might have some of them. She slow-gazed over rows of pews, the choir stall to one side and beyond it the altar. This was the first time she'd been here alone. The silence was profound, the air around her warm and heavy but not oppressive as it had been at the re-consecration. The atmosphere was soothing today. It felt calm. Eternal.

She walked slowly down the main aisle. It felt wrong to call out for Deacon Burns. She would find him if he was still here. Raising her head, she looked at vaultings and numerous stone and plaster faces thrusting out from cornices, each in an agony of ecstasy, then down to a huge, dark painting of robed figures, their faces upturned to the crucified figure, their arms stretched in supplication. Delaney wasn't the only paradox here: the church itself might feel restful but it was also a place of horrific imagery. She thought of Matthew Flynn's remains, left in the crypt somewhere below her feet, his killer hoping for an eternity of concealment but getting just a year.

Her eyes drifted sideways at a sound from somewhere behind her. Something soft. Like a footfall. She turned, looked

back at the door through which she'd come. It was still closed,
the aisle deserted. She walked on to the wide steps leading
to the altar, went up them and stood, captivated by the brassware, the lace, recalling what Delaney had said about the theatre
of the church. He was right. It was here in all that she was
seeing. She gently lifted the lace between her thumb and forefinger and held it, fascinated by its intricacy, her eyes slowly
traveling over the arrangement of brasses, stopping at a single
space within the array.

The bank manager pointed at information on the computer
screen. 'See? Mr Best came into branch to make these withdrawals, himself. Always in cash.'

'Pretty hefty withdrawals, sir,' said Corrigan. 'And at regular
intervals over the last three or more years. Did you discuss that
with him?'

The manager shrugged. 'I advised him that it wasn't wise to
take out money in that way. For personal safety reasons,
mugging, burglaries and the like, but he continued to do it.'

'Did you ask him what he needed the money for and why
in cash?'

The manager looked dismissive. 'That's not part of the bank's
policy. It was Mr Best's money. It was entirely up to him what
he did with it and how. I thought it might be gifts to relatives.
Some people like to dispose of capital whilst they're still alive
so they can actually see the benefit to others, rather than
bequeath it.'

'Wouldn't the IRS have wanted to know where the money
was going?'

He sent Corrigan a thin smile. 'It's HMRC here. He would
have been allowed to make gifts to relatives. Or charity.'

Corrigan regarded him with patience. 'In these sums and with
this regularity?' He waited, getting no response. 'This is a police
investigation, sir. If you have information pertaining to it, you
need to tell me what it is.'

The manager's mouth tightened. 'All I can tell you is that
Mr Best did mention to me some weeks ago that he was feeling
pressured by HMRC for information.'

'And?'

The manager raised his shoulders. 'I advised him to tell them where the money was going.'

'And?'

'That's it. When I heard what happened I assumed the pressure he mentioned had become too much for him. This bank dealt with Mr Best's finances to the degree required of it. I can't tell you any more, lieutenant. Is that all?'

'I guess. Unless you have evidence to show that this bank genuinely cared for one of its elderly customers. Which would be a nice thing, don't you think?' Corrigan left the office, the expression on the manager's face conveying that the expressed views and values of an American were of no interest to him.

Thirty minutes later, Corrigan came into the building he and his colleagues had spent several hours inside a couple of evenings before. He went directly to the glassed-in reception area and pressed the bell on the counter. He wanted to jog the memory of anyone here who may have seen something on the evening Alfred Best died but maybe hadn't realised its significance. The plump woman inside the office looked up, did a double take and came to slide open the glass.

'Lieutenant Corrigan, ma'am. You were on duty here the evening Alfred Best died.'

'Yes.' Her bright red mouth widened. 'You asked me some questions.'

'I remember you.' She flushed. 'One thing I didn't ask is how you register visitors on arrival. Could you show me?'

'Of course.' She lifted a large hardcover book from one side of the counter. 'What we do is make a note of them in this.' She looked up at him and smiled again. 'Actually, I have to enter your name.' He watched as she did so then turned the book around. 'See? We write down the names of visitors, time of arrival, who they're here to see.' She turned back to the page relating to the day Alfred Best died, lowering her voice. 'We had a death that morning. Mrs Lewis. A lovely woman. Ninety years old. Like I said, she died and her daughter and son-in-law arrived in the afternoon, very upset and distracted because it was so unexpected, despite her age. They'd been on holiday in the Lake District.' She pointed at written details.

'This is the entry for her daughter and son-in-law. Some visitors travel a long way so we like to keep registration brief. That way they can make the most of their time here.'

Corrigan pointed to a number on the same line as their names. 'Three? Why three?'

'That's a mistake.'

'Why a mistake?'

She shrugged. 'I thought they'd brought a visitor with them but later I found out that they hadn't. That's all we do if they bring additional people. Just give the number in each party. In case of fire.'

'You saw that visitor?'

'Yes, but as I say he wasn't with them.'

'What did he look like?'

She thought about it, shook her head. 'I can't really say. My focus was on Mrs Lewis's two family members. They were very upset so I accompanied them to her room.'

'What about this other person?'

'I don't recall seeing him again while they were here.'

Corrigan leant on the counter, lowering his voice. 'I understand the stress involved in that visit but it could really move our investigation on if you could give me even a vague idea as to what this man looked like.'

She looked up at him, pressing her red lips together. 'I don't remember much about him at all. I couldn't even say how old he— He was wearing a hat!' She beamed. 'I remember the hat.'

'What kind of hat, ma'am?'

'The kind actors wear. Like a fedora.'

'What about his voice?'

She shook her head. 'I'm sorry. I don't recall him speaking.'

'Where are the CCTV cameras?'

'There's one on the left of the entrance and one in each of the corridors but we've been having trouble with the system over the last few days. We've booked an engineer . . .'

'I'd like to see the external camera, please.'

'Of course.' She led the way outside and pointed to it mounted beneath one of the low eaves on the ground floor. Arms folded around herself against the cold, she eyed Corrigan as he pulled at a nearby drainage pipe, placed one foot on the wide sill of a nearby window and pulled himself upwards, placing his other foot on a nearby fence for balance.

He examined the camera then looked down at her. 'Is this the only external camera, ma'am?' She gazed up at him, nodding.

He turned back to it, examined it closely then reached into a pocket of his heavy jacket. Taking out a slender Maglite torch he shone its high intensity beam at the camera. Switching it off, he replaced it in his pocket and climbed down. He and the woman went back inside the building. 'I need to see the recording for the day Alfred Best died.'

'Oh dear. I'm sorry but there isn't one. It was around that time we started having a problem with the system.'

Corrigan was on his phone inside the Volvo. He nodded several times. 'I understand. I'm sorry for your loss and also grateful for your time.' He ended the call and looked down at a photocopy of the page from the visitors' book. Mrs Crosby, daughter of the elderly woman who had died on the morning of the day Alfred Best had gone out of a fourth-floor window into nothingness, had just described how shocked and upset she and her husband were on the evening they visited her mother's care home, having been summoned from holiday due to her death. Too shocked and upset to be aware of anyone beyond the staff members they had conversed with. He started the Volvo, thinking of the unknown male who had gained access to the care home by attaching himself to two distressed and distracted visitors. Whoever the guy was they had served his purpose, allowed him access to the inside of that building without drawing undue attention to himself. 'Which is exactly what you'd want if your plan was to throw somebody out a window.'

He reached for his phone, got Watts on its first ring and told him what he knew. 'Somebody they can't identify was here. No CCTV evidence. Either he got lucky and the system was down or he tampered with the external camera.' There was brief silence.

'The chief's going to love this,' said Watts. 'How about our chances of proving it was murder?'

Corrigan gazed at the well-lit, modern building, its external camera just visible. 'Not good.'

*　*　*

Hanson slowly lowered her hand until her fingertips made contact with crisp, white linen in the small space amid the decorative brasses. The material felt clean, smooth. She carefully removed her hand, stared at her fingertips, rubbed them together. No gritty feel. No dust. She took out her phone, raised it and took several pictures of the regiment of brasses and the space in the middle of them. She checked the pictures. They showed the detail, the various designs wrought in gleaming metal. All laid out with precision. Why one missing? Colin Chivers sidled into her mind. The kind of thief for whom the 'if it wasn't nailed down' phrase had been invented. But why would anybody take only one? Why not take all of them? Maybe this was a careful thief: steal by stealth, one item at a time. Particularly if he knew of the police activity around here. She studied the several brasses arrayed in front of her. It opened up another question: whoever had taken the brass had selected it from the middle of a group. Why *that* one? She looked again at the photographs she'd just taken. The first two were fine, the third slightly out of focus but each of them showed the space— She stiffened, her eyes moving to the extreme right of where she was standing, ears straining for sound or movement, rationalisations arriving from her amygdala to explain the stealth she was picking up from behind her: she was here on police business to see a man who was also here, on church business. Her rational prefrontal cortex wading in to support this prosaic logic, even as the air around her shifted. Shoulders rigid, core muscles in tension she felt the quick rush of air over the right side of her head, a blast against it then her shoulder, followed by a river of warmth and nothing.

Watts's eyes were on Hanson, sitting in the doorway of the ambulance, wrapped in a blue blanket as a paramedic shone a light into each blue eye, moved a finger in front of them then consulted with his colleague. They exchanged words, finger-pointing her head, her shoulder. Watts had had enough. He went to them. 'How is she?'

'. . . I'm . . . fine,' murmured Hanson.

'She's in shock,' said the paramedic with the light. 'Head and shoulder injury.'

Watts bent down to Hanson, lowering his voice. 'Doc? What

happened?' Seeing her eyes drifting, he straightened and turned to the paramedic who pointed to a man in paint-stained overalls standing nearby, watching them. 'He found her lying on the altar steps.'

Watts went to him. 'I want your name and your business here.'

The man in the overalls pointed across the church grounds. 'I'm painting Church House. The name's Bennett. Frank Bennett.' He nodded towards Hanson. 'She was asking me questions at lunchtime. When I got back here I did a bit of work then noticed her car still here. I wondered where she'd got to. I came across and had a look. That's when I heard something inside the church so I went in and found her.'

'See anybody else?' Bennett shook his head.

'Stay here. Don't go anywhere until told, right?' Bennett nodded as Watts headed back to the paramedics, keeping his voice low. 'Tell me her injuries.'

'Superficial cut to the right side of the head which I've treated. She was lucky.'

Watts gave him a level look. 'How'd you make that out?'

'It was a glancing blow. Her hair cushioned it, leaving only a minor wound. The blow continued downwards, striking her on the right shoulder. She'll have a bruise there but it could have been a hell of a lot worse.' Watts watched as the paramedic leant inside the vehicle and brought out Hanson's dark green parka which he held up in front of him. An area on the right shoulder was torn and bloodstained in places, thick padding protruding from it. 'This took the brunt. Like I said, lucky. She could have sustained a broken collarbone.'

Watts took the parka from him, his eyes on the damage, running his finger over several tears in the smooth, shiny material. 'Not the usual blunt instrument, then?'

'Nothing like,' responded the paramedic. 'Something with sharp points.'

Watts gazed towards Church House, seeing no visible signs of life. They both turned at the sound of a car arriving at speed, skidding to a halt and a door slam. Watts headed for the parking area beyond the church, the tall figure already out of his car and coming towards him in response to his earlier call. 'Hold on, Corrigan . . . Hey, take it easy! She's OK and she can do without more upset.' They'd worked together for nearly five years. He'd seen Corrigan's face in all kinds of policing situations. He'd seen it tense. He'd seen it cool and considered. He'd seen it focused. He'd never seen it looking like this.

'What's happened? Where's Kate?'

Her first name. 'Somebody hit her. Hang *on*. She's in shock. Right-sided minor cut to the head, right shoulder bruised. She's all right.' Corrigan brought both his hands to his mouth. Watts looked down to the chill grass between them for a few seconds then up. 'Come on.'

'Who's that?' asked Corrigan pointing to Bennett.

'He's painting the outside of Delaney's place. He heard something and went inside the church to take a look and found her. I've got his details. We'll get a statement off him.'

Hanson looked up as they approached then bowed her head. Watts hung back as Corrigan crouched in front of her and reached out his hand. Watts saw her take it, grip it tight. He knew her well enough to anticipate that by tomorrow she'd wish she hadn't. He looked at his two colleagues, their heads close together. Two people he had a lot of time for. He shook his head and got on his phone to ring Charlie Hanson.

Hanson was home and not pleased at being the focus of attention. She looked up at Charlie, his face full of concern, then at her two colleagues. The ache in her head surged. The only good thing was that Maisie wasn't here. She was going from school to Chelsey's house. 'Let's get something straight. I'm OK.'

Watts studied her face. It was pale, grey shadows beneath the eyes. 'Let's play it your way. Tell us what happened.' Thoughts and impressions poured into her head, jostling for attention, making it spin. 'It's . . . a bit mixed up. I'd gone there to see Richard Burns, Delaney's other deacon. I'd made a loose kind of arrangement with Delaney that I would see Burns sometime this afternoon. He told me Burns would be there, tidying up or something.' She frowned at the effort to focus. 'I was later than I'd intended. I got side-tracked by something else.'

'You were talking to Frank Bennett, the painter chap. He's told us. It was him who found you.'

She reached up, touched a place in her hair and winced. 'The church was unlocked when I got back there. I went in, expecting to find Burns already there.' She stared ahead, the scene inside the church still hazy. 'I remember walking inside and down the main aisle. It felt empty and . . . peaceful. I went up the steps to the altar and . . . I looked at the lace and the brasses laid out on it.' She looked up at them. 'Something I was seeing was . . . wrong. I can't explain . . .' She reached up again, touched her shoulder. 'I can't remember what it was . . . and then, it happened . . .' Half-realised memories shifted, the ache in her head intensifying. 'That's it. That's all I remember.'

Corrigan's eyes were fixed on hers. 'Did you get an idea somebody was there before you were hit?'

'Yes.'

'How?'

'I heard something behind me.' She frowned at the effort to recall. 'I was looking at the brasses and . . . I just sensed him there. And then, whoever it was came very close. Too close. I knew he was there to hurt me.'

Seeing Corrigan's lips compress, Watts intervened. 'You thought it was male?'

'Mmm . . . Much bigger than me. Taller. A change in the light or something.' She looked up at them. 'I'll call you if I remember anything else.'

She did, an hour later. 'I want to go back to the church.'

'OK,' said Watts, looking across UCU at Corrigan, mouthing her name to him. 'We'll go with you tomorrow morning and—'

'No, now. I need to sort out what happened.'

He looked at his watch, five forty-five, then at Corrigan. 'Give it a rest, doc. Relax. We've got the painter's statement. He seems on the level. Take it easy and—' He held the phone away from his ear, her voice spilling from it.

'I said *now*. Too much time's gone by already. I need to think. I need to be there. In that situation.'

'OK, take it easy—'

'If you give me any more advice, I'll scream, understand?'

'Yeah. You're back to normal. We'll pick you up. We've got an idea to put to you.'

*   *   *

They walked on either side of her into the church and up the
central aisle, Corrigan and Watts detouring, leaving Hanson to
continue on to the altar now in deep shadow. Reaching it, she
stood, looking straight ahead. Her eyes moved downwards to
the altar with its thick lace cloth, it's tall, slender candles, its
brassware, polished and gleaming even in this dull light, and
it's one small space. Memory yielded up a small gift. She reached
into the pocket of her overcoat and pulled out her phone. She
looked at the three photographs she'd taken of the altar. Despite
the fact that she was expecting it, a sound from the direction of
the main door caused her to flinch. Facing straight ahead she
felt rather than heard someone walking quietly, steadily towards
her. She swallowed, her eyes focused straight ahead, her breathing
under control, mind receptive. Her eyes moved to the left of her
then the right. He was close now. Very close. She turned as Watts
and Corrigan materialised from the shadows on either side.

'It wasn't Frank,' she said.

Corrigan went to the painter. 'Thanks for coming. I'll walk
you out.' Hanson and Watts watched a bewildered-looking Frank
being escorted to the door then Corrigan walking back to them.
Watts studied her. 'What did that tell you?'

'Whoever hit me was taller than Frank and he wasn't carrying
the smell of cigarettes or body odour. The man who hit me is
very careful about his personal care. Very clean. He wears
cologne.' She pointed to the altar. 'I've realised what's wrong
here. Look.' They gazed down at the objects on it, the candle-
sticks and numerous items of brassware. She pointed to the
space. 'It's something that isn't here.' She showed them the
photographs on her phone. Watts put on his heavy glasses as
Corrigan's eyes moved over the individual brasses, most of
them plain, one with four decorative points along its upper edge.
He reached out and placed his fingertip on one of them then
turned to look at them. 'At a guess we're missing a processional
brass with a sunray design. I went back to the care home earlier.
I don't think there's any way to prove that Alfred Best was
murdered, but if he was, it means we have a serial here.'

She looked up at him. 'And his attack on me suggests he's
out of control.' She walked a few steps down the aisle. 'We
need to locate Richard Burns.'

TWENTY-TWO

Hanson's eyelashes fluttered. Her eyes opened to seams of dull light beyond the curtains. She had arrived home the previous evening, ambushed by exhaustion, ideas still careening through her head. She had taken her first ever sleeping pill, supplied by the paramedics. She lay, coming slowly to life. Maisie. Work.

She got out of bed, pulled her robe from the chair and put it on, picking up a low rumble of voices somewhere in the house. Deep voices. She went downstairs and headed for the closed kitchen door, words drifting towards her. 'We've got officers out looking and a bunch of ideas as to how we might—' She pushed open the door. Corrigan got to his feet, his face full of concern. 'How're you doing, Red?'

She gave a careful nod, walked to the chair Charlie was holding out for her. 'Fine. I think yesterday has sneaked up on me.' She looked up at Charlie.

'All under control, Kate. Maisie's gone to school, and no, she doesn't know anything about what happened. I called your office and Crystal is taking care of things until she sees you.'

Hanson looked out of the wide kitchen windows at morning fog. 'What's happening? What are we doing?' she asked Corrigan.

'We got an early start. The chief has given us some extra help – they're out looking for Richard Burns. Nobody's seen him, including Delaney who we spoke to an hour ago. He hasn't actually seen Burns since he got back from the retreat. He phoned Burns' house while we were there. Got no response. We're going there in half-an—'

'I'm coming with you.'

They arrived at Burns' small terraced house. It looked deserted. Hanson waited as Watts checked its front door and blank-looking downstairs windows and Corrigan walked to the end of the row of houses and disappeared. He was soon back. 'Nothing. There's blinds down at every window back there and not a sound from inside. Wherever Burns is, it isn't here.'

'We're being watched,' said Watts, eyes sliding to the house next door. Hanson saw a curtain at a downstairs window fall back into place. He went to the door and thumped it.

After a short delay it was opened by a woman wearing a dressing gown and slippers. Watts showed his identification. She looked from him to Corrigan then Hanson. 'About time somebody called you in. It was bliss last night without him here. What are you going to do about him?'

'Who?'

Exasperated, she pointed at Burns' house. '*Him.* I've called the council about him and they've done nothing. He's been living next door to me for twelve months and now I'm on anti-depressants. During the last three months I've made complaint after complaint about him to the council and the agents but nothing's been done. See his windows?' They looked to where she was pointing. 'Brown paper that is. Stuck over every single window in the place. He plays religious music, runs the water at all hours. The noise travels straight through the walls. I've tried talking to him. I've threatened him with the law. You know what he called me? *Jezebel.* I've had enough.'

'Did you report it to the police?' asked Hanson.

The woman shook her head. 'No. He works for the church and I didn't want to make trouble. He seemed pleasant enough when he moved in, quiet and polite but he changed. I think there's something wrong with him.'

Watts looked along the row. 'All these houses are rented?'

The woman nodded and disappeared inside her house. She reappeared with a business card which she held out to him. Hanson looked at it. Agents' details. 'I'm at the end of my tether with him. Will you do something?'

'When was the last time you noticed him here?' asked Watts.

'I "notice" him every bloody day, that's what I'm saying.'

'But he's been away.'

She folded her arms, looked at him, head on one side. 'No, he hasn't. Who told you that? Every night it's the same, the chanting going on all hours. Except for last night.'

*   *   *

The manager of the leasing agency had been contacted and told to bring keys. He arrived, unlocked the front door, pushed it wide and stood, deep disapproval on his face, repeatedly tutting at what was visible until Watts told him he could leave. Now Watts was slowly pacing the small living room on his way to the kitchen, phone to his ear, listening as Delaney confirmed that St Bartholomew's had rented the house on behalf of Richard Burns. Hanson stood in the middle of the room, the only natural light coming from the open front and back doors. The neighbour was right. Every window was covered by heavy brown parcel paper taped to its frame. She heard quick footsteps on the stairs and Corrigan came into the room wearing forensic gloves.

'The two bedrooms look to be unused. The bathroom's pristine. There's enough personal hygiene products in there to start up our own drugstore. No cologne.'

'I want to see it.'

Corrigan led the way upstairs to the bathroom. It was small, all its fixtures scrupulously clean. The windowsill was crammed with bath and shower products. She opened a small cupboard. More products. Hanson glanced into each of the bedrooms. Like Corrigan had said, unused. They came downstairs, Hanson's eyes on the sitting room furniture piled in a corner, the odd swirls of black paint visible on both party walls. She looked down at the carpet, white powder sprinkled in lines forming a large square, in its centre a cushion, dented in its middle. Someone had recently sat there.

Watts returned from the kitchen. 'Wherever Burns eats, it's not here. Unless he lives on toast. All I can find is bread, butter, jam and a few tea bags. Nothing in the fridge but bottled water. Delaney should be here any minute.' He looked at the walls then went to stand by Corrigan who was studying the carpet.

'What's all this?' Hanson went onto her heels peering at the powder. She reached out a hand and touched it with a tentative fingertip.

'Careful, doc,' said Watts. 'You don't know what it is.'

She brought her hand to her nose. Straightening, she glanced at the piled furniture, went to it, knelt and looked beneath it. Reaching for the small object, she stood and held it up between her thumb and forefinger. 'Talcum powder.'

Watts stood, baffled. 'Why? What's Burns up to?'

'I'm guessing he used that to designate what to him was a 'safe' area within his own home. Looks to me as though Matthew Flynn and Callum Foley weren't the only ones who were frightened.'

They turned at a sudden loss of light. Delaney's bulk was filling the doorway. He came inside the small room which suddenly got smaller. Watts waited for him to speak. He didn't. 'Got anything to tell us about this place, Father Delaney?'

Delaney shook his head, his eyes sliding over the covered windows, the piled furniture and finally the carpet and its powdery lines, his facial expression one of disbelief. 'This is the first time I've been here. It's . . . I don't understand.'

Watts stared at him. 'Burns works for you. You see him most days. If you can't explain it, we're in trouble.'

'I'm sorry, I can't. I know that Richard has been spiritually troubled for a while.' Delaney glanced briefly in Hanson's direction. 'But the church is about acceptance. It doesn't believe in pathologizing people.'

Hanson was sliding back into unease where Delaney was concerned. 'Tell us about the retreat you say he's been on.' She watched him looking around the room, trying to bring sense to a place where there wasn't any.

'Richard has been somewhat distracted and under pressure. He appeared at times to be questioning his faith. It was clear to me that he was unsettled but he wouldn't confide in me or anyone else at the church. Which is why I arranged the three-week retreat for him. It's run by an organisation well known to the diocese. It paid for him to attend. He isn't the first to have used their services.'

'He never went,' said Watts.

Delaney stared at him, then at the room, shaking his head. 'I can't believe what I'm seeing here.'

'When did you first suspect he had mental health problems?' asked Hanson.

Delaney looked shocked. 'I didn't. As I said, I thought he was questioning his faith. That in itself would have a significant impact on anyone who is part of the church.'

Hanson looked at the covered windows, the room, a comment Delaney had made a while ago surfacing inside her head. Something about her labelling anyone who professed to hear the voice of God as mentally ill. That had been a reference to Burns. 'It's much more than that.' She pointed to the carpet. 'He felt the need to designate a place of safety for himself in his own home.' She indicated the windows. 'He covered those for the same reason. What was he so frightened of, Father Delaney?'

Delaney suddenly turned, made his way to the door. 'As I've already said, he did not confide in anyone at St Bartholomew's. You'll have to excuse me. The woman next door spoke to me as I arrived. I said I'd have a brief word with her.'

He was gone. Watts looked around, his gaze falling on the black swirls on two of the walls. 'Is this more of that devil stuff, like the graffiti at the church, the pentagram?' No one spoke.

Corrigan's eyes moved over the walls, the floor. 'What I'm seeing is a place lived in by somebody who has problems with reality.'

Hanson nodded. 'My guess is that Burns is experiencing hallucinations or delusions. Maybe both. Based on what we're seeing it's more than possible that Burns has developed paranoid schizophrenia.'

She turned to Watts. 'Any sightings so far?'

'Not yet.' He looked at her. 'But it looks like he's the one who hit you.' He gazed around the desolate room. 'Where does he keep his personal stuff?'

'I took a look in the cupboards upstairs. Nothing but a few items of clothing,' said Corrigan.

Hanson followed them up the narrow staircase and into each of the bedrooms. As Corrigan had said, nothing. They came onto the landing, Hanson looking around then up. She pointed. 'What's that?'

They followed where she was looking. 'Access to the roof space, by the look of it,' said Watts. He went into one of the bedrooms, came back with a chair and placed his foot on it.

Corrigan shook his head. 'Looks like a tight fit up there. Let me try.' He stood on the chair and pushed at the small, square section of ceiling above him.

'Careful, Corrigan. Burns might be up there.' Hanson watched, tense as Corrigan pushed at the access cover. It flipped upwards, over and fell inside the dark space. They listened. She watched as Corrigan pulled himself up and inside. 'OK,' he called. 'No one here! I'm sending something down!' A large holdall appeared in the space, end first.

'I'm ready!' said Watts. 'Let it go.' The bag came through the opening and into his outstretched arms. Hanson watched Corrigan lower himself from the roof space. 'What've we got?' he asked, brushing dust from his hair and clothes. Watts was kneeling over the unzipped holdall. 'Grab hold of some of these.' They did, taking papers, reading quickly, letting them fall.

Hanson looked up. 'Delaney told me that Burns used to be an accountant.'

Corrigan held up a printed list. 'These look to be his clients, back then. His main function seems to have been to help them evade tax.'

'See anybody familiar?' asked Watts.

Corrigan nodded. 'Yes. I do.'

TWENTY-THREE

Crystal brought three cups of coffee to Hanson's desk, handing one each to Watts and Corrigan. 'Here you go.' Hanson took hers. 'I need this. Any problems this morning, Crystal?'

'All sorted. Julian took your first year group for a guided tour of the library and showed them the computers upstairs and how to log in. Let me know if you need anything.'

'Nice girl,' observed Watts as Crystal left the room.

Hanson closed her eyes. 'Woman. She's twenty-two.'

'Don't get bitter, doc.'

She held out a hand. 'Give me that list of Burns' clients.' He handed it to her and she examined the names. Only one of them meant anything. Brad Flynn. 'What do we do?'

'We'll have him in. Richard Burns is our priority right now. If we find him, he can tell us what he knows about Flynn before we speak to him.'

'If you can get anything out of him,' she said. She sipped coffee, feeling better. Almost back to normal. 'What about Alfred?' She saw them exchange glances.

'I went to the care home,' said Corrigan. 'An unidentified visitor got inside the evening Alfred Best died but there's no CCTV or witness evidence that might help us identify him.'

'We've put that to one side for Upstairs to investigate,' said Watts. 'Can you imagine the chief's response if he knows we're following it up?'

She stared at him. 'But it has to be connected to our case. What about the behavioural evidence it's giving us? Whoever that unidentified male was, he managed to get inside that building, which tells us he's a planner. He got to that specific room without being challenged: he's cool under pressure. He took charge . . .' She stopped.

'What's up?' asked Watts.

'It's only just occurred to me. He went into that room knowing that Alfred's wife wouldn't be a problem. That she wouldn't call out, press a buzzer or whatever.'

'Because she's got Alzheimer's.'

'How did he know that?'

Watts frowned at Corrigan. 'Because . . . he saw it written down or he heard somebody say it.'

Hanson shook her head. 'He had significant cognitive demands on him when he arrived inside that place. If we're right and he was intent on murdering Albert, he had to tune into his surroundings, select someone he thought he could easily attach himself to. His mind was working overtime, keeping a low profile, avoiding challenge to his presence there. I doubt he had the cognitive capacity to search or listen for that kind of information once he was inside. He was there to kill and he had to be in and out whilst remaining unmemorable.'

'That's all well and good, doc, but it's all theory, not facts.' He and Corrigan stood.

'You're OK?' asked Corrigan.

She nodded. 'I've got one lecture and a couple of tutorial sessions and then I'm going home.'

* * *

She came into her house, closed the front door and let her bag and briefcase fall to the floor. She'd felt better as the day progressed but now she was out of energy. Charlie was meeting one of the lawyers he used to work with. Maisie was at hockey practice after which Candice was making dinner for both girls. *An hour or so alone won't kill you.* Dropping her coat onto the hall chest, she went directly to the kitchen, pressing the button to activate the blinds on the floor to ceiling windows. They lowered, blocking out darkness. *Snack and bath.* She fetched sourdough bread, cheese and salad and started constructing a sandwich, her focus on the knife as she sawed through the bread. In the process of spreading butter her head rose at the faintest of thumps from somewhere outside, just beyond the kitchen. She glanced down at Mugger snoozing under the table. 'I think one of your kitty girlfriends is here.' She murmured, unwrapping cheese, slicing it. Reaching for tomatoes, her hand was stopped by another thump, louder this time. She raised her face to the blinds covering the windows. Mugger was now on his feet next to her, his eyes also on the windows, ears up. Slowly, carefully, she sliced tomatoes, adding them to bread and cheese, monitoring the house, picking up its familiar creaks and boiler's click, the hum of the refrigerator. She laid the knife down and carried the food to the table, eyes on the place behind one of the blinds where the sturdy door handle was situated. Once it was pushed down, the wall of glass doors folded and slid, opening the kitchen, the whole house to the garden. It was locked. Wasn't it? Scuffing, scrapes, followed by a sound she knew: an insistent tugging of the handle. Plate and sandwich fell from her hand to the floor, cheese, tomatoes, bread, china shards scattered around her feet, slid across tiles. Mugger shot into the narrow space between washing machine and dryer. Hanson gazed frantically around the kitchen. *Phone. I brought it in. It's here! Has to be . . .*

She found it in her trouser pocket, lifted it to her ear, her eyes on the door, whirling at a sound from the hall. Eyes wide, she grappled for the bread knife, clutched its handle close to her chest, blade pointing towards the hall door, heart racing.

'Hi, Mom!'

Dropping the knife onto the counter, she bent to pick up the wreckage from the floor as Maisie came into the kitchen.

'Wow! Looks like a food fight.'

Within ten minutes with Maisie's help she had the kitchen tidied. She checked the garden door. It was locked. *What happened is that you over-reacted to ordinary night time garden noises.* She walked from the windows, turned back and stared at the lowered blinds.

TWENTY-FOUR

Inside her university room on Monday morning, Hanson was listening to two pleasant voices coming to her in waves, loud-soft, loud-soft. Earlier she'd told Maisie to stop shouting, then realised it was she who was out of kilter.

'What do you think about my proposal, Professor Hanson? Is it something you would be interested in supervising?' Hanson returned to the tentative voice of the potential research student who was earnestly gazing at her.

'It's excellent, Laura. It fits with and potentially extends Julian's own research.' She smiled across at him. 'Which means you have a ready-made collaborator.' She saw the quick smile pass between them and checked her watch. 'Sorry, but I'm due somewhere. Take the textbooks you think might help and I'll see you here again in say two weeks?' Laura gave an enthusiastic nod.

'How's the case developing?' asked Julian. He caught Hanson's quick glance at Laura. 'Laura understands what you do at headquarters is confidential.'

Hanson's eyes went to the flip chart, checking that she'd covered it before Laura's arrival. She started to load her briefcase. 'Could be better.'

'Remember The Murder Group, Kate?'

She did. Around four years ago, members of one of the intellectually quickest tutorial groups she'd had, Julian among them, had started it, studying homicide cases in the media and raising credible suspects, as shown by the subsequent arrests reported in the newspapers. She looked at their expectant faces, guessing what they were thinking. 'Sorry, no. Not this case.'

The phone rang as Hanson arrived in UCU. Watts reached for it. 'Unsolved Crime—' He listened. She and Corrigan saw disbelief arrive on his face. 'We'll be there.' He put down the phone. 'One deceased. Sutton Park.'

'Richard Burns,' she said.

Watts was on his feet. 'Think again, doc.'

They got out of the Range Rover into silent chill and headed down a wide track between rows of tall evergreens. They came into the clearing where officers were gathered, some in forensic suits, one standing with the pathologist, looking at something grey lying on the ground near their feet.

Chong looked up as they approached. 'Want to take a look?' She unzipped the grey body bag and pulled the sides apart to expose the face: Diana Flynn, eyes closed, blonde hair barely ruffled, lips bluish, throat intact. Chong re-zipped the bag and nodded to her assistant and a forensic worker. 'You can take her now.' She reached inside her case and turned to Hanson and her colleagues, holding up a half-full brandy bottle shrouded in plastic. 'A mix of this and Valium.' They stared at the bottle.

'You're sure?' Watts asked. He got a clipped response.

'Yes, or I wouldn't be saying it, would I?' She replaced the bottle inside the case. 'She must have arrived here early this morning.' She pointed to the case. 'We collected an empty Valium packet from near the body. It looks like she chose what she thought was a good spot on a Monday. Off the main tracks and not visited much in November. She took the tablets with the brandy. Her breathing slowed. She became sleepy, blood pressure dropped, pulse dropped and she became comatose.' She turned, watching the body bag being slid inside the black estate car. 'What more do you need to know.'

'Has Brad Flynn been informed?' asked Hanson.

'Not yet. He wasn't at the house this morning. I rang Dominic Flynn. According to him, his father had scheduled several business meetings in the city. We didn't tell him why we wanted his father. We're still trying to locate him.'

'No evidence on her body of a struggle?' asked Watts as Chong reached inside the case again.

'Given what I've just said, what do you think?'

'Note?'

She straightened, holding out an evidence bag. 'Here. Short and to the point. A reward for your first sensible question.'

Hanson was in her room, her eyes fixed on a copy of Diana Flynn's suicide note, the original of which was being processed for prints. It was hardly a note and it hardly needed copying: a name, chaotically written, probably as Diana ingested much of the substances which killed her. Hanson sat back, letting it fall onto the desk, her eyes on its message: Brad Flynn – you should have— Knowing that the woman who had written those words had destroyed herself gave them an awful finality. To Hanson they crackled with blame. She rested her head back and stared towards the window, recalling the scene at the park that morning, thinking about Brad Flynn's complaint against her and the unlikelihood it would carry weight, given that he himself had become a person of interest in the last day or so. She started at Crystal's voice.

'Want anything before I take this stuff to Admin, Kate?'

'No, thanks.' Crystal looked at her watch. 'Don't forget your lecture on antisocial personality to the second year undergrads.'

Hanson was on her feet. 'Damn!' Waiting for the unsteadiness she'd had since the attack on her to settle, she grabbed files and her laptop, headed for the door. 'What would I do without you, Crystal?'

'Survive just fine.'

Watts parked the Range Rover at the end of a row of cars in the space marked with a large yellow 'No Parking' cross and headed for the School of Psychology entrance. He hadn't taken to the place the first few times he'd come here but now he liked it. Red brick. Solid. He felt at home here. He walked up the steps, ignored the lift because he'd got stuck in it once, and took the stairs. He felt heavy, weighed down by the nightmare of a day he'd just had, guessing that Hanson's had probably been as bad. He was later than he'd anticipated but he knew she was still here. Her car was outside. Not that he had any good news for her. They still hadn't located Burns. He thumped the door, got a response and pushed it open. 'How you doing, doc?'

He looked across the room to where she was sitting at her desk, the low sun shining through the window, flaming her hair. She looked up at him. 'About the same as you, at a guess. You look shattered.'

He sat heavily. 'Go for it: "lose weight. Take exercise. How's your blood pressure." Let's get it over with.'

'I was about to offer you a drink. Tea? Coffee?'

'I'll have tea. Three . . . No. Make that two sugars.'

Hanson went into Crystal's room and he glanced at the notes on the flip chart. Hauling himself up, he went to it, his eyes moving over the words. Typical of the doc to have everything included, everything categorised, everything . . .

'Here you go.'

He turned and took the mug from her. 'Ta.'

'Anything to report?' He took a mouthful of tea. Shook his head. 'I've got officers still out looking for Burns under Corrigan's direction. I gave Chong time to settle, do what she does, then went down to the PM suite to check if she was still convinced it was suicide. Got chewed out because she reckons she'd already said it's textbook. Came back to UCU. Located Brad Flynn at his city office. Broke the news of his wife's death. Phoned for a car to bring him to headquarters to identify her.'

She looked at him. 'Why didn't you transport him?'

'Call me over-sensitive if you like, but I didn't fancy being in a car for half an hour with a bloke who's just been told his wife has topped herself.'

'Carry on.'

'He confirmed identity of the body. I said we'd want to talk to him sometime. The son came to collect him. He didn't look a lot better. Said he knew his mother was still very upset at Matthew's death but he thought she was handling it. He didn't have much else to say. They left and I came here.'

'Busy day,' she said. 'Did you disclose the note to him?' He gulped tea. 'He didn't ask if she left one, so no, not yet. What you up to?' She pointed to the copy of Diana Flynn's note on her desk. 'What do you make of it?'

'Not a lot to make is there? Maybe she was starting a goodbye to him, but the pills and stuff took over and she never finished.' She looked down at it. 'I'll tell you what I think, shall I? I see blame. Accusation.' She looked across at him. 'Pity she didn't have a chance to write more.'

He came to the desk, lifted the note. 'You don't think she was blaming him for Matthew's death?'

'I don't know.' She watched him as he drained the mug. 'I might have had a prowler at my house the other night.'

He stared down at her. 'Oh, yeah?' She told him about it. 'Who have you reported it to?'

'You.'

'I'll put one of our extra officers outside your house.'

She shook her head. 'No. We need as many people as possible out looking for Richard Burns.' She glanced at the note. 'Will you be getting Brad Flynn in for interview?'

'We'll wait a day or two, in view of what's happened.'

A few minutes after Watts left Hanson was on her phone. She needed her caller. Needed some ordinary, normal time. A break from mayhem. What she'd just heard held promise. 'So, you're over this way tomorrow?'

'I'm taking a course at the cooking school at The School Yard. I'll be learning how to pimp my vegetables.'

She smiled at her friend Celia's words. 'Steaming works for me. Meet me for lunch, Cee. *Please*. I need some downtime.'

'OK, but it'll have to be at twelve. How about the Boston Coffee Shop?'

'See you then.'

TWENTY-FIVE

Following a morning of non-stop lectures, Hanson was inside the busy coffee shop, Celia scrutinising her. 'You look tired.'

Having eaten a salad, Hanson now took a large mouthful of

carrot cake. She hadn't told Celia about the attack on her and
wanted to shift attention from herself. 'How's the cooking course
going?' she asked, indistinctly.

'Great. Not your kind of thing but useful as a subject-change.'
She gave Hanson a quick grin. 'How's work going, professor?'

'Getting used to the difference in workload. Less students
but more opportunity for research.'

Celia leant on the table, bright-eyed. 'And how is the force?
Still with you?'

Hanson knew only too well the object of the enquiry:
Corrigan. She kept her response neutral. 'We've got a case I'm
not going to tell you about, except that it's a mess.'

'I read about it. Remains interred at a church. I'm profoundly
grateful for not hearing the details. How's The Corrigan?'

'Leave it, Cee.'

'OK. How's Charlie?'

'Fine. I don't want him to leave.'

'He's got his own life, Kate.'

'I know.'

'And you need a life.'

'If I'm not mistaken, I already have one.'

'I'm talking about a full life, with somebody who adores
you . . .'

Diana Flynn slipped inside Hanson's head. 'In my experience,
relationships start out on a high then break down with a lot of
lying, bad feeling, conflict, blame—'

'Corrigan is *not* Kevin.'

'I didn't say he was.' She sipped coffee. 'I know more people
who are divorced than aren't. Actually, I will mention the case
because it's a maelstrom of emotions. Or it was for the woman
who died yesterday. I think the only relationships in her life
which were rewarding were those with her sons. And even
those were probably difficult at times.'

'Sad.' She looked at Hanson. 'What can I say? Life's a
challenge. I'm here right now because husband is working and
children are hopefully learning, I'm anticipating a battle about having
my mother over for Christmas and the sibling rivalry in our house
has to be seen to be believed and is driving me *nuts*.' She pulled a
slice of carrot cake closer. 'This is my way of "getting by".'

Hanson's phone buzzed. 'Hang on, Cee.' She answered it. It was Watts. 'Hi.' She listened, nodded. 'I'll be with you in fifteen minutes.' She cut the call and stood, reaching into her bag for her purse. 'Sorry. I have to go.'

Celia looked up at her. 'Kate, I know your stand on commitment but I also know you. Life gets messy for most of us at times. By not accepting that you're missing out.' Hanson placed money on the table. Celia shook her head. 'Lunch was on me. Say hi to the force for me.'

The dark blue Bentley was on a trailer parked some distance from the entrance to headquarters when Hanson arrived, one of its wings damaged. She went straight to UCU. 'Where is he?'

'Police surgeon's taking a quick look at him,' said Corrigan. 'He ran his car off the road into a fence. He was breathalysed at the scene. We're planning to have a brief talk with him before his son arrives.'

She looked from Corrigan to Watts. 'Can you do that?'

'Yes. He's a person of interest, not a suspect. He's agreed to talk to us.' The desk phone rang. Watts picked it up. 'OK. We're on our way.'

She watched them go. Five minutes later, she followed them to the first floor. Inside the observation room, she got her first look at Brad Flynn. He was staring across the table at Watts and Corrigan, looking exhausted and to her, drunk, an area of redness on the right side of his forehead.

Corrigan spoke. 'You're free to leave but we'd appreciate a brief word with you before you do. Just to check you're OK.'

Flynn shrugged. 'Would you believe I don't drink much?' He raised both hands. 'Yes, I was speeding. I knew I was over the limit but I had to get home. That's it.' His hands dropped and he sat back, seemingly satisfied with his own logic.

'You've had a lot happen in your family in the last week,' said Watts.

Flynn stared at the table between them. 'That's one way of describing it. The whole family, everything, was fine. Now it's all fallen apart. I didn't always do right by Diana, I know that, but I really tried with Matthew. Dom I never worried about.

He's straight forward, quick minded. I understand him. Matthew, I never did.' He lapsed into a brief silence. 'He was always a mystery. I didn't pressure him. Just let him do his own thing. Trouble was, he didn't seem to want to *do* anything. He never wanted anything. That, I didn't understand. I supported him but half the time he refused what I was offering. We had no common ground. I used to end up getting angry with him.' He ran his hand across his slick forehead, drank water from a cup provided by Corrigan. 'Dom didn't get Matthew either. He thought I indulged him. First it was the drugs, then it was . . . something else about him that worried me. Not that it matters now.' He looked up at Watts and Corrigan. 'I'm talking to you because I want that psychologist off this case.' Hearing this, Hanson stiffened. 'She upset my wife who's now killed herself. Don't tell me there's no connection. My name carries weight in this city. By the time I've finished telling the vice chancellor of her university what she's done to my family, she'll have no job left.' He paused. 'Did you know, I'm up for an honorary doctorate?' Standing at the glass, Hanson realised she was shaking. She made herself listen to what Corrigan was saying.

'While you're here, Mr Flynn, can you confirm whether you ever heard of or met somebody by the name of Callum Foley?'

Flynn put a hand to his forehead, not looking at him. 'No. Who is he?'

'He was around the same age as your son, Matthew. They attended the drug counselling group together. Did either of your sons ever mention anyone of that name?'

Brad Flynn frowned across the table. 'No. Neither of them.'

'How did you find out that St Bartholomew's ran a drug support group?'

Flynn gazed at him. 'I didn't.'

'Yes, you did, Mr Flynn,' said Watts. 'We've gone through the records. Found your name as Matthew's referrer.'

Flynn looked fuddled. 'I don't recall. It was a long time ago.'

Hanson saw doubt on Corrigan's face, outright suspicion on Watts's. She watched Flynn's face clear.

'I think somebody from the church came to the office, looking for hand-outs, you know how they do. He told us about what the church did. The business community supports charitable stuff so Dom and I both gave him a cheque.' He shrugged. 'Tax deductible.'

'Give us the name of the person who came,' asked Watts.

'Not a clue.' He stood, still unsteady. 'I need to get home.'

Corrigan also stood. 'I'll check if your son has arrived.'

Hanson watched her colleagues walk Flynn from the room. Had he forgotten who it was from the church who had called at his office? She recalled what Robbe, Matthew's years-ago teacher had said about Brad Flynn. That his financial support of the school meant he felt entitled to exert pressure on him to adjust Matthew's grades. *He doesn't remember the name of whoever called for donations. What he does recall is that his donation was tax deductible.* She left the observation room. *A businessman through and through.*

They returned to UCU. 'Don't let Flynn upset you,' said Watts, eyeing Hanson. 'He hasn't got a clue what he's saying.'

Hanson knew different. 'He thinks I'm responsible for his wife's suicide. He wants me to feel as bad as he does.' She paused. 'I shouldn't have implied anything about an affair to his wife when I saw her. I should have waited. I was too quick to get in there. Too focused on the case. I have to go.'

Hanson was back in her room, immersed in student papers when Crystal appeared holding an email. 'Hi, Kate. Urgent message from the vice chancellor.'

She stared at it in Crystal's hand as if it were a viper. Brad Flynn had lost no time getting onto the VC. Another thought followed. Or had the VC somehow heard of Maisie's assault on another student? 'I'll have a strong coffee then go and see him.'

Crystal frowned. 'Why? He only wants key details of your PhD students' research areas.'

Hanson took the email. As Crystal returned to her office Hanson logged into the desktop and gave the VC the information he'd requested. She took a deep breath. *Get going. Back to square one with the case while you've still got both of your jobs.*

Seizing a sheet of paper and with occasional quick checks of the flip chart she listed all the possible leads she and her colleagues had amassed during the investigation of Matthew Flynn's murder: his drug caution, the drug group, Callum Foley, the reported harassment Matthew had experienced in his neighbourhood. She opened her notebook. There was something else, less a lead, more a puzzle: Matthew's scarf around his neck in death, devoid of bloodstains. She leant back on her chair, her eyes on the words. She returned to the harassment. They had no confirmation that Matthew Flynn was gay. The woman he had worked most with hadn't said so. She'd told Hanson he had a girlfriend. Said it with no trace of surprise which surely she would have shown if she'd assumed or knew he was gay? Hanson's eyes were back on the flip chart. Matthew had never reported any of the incidents of physical harassment. It was his brother, Dominic who had done so, following Matthew's disappearance. She frowned at the meagre descriptions of the attacks, the reference to theft, the targeting of Matthew twice in daylight by the same youths. Watts's criminal contact had not been impressed by the reported harassment incidents. Considering them now, neither was Hanson, but for a different reason. If they were not reliable, why would Matthew Flynn fabricate them?

She read the references to the inverted crucifix tattoos and the plant residue on the remains of both Matthew and Callum Foley. They'd had a shared fear. Of what? Had somebody threatened them? Drugs. Had they angered someone involved in the illicit drug trade as Watts had suggested? But, if that was the case, what kind of protection did they imagine they would get from inverted crucifixes and plants? She clasped her hands at her mouth. Devil's Claw. Were they fearful of something neither of them understood? Had they been made fearful? She recalled the pentagram Delaney had told them was daubed on the church door. Her eyes drifted over the many lines. Did evil live somewhere in this case? Hanson gave a vehement headshake. She had no time for evil as a concept but it had to be considered. Others believed in it. It was what the evidence was telling her. She glanced to the window and the bright, cold day beyond it. *I need to get out there. Walk the campus. Cut the thinking. Move. Breathe.*

'Back in half an hour, Crystal!'

Hanson was back in her room, standing before the flip chart. Whatever this killer's motivation, he was now out of his own control. She picked up the marker and wrote names. Not suspects because she and her colleagues didn't know enough to identify any. These were persons of interest, a broad net to gather the possibilities together: Brad Flynn. Richard Burns. Jeremy Fellowes. Father Delaney. What about Will Graham? Zach Addison? Their being on remand recently had raised doubts about their involvement in the murder of Alfred Best but without a full understanding of this case she was taking no chances: everyone needed to be considered.

Hanson stared at the names, thinking of Brad Flynn. If this case was about money, there had to be a lot of it. She looked at other names. Most of them had withheld information. Possibly because they'd forgotten it, maybe not. She looked at one name in particular. *Let's start at the top.*

She picked up her phone, selected a number and waited.

TWENTY-SIX

Watts parked next to Hanson and opened her passenger door. This was typical of the Doc. Whatever she wanted, she wanted it now. Huffing, he lowered himself inside. 'Next time you buy a car, think "bigger".' He settled himself, almost filling the available space. 'OK. What's set your underwear on fire?'

She reminded him of the Flynn family's lack of openness about its contact with the church, plus Delaney's own omission. 'As soon as Delaney was aware whose remains were in the crypt he should have told us right then what he knew of the Flynn family. He didn't. He has to tell us now.'

Watts looked across at Church House on its high ground, all red brick and black paintwork. Victorian as an antimacassar and as inviting as the headstones a few metres away. He looked at her. 'Right. Let's get it done.'

They approached the house, went up the steps to the veranda and on to the front door. Watts jabbed the bell. They heard it ring inside, then nothing. He jabbed it again. A shadow appeared on the other side of the glass beyond the heavy, lace curtain. It slowly approached, getting bigger. The door was opened by Gorridge, her face set. 'No need to ring twice. We're not deaf. What do you want?'

Watts had had a hard day so far and this woman who looked like she'd forgotten to shave, wasn't improving it. 'We're here to see Father Delaney. Tell him.'

She gave him a furious glare. 'He's in but he's busy!'

A voice drifted down the hall towards them. 'Who is it, Mrs Gorridge?'

'It's them from the police. Shall I let 'em in?' Getting an affirmative she stood aside. 'Hurry up! You're letting the heat out.'

They came into the hall and Watts glanced at Hanson. She got his drift. What heat?

'Wait *here*,' said Gorridge with a direct look at Hanson.

They watched her walk away, huge hips and thighs encased in leggings patterned this time in a riot of yellows, reds and greens. She opened the door of the room which Hanson knew was Delaney's study. They waited in the heavy silence, the housekeeper's words drifting towards them through the open door. 'It's that fat bloke, the detective, and that posh woman who thinks she owns the—'

'Thank you, Mrs Gorridge. Leave it with me.'

Gorridge emerged with a last sharp look at Hanson as she stomped in the direction of the kitchen. Delaney appearing in the doorway of his study, motioning them with his hand. 'Please. Come on in.'

They walked across the wide hall and along the passageway into the study. Watts got straight to what was on his and Hanson's minds. 'Tell us about your connection to Brad Flynn and his business interests, Father Delaney.'

Delaney's eyes moved calmly between them. 'We've been

fortunate very occasionally to receive a donation from him. Once, twice, he's advised us on raising money.'

Watts wasn't about to leave it at that. 'You didn't tell us that Flynn has a connection with this church.'

He responded, his tone easy, patient. 'That, detective sergeant, is because he doesn't. He's not a member of this congregation. He has never visited the church itself but as one of the city's foremost entrepreneurs, what he has done is make donations, as I have just acknowledged. It was on one of those occasions that he advised me that St Bartholomew's could benefit from being organised and run on business lines. A simple, throwaway remark as far as he was concerned, I'm sure, but knowing of his success I thought about it. It took months of hard work on my part to apply what he advised to this church.'

'So why not mention that at the outset?'

Delaney's fleshy face took on a long-suffering look. 'Because those instances were barely contacts. His name was on my list of potential donors. I phoned him twice, I believe. He was kind enough to agree a donation each time. Relatively modest sums, as far as I can recall – a couple of hundred pounds each time. He also offered the advice I've described. That was the sum total of my contact with him. Prior to Matthew Flynn's remains being found here, I was not even aware that he *had* sons.'

Watts wasn't satisfied. 'As soon as you knew the identity of the remains, you should have mentioned this contact you had with Flynn.'

'There was nothing secret about it,' protested Delaney. 'Nothing clandestine. The donations were entered into our financial records.' He looked from Watts to Hanson, perturbed now. 'It simply did not occur to me as being relevant.'

'We make that kind of judgement,' snapped Watts. 'When did this advice-giving happen?'

Delaney gazed towards the ceiling. 'St Bartholomew's has been run on business lines for at least five or six years so it was prior to that, obviously. I don't remember precisely when.'

'Did Mr Flynn mention his personal life at all? His family?'

Delaney looked exasperated. 'I just told you, detective sergeant, I know nothing of his family. My focus was always on

St Bartholomew's. His advice felt somewhat alien to me at the time but we've seen the benefits.'

Watts filled the silence. 'You've heard the news about Mrs Flynn's suicide?'

Delaney's eyes widened within their pouches. 'Was that his *wife*? I heard a report on the local radio but I didn't make the connection. How dreadful. No one's life is theirs to destroy. Life belongs to God. He calls each of us in his time.'

'Alfred Best,' said Hanson. 'Tell us about him.'

Delaney looked puzzled. 'What about him?'

Watts saw Hanson lean forward, her eyes on him, thinking that if Delaney knew what was good for him he'd better give her some real answers. 'Tell us how it is that Alfred had a significant personal fortune yet when he died he was virtually impoverished.'

Delaney shook his head. 'That, I cannot tell you. Alfred gave freely of his time here and, yes, he made financial gifts to the church. Modest ones, I assure you. I was aware that he was a little concerned about money during this last year. I assumed that his wife's care was a heavy financial burden. When I last spoke to him some weeks ago, I suggested he stop all donations to the church. I also assured him that the church would do whatever it could to provide for him in future.' He gave each of them a direct look. 'That is one of the benefits of running St Bartholomew's as a business: we invest in projects and also in people. When those people need our help, we have the funds to do so.'

They were outside, a stiff wind blowing. Watts looked up at the house and the scudding clouds. 'I'm not sure what to make of him. How about you?' She stared across the open land. 'Assessing a minister of the church is a new experience for me. He sounds sincere but I can't decide if what he says is *him* talking, or just words and phrases that are part of his job.' She frowned. 'And then there's this business in America. He's a paradox. What do you think of his explanation as to why he didn't tell us he knew Brad Flynn?'

'Like you just said, he talks a good talk but afterwards you're left wondering.'

* * *

Hanson was half-heartedly gathering up textbooks and files inside her room. She carried books across the room, distributed a few to shelves, then dumped the rest on the floor and went directly to the flip chart. She'd already added what she and Watts had gathered from Delaney. Her eyes skimmed the black words, drifted down to the photographs, to Matthew's 'in love' face, according to Crystal. *This was never about drugs. Yes, drug cautions indirectly led Matthew and Callum to their deaths in a way we still don't understand. No, this is about money.* She frowned at everything she'd written in the last few days. *Three people dead. Matthew. Callum. Alfred.* After meeting Callum's mother, her sympathies were with Callum who probably never had a chance. *That isn't all I know about him. I know he was a friend to Matthew Flynn. He'd supported Matthew at the tattoo parlour, as any friend might. There was good in Callum Foley. We know there was good in Matthew: he was kind. Someone who did his best. Not materialistic. Naïve. And both he and Callum were united by a shared fear.* Hanson stood, her eyes fixed on her notes. Alfred was also a good person. Kind.

She went to the window, watched leaves hurling themselves across the campus. There had to be something else, something she couldn't see or didn't know about which had led to those three deaths. She looked up at sullen clouds. Why did people kill? She didn't need to search for answers. Her training, her job, told her: for pleasure, greed, jealousy, resentment, rage.

She turned from the window. They also killed out of fear. She was back at the flip chart. *Most of those reasons presuppose a relationship with, or at the least some knowledge of, all three victims. Maybe we need to widen the investigation beyond the church?*

She got her coat and other belongings and went to the door. Switching off the light she looked at black words on white in the failing light. No. They already had their link: St Bartholomew's Church. All three victims were associated with it.

Charlie was out for the evening with one of his ex-colleagues. She'd agreed with Maisie that they have a 'girls' evening, which these days involved Maisie purloining all of Hanson's bath and hair products. Hanson had given herself a pedicure, after which she'd painted Maisie's toenails bright red, refusing to do the same to her fingernails. 'Maisie, stop the constant pushing, please. You know that it's school tomorrow.'

'Nobody will notice!'

Hanson held up a pale shell pink polish. 'My one and only offer.'

Maisie eyed it and pulled a face. 'Mom, has anybody ever told you you're a total control freak?' *Your father. Many times.*

Hanson jiggled the bottle. 'Yes or no?'

Maisie submitted her fingernails to a thin layer of shell pink. 'When I'm eighteen I'll, like do super-mad stuff. Go crazy. Have weird hair and everything and then you'll realise what you did, Mom: kept me down, like a prisoner, suppressed my personality and you'll be well-sorry.'

'There you are,' said Hanson, head on one side, eyeing the small, glossy nails. 'They look nice.'

Maisie scrutinised them. 'Yeah, but I'm having only black nail polish when I'm older.'

Hanson put the manicure accoutrements back into their little bag. 'Sounds dramatic. Want a snack before bed?'

TWENTY-SEVEN

In his head he was running like the wind, gazelle-like through early-morning mist towards sanctuary. He beat against the door, desperate now. It stood, immutable. He flattened his back against it, chest burning, eyes wide, his breath billowing from his mouth. Terrified, his head spun towards a disembodied voice telling him to stop. He needed sanctuary. One he himself had made. Pressing his fist to his mouth, panicked now, he sprinted among the headstones to the only place he would be safe: home.

'He's on the move, sarge! Look!'

Watts was out of the car, swearing under his breath. He hissed to the young constable. 'Are you thick or just wanting to make a bad situation worse? *Shut* it!'

He and Corrigan headed in the direction of raised voices, a short, plump man accompanying them.

'The moment he's detained, I must be allowed to go to him.'

They nodded. As far as Watts was concerned the psychiatrist was welcome. They reached the parking area which was full of official vehicles, their lights picking up a thin male, his eyes wide, turning this way and that, clearly disoriented. Like a cornered animal, thought Watts as several uniforms took hold of the man and brought him to the ground. Watts shook his head. It had been relatively easy. It could have been a fiasco. If it had been, they'd all have been for the high jump. He followed as Corrigan accelerated towards the distressed figure on the ground. Watts nodded to the gasping psychiatrist just catching up. 'He's all yours.' They watched him approach the now prone figure, kneel, and place his hands gently around the man's head.

'Richard? Richard, this is Dr Solomons, remember? I've come to look after you.'

Corrigan had rung to tell Hanson of Richard Burns's arrest early that morning. She had gone directly to headquarters' custody suite to look at Burns, his psychiatrist still in attendance. She took in Burns's thin stature, the unkempt hair, the lower face covered with several weeks' growth of beard. She recalled the attack on her inside St Bartholomew's Church. A careful, planned, silent attack by someone who was clean and wearing cologne.

'Say it: You don't like Burns as your attacker.' They were back in UCU and this was the second time Watts had said it.

'He is not the one. You *saw* him. He's got a significant mental health problem.'

'Tell us something we don't know. We went to his house at five this morning, fetched his medication, got in touch with his psychiatrist who filled us in on the hallucinations, the paranoia.' He stared at her, pugnacious as always. 'Think about it. You went to that church expecting Burns to be there. You saw the state of his house. He's as mad as a bloody hatter. We need to at least consider him as the one who hit you.'

She closed her eyes, momentarily blocking out Watts's

determined face, the jabbing forefinger. 'It was *not* Burns who hit me inside that church.'

'I don't see how you can be that sure.'

'It's what my senses told me at the time and I've since told you. Whoever it was, he was physically clean. Yes, we saw a lot of evidence in his bathroom that Burns set great store by personal cleanliness but now we know that his mental health has declined. He's ill-kempt, his behaviour is disturbed. Whoever hit me was clean, silent and wears cologne.' She hesitated. 'And of heavier build.'

Watts went heavy-footed to the board, circled two names already written there with his forefinger and returned to the table. 'OK, brass-tacks time. We've got Burns, who you don't like for the assault on you but there's also Delaney. It's his church. He lives right there. He told you Burns would be at the church. It could have been Delaney who set you up, hit you and was back inside his house in minutes.'

She shot him an exasperated look. 'Delaney coming up behind me would have been like an eclipse!' She paused, recalling how light on his feet she'd observed him to be for such a huge man. He didn't have personal care problems either. But did he wear cologne? She couldn't recall.

The door opened. Corrigan came inside, papers in one hand. He spread them out on the table, pointed at a brochure, on the cover of which was a photograph of a modern building set in pastoral landscape. 'This here's the place which runs retreats for the clergy.'

'Don't tell us,' said Watts, looking sour. 'All the gruel you can eat and your own personal cat-o-nine-tails.' He picked it up, glanced through it, brows climbing. 'Blimey. It's like a five-star hotel.' He held it up. 'Look, doc. A bathroom fit for somebody like Burns with "personal issues".'

'I've been on the phone to them,' said Corrigan. 'They've confirmed that Richard Burns was a no-show for the whole of the three weeks.' He looked at Hanson. 'His neighbour was right. He was home. I also phoned Delaney who sounded surprised when I told him. Said he'd persuaded Burns he needed the break and to look on it as a vacation. He described Burns as looking forward to going.'

Watts grunted, his eyes on Hanson. 'Delaney knows Burns has serious mental health problems and is potentially dangerous, yet he told you that Burns would be inside the church that afternoon. He let you walk straight into a risky situation. I want proper answers from him and not wrapped up in the kind of chat he gives his congregation or us the other day.'

The door opened and a young, blonde constable leant inside, giving Corrigan a wide smile. Hanson rolled her eyes. 'Sarge, the chief asked me to tell you he's instructed that Richard Burns be released into the care of his psychiatrist.'

'Ta.'

'He also wants to see you and the lieutenant.'

Watts stood. 'You couldn't find us, right Barb?' They headed for the door.

In the afternoon's fading light, Hanson followed Corrigan's Volvo onto the parking area, pulling up facing the open land and its headstones, the church to her left, Church House on the right. There was no car parked outside the house, no lights visible inside. She opened her door, hearing distant traffic in the stillness.

They walked the path, headstones on either side and up to the house sitting on its high ground, up the steps and onto its wide veranda where Corrigan rang the bell. Getting no response they watched as he went around the side of the house. He was back within a minute. 'Nobody home. No lights. Nothing.'

'Where might he have gone?' said Hanson. 'His housekeeper isn't here either. There's no car.'

Watts walked back down the steps to scrutinise the house frontage. 'He could be out doing some of that outreach work he told us about.'

'I didn't get the impression he's that hands-on.'

'The housekeeper doesn't live in?'

'No. She lives locally.'

'Where?'

Hanson frowned, sifting memory for the small detail which at the time hadn't seemed relevant. *What was it? Something incongruous. Something which didn't fit Eunice Gorridge in any . . .*

'Primrose Way. Delaney said it was local to here.'

'We'll find her. Ask where he is and what she's got to say about him.'

'Good luck with that,' murmured Hanson.

'If we get no joy from her, we'll come back here to see if he's turned up.'

'Let me know what you find out, if anything.' She went with them to the Volvo, searching the pockets of her overcoat, watching Corrigan tap Primrose Way into the satnav.

'Where you off to now?' asked Watts.

'The university to collect some work then home, with a quick detour to headquarters. I've left my phone there.'

Watts waved a large hand as the Volvo's engine roared into life. 'If you see the chief and he asks you where we are, you know nothing.'

As soon as Hanson walked through the door of UCU she saw her phone lying on the table. She checked it for messages from her colleagues. Nothing. *Knowing Gorridge's antipathy for the police and virtually everybody else, she'll be as unhelpful as possible for as long as possible.*

Dropping the phone into her bag she headed out, lingering at the board's blank surface, resisting the temptation to start it up. She needed a break. She was going home. Walking through reception on her way to the main doors she was stopped by someone calling her name. Gus Stirling from Upstairs. She turned. 'Hi, Gus.'

He beckoned her. 'Just the person I'm looking for. Have you got five minutes?'

She followed him upstairs listening as he told her about the ongoing problems he and his team were having with their review cases. 'That's why I was looking for you. Cold cases are your territory, Kate, and I don't mind admitting we're floundering. We need some advice.'

She followed him inside the squad room where several officers were engrossed at screens or reading hard data, the atmosphere low-key. Gus pointed to information written on two large glass screens, the pressure he was under quickening his delivery. 'The two abduction cases: Zoe Wilson, aged thirteen when she was taken six years ago, Rosie Mahoney, seven years old when she disappeared eleven years ago.' He pointed to two photographs pressed to the screen, one of a dark-haired, teenage Zoe, next to it that of a small girl of about five or six with pale blonde hair and wide blue eyes. Eleven years. A long time. Too long for a good outcome. 'No connection between the abductions?' she asked.

'None identified at the time or by us so far. Zoe disappeared from a fairground. No known witnesses. Rosie was small for her age when she disappeared from outside her house. A single report of her being put into "a large car", never verified. That's about all we've got.'

Hanson absorbed the limited detail. 'No CCTV?'

'No.'

She turned to Gus who looked worn. She understood. 'I'm sure you're doing all the right things, Gus: re-evaluating all the known facts, following up the slimmest of leads, which is what UCU does but it doesn't always pay off.'

He looked dispirited. 'I'm sorry, Gus. I don't see that I can add anything.'

She looked at the second screen. 'This is your other review?'

'Yes. The rape series for which we've also got nothing. No DNA, no witnesses.'

'What about the victims? What's their response to the review?'

'Two have refused to help us. They don't want to go through it all again, which I understand. The other two are very willing and we've got female officers wanting to work with them, but we need to get the best and smallest details from them and that won't be easy.'

Hanson nodded. 'I'll give you some current research information on ways of talking to sexual crime complainants which can help cue them into the detail of their attackers' behaviour. Have you done any geographical profiling of the areas of the attacks?'

'We could do with some guidance on that.'

'I'll let you have it sometime tomorrow.'

She went out of the squad room, down the stairs and out, Gus's thanks following her. UCU was still floundering, she was out of ideas and no one was coming along any time soon with offers of help. Starting her car she headed towards the university. Like Gus, they badly needed some momentum. She drove, a rhythm starting up inside her head. An earworm: Zoe – Rosie. Zoe – Rosie. Zoe – Rosie. Zoe— On impulse, she changed direction and headed for St Bartholomew's. Delaney may have returned and her colleagues might have achieved the impossible, prised information from Gorridge and be back there now.

She came onto the church grounds, stopped the car and looked around the deserted parking area. The repetitive rhythm was back: *Rosie – Zoe – Rosie – Zoe – Rosie . . . God, I'm tired.* She glanced across to Church House. It was as closed-looking as when she and her colleagues were last here an hour or so ago. She looked at its upper floors, away, then back, eyes fixed on one window. Switching off the engine, eyes still fixed, she got out into silence and falling darkness. It was there again. In the upper window. Robbed of all colour in the moonlight. She gazed at the house, bulky on its high ground. Matthew's face as it looked in death was inside her head again. Its avidness. Its expectation. She still didn't know what Matthew wanted of her. She got a sudden, irrational certainty that there was something here, inside this house, waiting to tell her.

Approaching it, eyes still on the window, her heart squeezed. The watcher was still there. Reaching the veranda steps she looked up again. The glass was now covered by something. Hanson put all critical thinking on hold, knowing that if she gave the situation a second's thought she would be heading for her car. The repetitive beat was back. *Zoe – Rosie – Zoe – Rosie . . .* Raking her fingers through her hair, tension spiralling, she went up the steps to the front door. She placed her hands against its cold, black-painted surface. It moved. She snatched them away. *Run. Get away! Now! Zoe – Rosie . . .* She dug inside her pocket, gripped her phone. Since this case had started, Matthew Flynn had been trying to tell her something. If the answer was here in this house, she and her colleagues had to have it. There might never be another chance. Pushing the door she came into the shadowy, dark-painted hall with its palm-hand walls, stairs facing her. She flinched at the front door's soft click behind her. In the darkness a narrow seam of light showed at the edges of one of the doors beyond the hall. The door of Delaney's study. He was here! He had to tell her all that he knew.

The only sounds her own swallow reflex and a rhythmic thump she realised was her heart, she went to the door, put her head close to it. 'Father Delaney? It's Kate Hanson.'

Silence. Reaching down for the handle she pushed open the door. A fire was burning low in the hearth, the room warm, heavy, red, velvet curtains drawn across its window. He was sitting on the high-backed chair, facing his desk.

'Father Delaney?'

She went slowly to him, turned, looked down at him, just one coherent thought in her head: the headquarters' forensic artist knew what he was doing when he produced the anatomical sketch of Matthew Flynn's throat injury. She was looking at one exactly like it, real, visceral, sickening, the high-backed chair the sole support for Delaney's head. Cold, shocked, her eyes moved slowly over the bloodstained carpet, looking for what had killed him, not finding it. The desk was mired in blood, splashed and splattered over the papers on it: handwritten records, payments-in, payments-out, lists, dates, certificates for shares. Bonds. Initials: A.B— *Alfred*? Seeing it all, she knew. St Bartholomew's was not a church. Its foremost task was profit through business acumen and the wealth of its elderly parishioners. Hanson gazed at Delaney's face, the eyes still open, the plumpness slack now, dull and grey. He'd led it all. Corrigan was right. Delaney had played games with her: about Burns and about himself in his mocking challenges of psychology, his manipulation of the congregation at the re-consecration. His past had followed him here. She and her colleagues knew the sexual enigma that he was. Now he was dead.

A sound on the upper floor jerked her head upwards, the two-name tempo back, quicker now: *Zoe – Rosie – Zoe – Rosie*, matching the blood-beat inside her head. Taking out her phone she sent a brief text to both her colleagues.

Leaving Delaney's corpse, she walked out of the room and across the hall, senses on high alert. She was stopped by a small, sweet sound which stirred the hairs at the nape of her neck. 'Oranges and lemons, say the bells of St Clements . . .

You owe me five farthings, say the bells of St Martin's . . .'
She stood, one foot on the first stair, the two-name pulse in her
head now a thunderous drumbeat, her subconscious giving up
what it knew: *Zoe! – Rosie! – Zoe Wilson! – Rosie Ma—* Facts
on a glass screen rushed to her head: a small girl, missing for
eleven long years. Delaney the towering figure, the sexual
enigma would have needed someone, a business partner,
personal fixer to obtain what Hanson knew was waiting for her
here

She went silently up the stairs to the landing, guided by the
ethereal voice, past several closed doors to one she knew opened
onto a room at the front of this house. 'I owe you five farthings
say the bells of St—' The voice stopped as if a switch had been
pulled. Hanson watched her own hand reach for the doorknob,
turn, then release it. The door swung wide. In front of her was
a poor, cold cell, ragged lace over the window, bare floor, the
one item of furniture apart from the bed an incongruous white-
painted dressing table, exuberant in design, Hanson herself,
pale, large-eyed, reflected in its small, asymmetrical-framed
mirror. A window, according to Crystal one afternoon a hundred
years ago. A pale, thin female, blonde, barely more than a girl,
was facing Hanson, eyes wide. Hanson saw them dart to the
narrow bed and its thin blanket, a single pathetic barrier between
them. She wanted to weep. *How could anyone treat another
person like this?* This person had a name. She had seen it written
up in Gus's notes. She'd seen the years' old photograph.
Mahoney. Had Matthew used it as a pet name? Or was it his
approximation of something, half-remembered by this girl? Face
calm, her movements minimal, Hanson took two steps into
abject privation and stood.

'Hello Honey,' she whispered.

Thin hands rushed the pale face, the soft voice plaintive,
breaking. '. . . Matthew?'

Hanson put her phone to her ear. Dropping her voice, she
gazed at the waif-like figure and the cheerless room. 'Gus? It's
Kate Hanson.'

'Hi, Kate!' His voice was strong, from a world of warmth
and light and caring. 'You've found something else to help us?'

Hanson nodded. 'Yes. I'm with Rosie Mahoney.' She listened

to stunned silence, seeing a flicker of recognition in the small, white face.

'*What?* . . . Where?'

'Church House.' She gave the address. 'Watts and Corrigan know it. They should be on their way.' Ending the call she took two tentative steps towards the young woman, keeping her voice low. 'I need you to come with me, Honey. It's time to go.' *Time to go home.* Honey's eyes darted away from her, one thin arm reaching out to snatch the blanket, pulling it against herself as if her life depended on it. It probably had at times if this awful, frigid box had been her world for much of the last eleven long years.

The enormous eyes fastened on Hanson, voice scarcely audible. 'I can't. She won't give me dinner. She'll take my blanket.' She folded her thin arms around it. 'I can't leave my father.'

Gorridge. Delaney. Hanson understood. Eleven long, captive years, with rare outings once her bond was so strong that she came back to where there was no comfort, no pleasure, no tenderness. Until a young man had somehow discovered she existed. A young man who had maybe grown to love her. Had Matthew planned to rescue her using money he had saved, maybe stolen, some of which he'd given to street-wise Callum Foley in exchange for his help? Or had he died simply because he knew she existed?

Hanson held out her hands, still using the name Matthew had given her. 'Honey, my name is Kate. Trust me. Come with me. Now.'

Her eyes on Hanson's face, Honey stayed where she was and Hanson knew she was seeing traumatic bonding. Rosie Mahoney had survived the last eleven by aligning herself with her captors, living with deprivation and abuse as a means of survival. It had kept her captive. She shrank back as Hanson came around the bed, placed her hands around the thin, frigid upper arms and pulled her slowly, gently towards the door, making soft, encouraging sounds as they crossed the room and onto the landing, Honey shaking with cold and shock, face contorted by fear. Hanson took off her overcoat, put it around the thin shoulders.

'It's OK, Honey,' she whispered, gently lifting the white arms and slipping them inside the sleeves, quickly tying the belt around the small frame then taking her hand. 'It's time to go now.' Honey pulled back, eyes huge. Hanson held both her hands. 'I'm going with you, Honey. We're going together. Down these stairs, see? I've got some good friends. They're coming to help us.'

They'd covered four of the stairs when Hanson stopped, listened. From somewhere distant on the ground floor she heard steady, determined footfalls on a solid floor, coming closer. Honey shook convulsively, whimpered. The footfalls halted. She turned Honey's face to hers, placing a finger against her own lips then peered over the bannister. The footsteps started up again. Honey began to cry. Hanson couldn't see anyone. She looked at the few steps she and Honey had covered so far. No point going back. They would be trapped. The front door. They had to get to it.

She turned to Honey, put her hands on the slender arms within the thick sleeves. 'Honey?' she whispered. 'I want you to sit on this stair and stay here. I'm going downstairs but I'm coming back for you.' She took the small, pale face in her hands then raised her finger to her lips again.

Going quickly, quietly down the stairs, almost to the last one, she stopped and listened. She'd come to this house with three suspects in her head, one of whom she'd found dead. It had been a meeting of minds, in which greed for money and for power grew to be an obsession until one of them became a killer. He was now downstairs, his moral compass obliterated, beyond caring if he made another victim. Or two. He would destroy both Honey and her as surely as he had the others. The footsteps were close now. Looking up, she saw Honey clutching the staircase spindles, eyes frantic. She turned and looked down. He was here. At the bottom of the stairs. Looking up at them.

Hanson faced him. He was holding the processional brass with its sunray design in one hand, tapping it against his other, both bloody.

'You don't seem surprised,' he said.

'No. I'm not.'

He jabbed the brass towards her. Honey whimpered as Hanson quickly backed away from him. He studied her. 'If you were really smart you wouldn't be here. Why aren't you surprised?'

'Because I've thought a lot about you.'

His lips curled. 'Go on.'

'I know that you're controlling, ambitious and greedy. You're also full of rage. It was the rage that led me to realise it was you.'

He looked past her. Honey whimpered again. 'I see you've found Delaney's dirty little secret.' *Engage him. Keep him talking.* 'And yours.'

He gave her a cold look. 'You're way off track there. I've got zero interest in children.'

'No. Money was your motive for bringing her here. Delaney paid you. You and he devised a moneymaking scheme to separate wealthy, elderly parishioners from what they had. You killed Alfred, probably because he was threatening to expose you. I'm only surprised that given the ages of some of the congregation, their wealth, you didn't kill more.'

'There are no more,' he said. 'Delaney was a greedy bastard. He wanted everything the old parishioners had and me to get rid of them. I put him straight on that: "Choose the oldest because they're least likely to notice the money going, and onto the next".' He smiled. 'I was right. They never noticed, they were pleased to be 'chosen' for the committee until they eventually died of natural causes. It was just another business venture. We steadily drained their accounts. Amazing what some of these old people had stashed away.'

She looked at him, cocksure, willing to talk. She knew why. She and Honey weren't leaving this house. 'You are amoral.'

'And you're not listening.'

Hanson recalled her colleagues' description of Brad Flynn's words to his wife minutes after they'd been given the news that one of their sons was dead: 'You're not listening. I need food.' Some acorns fell a long way from the tree. Others stayed close. Delaney had said 'sons'. How did he know there was more than one, if he didn't know anything about Brad Flynn's family, as he'd claimed?

'Why Callum Foley?' she asked.

'He and Matthew first met at the drugs group. They became friends. Matthew was a pushover. Really impressed by the deacon who ran that group. He started taking an interest in the church. I heard him and Foley arranging to go to a service together. My business interests were taking off here. I was coming and going as I pleased. I didn't want Matthew hanging around.' His face darkened. 'And somehow he found out about *her.*' Honey shrank from him as Hanson stood between them. 'Foley was no good. I thought I could pay him off with a few pounds, until I realised that he was helping Matthew get inside this place to see her. I never expected that. This whole place was *my* business interest. Not some handout from the great Brad Flynn!'

'You procured a six year old girl for Delaney.'

He stared at her. 'It was a *job*. A favour I did for Delaney. You're judging me but you're wrong. You don't know what you're talking about. Delaney wasn't into sex. Not like most of us know it. He liked to *look*. That's all it was. That was his *thing.*'

Something clicked inside Hanson's head: Delaney excusing himself to go and answer a phone she hadn't heard ring, leaving her in his study feeling odd, cold and uncomfortable. "Take your coat off", he'd said. Now she knew. He'd gone to the next room to watch her.

'What he most wanted was a young girl. He had some sort of brush with the law years back. He wanted a girl young enough to accept him and what he wanted. Someone who would submit and never complain.'

'Why keep her in the abject conditions I've seen up there?' asked Hanson, holding on to her anger, needing to prolong the conversation.

He shrugged. 'I don't know anything about that. Delaney's housekeeper had responsibility for looking after the kid from the start. The kid got to thinking of Delaney as some kind of uncle. It worked all right except that that stupid cow, Gorridge left keys lying around, sometimes forgot to lock the place.' He pointed upwards to Honey who buried her face in Hanson's coat. 'But it didn't matter. By the time she was about twelve, thirteen, they started to let her out occasionally. She never ran. Never tried to get away. What does that tell you? She felt alright here.'

Hanson's voice shook. 'She was not *"alright"*. She formed

a bond with Matthew and you took that away from her by killing him.'

He gripped the brass tight. 'I told him she was Gorridge's niece. It took him ages to grasp that she wasn't. And what does he do when he does realise? He comes to tell *me* about her. Said he was worried. Ask *me* what I thought he should do.' He came closer. 'Matthew was a naïve pushover. I guessed Foley was the same. I started to frighten them off. Delaney had told me about vandalism at the church. I talked to them about it. Played up the satanic bit, gave them some plant crap said to protect people from the devil. It worked on Foley. He believed all of it, but I underestimated Matthew.' He glanced up the stairs. 'By then he'd got it bad for her. He wouldn't listen to me. He still hadn't worked out how she came to be here but I knew it wouldn't be long before he did.' His eyes settled on Honey. 'Or *she* told him.'

Hanson stared at him and somewhere inside her head a dam breached. Her voice shook. 'You abducted her, took her away from her home, her family, her *life*. So that Delaney could keep and groom and use . . . You *bastard*.'

He gazed at her, mock-shocked. 'Oh, dear. You seem upset.'

'There were never any attacks on Matthew, were there? You invented them.'

'I thought it a good idea to have a couple of suspects available, just in case Matthew's body was ever found. Delaney had told me about the crypt. He helped me put him in there. I thought that was the last of Matthew. That he'd be in there for keeps. And he would have been, but for those idiots breaking in!'

His words triggered a memory. 'You were at my house.'

He gave her a dismissive look. 'Not me. That was Gorridge, wanting to scare you off. A woman who runs on jealousy, rather than brains where Delaney's concerned.'

'Tell me how you live with yourself,' she whispered. 'You destroyed your own brother.' Above their heads, Honey whimpered.

'I call it collateral damage,' he snapped. 'He just knew too much.'

She gazed at him, shaking her head. 'That's not true. You resented Matthew way before that. You saw him as wasting his opportunities. Yet for every opportunity he threw away or back in your father's face, he was rewarded with more. That's how *you* saw it. You had to work and work to get your father's recognition, his approval, but it was never, *ever* enough, was it? The time, the love, kept going to Matthew who was—'

'A bloody waster!' he screamed at her, his face livid. Above them, Honey began to sob. To keep him talking was her and Honey's only hope. 'I don't believe you!'

'Then I'll tell you. He never did anything that *mattered*. He just carried on, doing what *he* wanted to do, working at no-account jobs and never giving a damn about anything. And the old man? He just took it!' He came closer, pointing at her face with the bloodied brass. 'What you just said is right. Dad *rewarded* him for being an idle, selfish sod. And me? I had to *buy* my first car. Off my own father who was worth millions. Buy it!'

Hanson looked directly into his eyes. 'You could never be sure, could you, that if you'd done the same as Matthew he would have loved you as much as he did him?' She studied the good-looking face, the well-cut clothes, the styled hair, smelled his cologne. He'd struck her inside the church, this resentment-filled man whose primary love was for himself. Yet, she knew it wasn't quite so simple, so clear-cut as that. 'Matthew was wearing his scarf when he was found in the crypt. It wasn't bloodstained.'

His eyes narrowed on hers. 'So what? I just threw it onto him. No loose ends to worry about.'

She gave a slow headshake. 'You *placed* that scarf around your young, dead brother's neck. A last subconscious gesture of caring. Despite the rivalry you felt towards him and all that resentment, once he was dead you felt something else for him, didn't you? Something your resentment couldn't allow you to admit.'

She saw his face flare as he heard what he dared not acknowledge to himself. Honey screamed as he came for Hanson, face contorted, the sunray brass raised. 'People, families, the church. I see them all for what they are. They're all a sham, including *you*. You haven't caught me. You didn't have a clue.'

Keep him talking. 'I'm here, aren't I?'

'Yes. But you didn't know it was me.'

'You're right. I didn't know for a long time. I should have realised much earlier.'

'Liar! You and your police pals didn't have a clue. Admit it!'

'I did think it was your father.'

He gazes at her. 'The great Brad Flynn. Why?'

'Because of what I saw in the crime scenes. The control. The calculation. But then I changed my mind.'

'Why?'

'The rage I was seeing got me thinking. And then I knew.'

He pointed a finger at her. 'No. No, you didn't. I don't do that kind of stupid, immature stuff. I'm a player. A cool negotiator. Like *him* but better. More.'

She watched him raise the brass above his head, face contorted as the front door exploded into pieces. Hanson rushed up the stairs to Honey, held her as she screamed and shook and officers filled the hall, Corrigan first, his fist making contact with Dominic Flynn's jaw, sending him unconscious to the floor. Giving his hand a brisk shake, he came up the stairs two at a time, knelt in front of them.

'OK, Red. You can let her go now. Gus has brought a couple of non-uniform female staff with him. Let them take her.'

Hanson shook her head. 'I can't. I can't open my arms.'

TWENTY-EIGHT

The jubilation from Upstairs was still evident but it had quietened now. Hanson was with her two colleagues inside UCU. They knew all that she knew. They'd talked it through until the words ran out. Hanson was thinking of their struggle to find motive in this case. In the end it had been a mix of motives reflecting the needs of each of those responsible to varying degrees. Delaney's greed. Brad Flynn's ambition in introducing him to Dominic and creating a deadly synergy within which both Delaney and Dominic stripped people of their money. Now there was justice for Matthew, for Callum

Foley and Alfred Best. Will Graham and Zach Addison were awaiting sentencing for their drug offences. Eunice Gorridge had been charged with aiding and abetting abduction. Spencer Albright had reappeared in the last few hours and made a statement about seeing a young girl inside Delaney's house. 'He was a Father. I knew that wasn't allowed', following which he'd made himself scarce. Very wise. At the local hospital Mr and Mrs Mahoney were anxiously awaiting their first meeting in eleven years with their daughter. Hanson knew that what they were facing wouldn't be easy, but at last Honey – Rosie – was going home. Exhausted, seeing the same in her colleagues' faces, Corrigan occasionally flexing the fingers of one hand, she stood, every muscle screaming. She put on her coat, shouldered her bag and went to the door.

She'd reached the car park when she heard someone coming after her. She turned. It was Corrigan. He stood in front of her, gentle fingers on the place in her hair where Dominic Flynn had struck her inside the church. She leant against him. He folded his arms around her, then let her go. She walked away then turned to him.

'Ring me, Corrigan.'

He looked at her for what felt like a long, warming time. 'I was already planning to.'

She walked to her car in the cold, clear evening and got inside. She needed to see Maisie. And Charlie. He was leaving soon. Going back to Worcester. She started the engine.

We all need to go home.